ChoirMaster

ChoirMaster

A MISTER PUSS MYSTERY

MICHAEL CRAFT

QUESTOVER
PRESS

Design and typography: M.C. Johnson
Cover images: Adobe Stock
Author's photo: TimCourtneyPhotography.com

Library of Congress Cataloging-in-Publication Data

Craft, Michael, 1950–
ChoirMaster : a Mister Puss mystery / Michael Craft
    ISBN: 978-0-578-52330-9 (hardcover)
    ISBN: 978-0-578-52375-0 (paperback)
    BISAC: FIC011000   Fiction / LGBT / Gay
                FIC022110   Fiction / Mystery & Detective / Cozy / Cats & Dogs
                FIC022100   Fiction / Mystery & Detective / Amateur Sleuth

First hardcover and paperback editions: October 2019
Questover Press
California • Since 2011

A marriage of convenience. A crisis of faith. A talking cat. What could possibly go wrong?

In the idyllic little town of Dumont, Wisconsin, the historic but financially troubled St. Alban's Episcopal Church has a new rector who plans to turn things around, a woman named Joyce Hibbard. Local architect Marson Miles puts two and two together and figures out that Mother Hibbard's husband is none other than his long-ago college friend, Curtis Hibbard, who is now a prominent New York attorney. And unless Marson is mistaken, Curtis and Joyce must have a marriage of convenience.

Mother Hibbard wants to build a fabulous new church to replace the crumbling St. Alban's. Local philanthropist Mary Questman wants her friend Marson to design it. And Mother Hibbard's husband *really* wants the hunky young choir director, David Lovell. But then, in a god-awful development, someone turns up dead.

It was murder, all right, and suspects abound. Once again, Marson's dashing husband, Brody Norris, steps into the role of amateur sleuth and sidekick to Sheriff Thomas Simms. And once again, Brody himself gets a bit of help—from Mary Questman's exotic cat, a chatty Abyssinian named Mister Puss.

CHOIRMASTER
Mister Puss Mystery #2

"Craft's prose, with its affectionate digs at gossipy Episcopal parishes and affluent gay culture, is cheery in a way that keeps the novel from ever getting too dark, even with the murderous subject matter ... Compellingly odd ... this cozy setting with its nosy inhabitants makes for a lovely place to spend a few hours trying to figure out whodunit and why. A satisfying mystery, pleasantly told."

— *Kirkus Reviews*

"*ChoirMaster: A Mister Puss Mystery* pairs a talking cat's tale with a crisis that circles around marriage, faith, and a troubled Wisconsin church. The narration moves between perspectives and incorporates different character perceptions and experiences, creating a fluid, multifaceted story ... Readers looking for a murder mystery that goes beyond a whodunit to probe the hearts, minds, and lives of small-town residents will relish the realistic setting, diverse characters, and quirky cat profiled in *ChoirMaster* ... An intriguing, fast-paced story ... a satisfying series addition standing nicely on its own four paws."

— *D. Donovan, Senior Reviewer,*
Midwest Book Review

FLABBERGASSED
Mister Puss Mystery #1

"What an elegant mystery. What an absurd idea made irresistible and almost mystical at the hands of a gifted writer. A talking cat? Yes … Mister Puss. The best cat in all of modern fiction."

— *Ulysses Dietz, Backlot Gay Book Forum*

"Crisp, lively prose … an exuberant murder mystery … delightfully offbeat."   — *Kirkus Reviews*

"One of the most intriguing introductions seen in the mystery genre … *FlabberGassed* is quirky, original, and a delightful read."

— *D. Donovan, Senior Reviewer, Midwest Book Review*

"Craft's return to the genre of gay mysteries is handled masterfully … At turns humorous, sexy, and even poignant."   — *Keith John Glaeske, Out in Print*

"Dumont could very well become as beloved by its fans as St. Mary Mead and Cabot Cove. Fans … will find much to enjoy in *FlabberGassed*."

— *Kristopher Zgorski, BOLO Books Review*

"I gave myself over to Craft's delightful prose and warm wit, finding myself charmed by this quirky and insightful mystery."

— *John Copenhaver, Lambda Literary Review*

Gregorian Cat Chants

Soft, atonal trope
mere whiskers of sound
float eerie through hallways
fill spaces in rooms

meaningful vibration
in a low register
felt as well as heard
by the man the cat trained.

— *Lynn DeTurk*

CONTENTS

PART ONE

Mother Hibbard's Husband

Mister Puss sneezed.

In the upstairs bedroom of the grand old house on Prairie Street, Mary Questman dabbed behind her ears with a crystal perfume stopper, holding it by its decorative pair of frosty, kissing doves. She then returned the stopper to the antique Lalique flacon that contained her L'Air du Temps—her fragrance of choice for nearly half a century. Tapping the dauber into the bottle, nice and snug, she turned to the cat who sat on her dressing table, framed by a shaft of late-morning sunlight that angled across the room through tall, lacy curtains.

A svelte Abyssinian with a regal bearing and a silky coat of deep auburn, Mister Puss followed Mary's every movement with his golden, almond-shaped eyes. Mary leaned her head close to the cat's snout, close enough to hear the first rumblings of his purr. The downy fur of his chin brushed toward Mary's ear as she told him, "You've been sneezing quite a lot lately."

You've been laying it on thick lately.

"I have?" she asked with a note of concern. The dainty stool on which she sat creaked beneath her as she backed off a few inches.

Her concern did not stem from hearing a voice emerge from the cat's purr—heavens, no. It had been about a year since that fine spring morning when, as if out of nowhere, Mister Puss had appeared on her back porch, stepped inside through the screen door, and entered not only Mary's home but also her life. Within an hour of his arrival, Mary first heard the voice, or thought she did, when the cat lulled her into a drowsy state, like a waking trance, with his purr thundering near her ear. Was she amazed? Certainly. Skeptical? Of course. But with the passing of days, then weeks, Mary became so accustomed to communicating with Mister Puss that she ceased to wonder—or even care—if there might be a more rational explanation for what she was hearing.

Today, therefore, at the dressing table in her bedroom, Mary was not concerned in the least about hearing her cat speak. Rather, she was concerned about what he had said. His admonition regarding her perfume—that she had been "laying it on thick"—made her worry that her years were catching up with her, that she was growing absent-minded, that her senses were failing, that she could no longer properly sniff when enough L'Air du Temps was enough.

A lady never lies; she was just past seventy. Just a tad. Not so old, not really, not these days. In fact, she'd felt *reborn* a few years back when Quincy Questman, her wealthy husband of forty-odd years, had died, freeing her from his shadow and allowing her to march forward and build a life of her own, a fulfilling new life defined by the arts and literature and philanthropy. Why, she had barely set forth into this rousing new era of mature vibrancy, so there was simply no useful purpose in fretting that she was losing her marbles.

Except, she'd been gassing her cat. Mister Puss stared at her, looking a bit forlorn, blinking a gummy film from his eyes, as if in the throes of hay fever.

"I'm sorry," Mary cooed. She touched a fingertip to her tongue, then rubbed the dab of spit behind both ears, rinsing away some of the perfume. "There now," she said, touching the cat's nose with her moist finger, "is that better?"

Mister Puss stretched his barbed tongue to taste the velvety pad of his nose. Bug-eyed—he looked as if he might gag—he hopped down to the floor.

Oblivious to the cat's distress, Mary pushed her stool back from the dressing table and stood to check herself in the mirror.

She looked fine. More than fine, she thought. Her nubby silk suit, dusty blue, worn with a matching pair of suede Ferragamo kitten heels, was perfect for a ladies' luncheon in early May at the Dumont Country Club. Her book club met there on the second Tuesday of each month, and today they had more to discuss than their usual critique of the latest best-seller. They were in the final stages of planning for their first group excursion, a full week down in Chicago, where they would attend a famed writers' festival featuring scores of big-name authors in a whirlwind schedule of readings, signings, and book chat. It would be heaven.

The adventure would begin in ten days, plenty of time for Mary to prepare for her departure, but she had already begun to assemble her vintage set of fine Hartmann luggage, originally made right there in Wisconsin by a Bavarian trunk maker. (Her late husband's family, whose fortune was rooted in the area's timber, was said to have connections to the Hartmanns dating back to the early 1900s, so the Questmans' loyalty to the luggage brand never wavered.) Mary had set out nine or ten pieces of classic leather-and-tweed cases, duffels, and carry-ons—nothing with wheels, thank you. She wouldn't need them *all*, but for now she wanted to weigh her options before the sorting and packing began.

Mister Puss cruised the bedroom, sniffing the suitcases on the floor. Then he jumped onto the brocade settee where one of the smaller bags was propped open. He hopped inside and broke into a purr.

"Now, what do you think you're doing?" said Mary, pulling him out. She cradled him near her shoulder.

Going somewhere?

As Mary descended the wide walnut staircase of her gracious

home and passed through the front entry hall, she smelled something familiar and tantalizing—and slightly pungent—wafting from the kitchen. Berta, her longtime housekeeper, had apparently finished her morning chores early because, when she did so, she often baked treats before heading home for the afternoon. Sometimes, she prepared lunch for Mary, but Mary would be lunching at the club today, so Berta was baking.

Mary warbled, "Something smells *wonderful*," as she waltzed into the kitchen.

Berta turned from the sink, where she was scrubbing the steel bowl and wire whip from a rugged old stand mixer. "Your stash was running low, but now you'll have something nice when you get back from your meeting."

"I think I'll wait till tomorrow—when you can join me."

"Suit yourself. I won't say no." Berta returned to her task, clanging the bowl in the porcelain sink. Her knotty hands glowed red from the hot, sudsy water.

Although Berta and Mary came from two different worlds, they had developed a deep bond over the decades, especially since Berta had joined Mary in widowhood. While Mary was a quintessential lady by virtue of her upbringing, deportment, and considerable means, Berta was a brusque, sturdy woman who knew the meaning of work and the challenges of a servant's limited income. While Berta was some ten or fifteen years younger than Mary, she was wiser to the world. While Berta's attire was as drab and undistinctive as her features, she had a sarcastic sense of humor that could match the jolly wit of the polished matron who employed her.

But now, as both women began to contemplate the prospects of later life, they discovered a growing commonality that overtook their differences. Neither woman had children, and both had lost their husbands to lengthy illnesses. Although employed as a housekeeper, Berta had grown into the added roles of Mary's caretaker and companion. And Mary, in turn, had found unexpected satisfaction in becoming Berta's provider and protector. It worked, this patchwork sisterhood. Plus, Berta had introduced Mary to the occasional pleasures of pot, usually baked into afternoon treats.

Berta asked over her shoulder, "How did His Majesty take the news?" The housekeeper had tolerated the arrival of Mister Puss, but she made little effort to conceal a certain resentment for having taken on extra duties as lackey to a cat.

"I couldn't bring myself to tell him." Mary shambled over to the heavy oak kitchen table and sat. An enormous lamp of hobnail milk glass hung low over the round table and anchored the room, which had a homey appeal that contrasted with the studied elegance of the rest of the house. Mary added, "He asked if I was going somewhere."

Berta rolled her eyes. She and Mary had reached a respectful impasse regarding the plausibility of the cat's speech. The housekeeper had given up questioning her employer's claims of communicating with Mister Puss, but that didn't put an end to the eye-rolling.

Mary breathed a petite sigh. "I'm not sure how to tell him I'm leaving town for a week. And since *you're* going with me, he can't stay here at the house."

Berta reminded her, "Brody said he was happy to cat-sit."

Mary nodded. "Mister Puss does seem to like Brody." With a chuckle, she added, "Everyone likes Brody."

Berta's eyes slid to the open doorway from the front hall. "Well, speak of the devil. Good *morning*, Your Majesty."

Having completed his inspection of Mary's luggage, Mister Puss sauntered into the kitchen, ignoring Berta, sniffing in the direction of the oven. Though he had grown accustomed to the distinctive scent of marijuana, his scrunched face made it clear he still didn't like it.

Mary made a kissy sound and patted her knee, which summoned the cat to her side. Mister Puss leaned in and swept Mary's ankles with the length of his body while Mary checked her purse for her keys.

"Almost forgot," said Berta, moving to the table with a small stack of envelopes and circulars. "The mail was early."

Setting her keys aside, Mary sorted through the stack, finding nothing that required immediate attention. But one of the items caught her interest—a note-size blue envelope addressed to her in a graceful hand, bearing the return address of the rectory of St. Alban's Episcopal Church in downtown Dumont. Berta handed Mary a well-polished sterling butter knife, with which Mary slit open the envelope. Unless she was mistaken, it was perfumed. She gave it a sniff, not recognizing the fragrance. Mister Puss jumped up to the tabletop, and he too sniffed the envelope. He sneezed.

Mary removed several sheets of folded blue note paper and skimmed the handwritten letter. She said, "Listen to this."

Berta pulled out a chair and sat at the table. Mister Puss settled near Mary's elbow and began to emit a soft, steady purr as Mary read the letter aloud:

Dear Mrs. Questman,

I understand that your family's valued membership in the St. Alban's community goes back for generations, but I do not believe we have yet had the opportunity to meet, so I would like to introduce myself. My name is Joyce Hibbard, and as you may be aware, I have recently stepped into the role of St. Alban's new rector. I feel both honored and blessed to be entrusted as shepherd of your historic parish.

As I'm sure you will agree, the beauty of Episcopal teaching rests in its sense of balance—on the one hand, we have a deep sense of roots and tradition, while on the other hand, we have a progressive vision that embraces the realities of change. Here in Dumont, St. Alban's finds itself at something of a crossroads, and our parish vestry has begun to discuss important ideas regarding our future direction.

Since the Questman family has played such a significant role in St. Alban's past, I would very much welcome the opportunity to discuss with you our plans to move forward. You may call on me at the rectory anytime at your convenience, or if you prefer, I would be happy to visit you at your home.

In addition, the vestry—our governing council—will hold an important meeting this Thursday evening at seven o'clock, which the entire congregation is encouraged to attend. Many of your fellow parishioners have expressed regrets that they have not seen you at services for many months, perhaps a year, and I am certain it would be their great joy to welcome your return to the bosom of our church family. May we count on your being with us on Thursday?

I have heard so many lovely things about you, Mary. (May I presume to call you Mary? And I hope you will think of me as Joyce, rather than Mother Hibbard!) I look forward to the pleasure of meeting you soon.

Yours in Christ,
The Rev. Joyce Hibbard, Rector
St. Alban's Episcopal Church

Mary folded the pages and returned them to the envelope. "Well, now," she said, "what do you make of that?"

"A little too flowery for *my* tastes," said Berta.

Mister Puss, still purring, reached his paws to Mary's shoulder and stretched his snout to her ear.

Hold on to your wallet.

1

Traipsing down the spiral metal stairs of a converted downtown loft we called home, I found my husband, Marson Miles, busy preparing for the day—brewing coffee, buttering toast, puttering with placemats and cutlery at the granite-topped kitchen island that separated the cooking area from our two-story living room. Our sleeping space was upstairs, on the mezzanine of a former haberdashery that had long ago been shuttered, ripe for repurposing by two architects who, two years earlier, had set out to build a life together. We were also business partners.

"Brody," Marson asked me, "could you check if the paper's here yet?"

"Sure."

I opened the front door and stepped out to the sidewalk on First Avenue, the main drag of our quaint little burg in central Wisconsin—not the sort of setting that would conjure even an inkling of impending menace, let alone murder.

A bright spring morning hinted of the summer to come. By seven o'clock, dawn was long gone and the sun had already spent some two hours warming the sky, greening the trees, and prodding the birds to mate and sing. Ah, nature.

I sneezed.

Snatching the rolled copy of the *Dumont Daily Register*, I darted inside and thumped the door closed.

Marson liked to fuss. By instinct—as well as by profession—he had a passion for precision and an eye for detail that some might deem stodgy. I, however, found his obsessive quirks to be among his most endearing traits. He was a designer to the core, and I not only loved him but learned from him.

Older than I by some twenty years (or so), Marson always took pains to dress well (jacket and tie at the office), to communicate clearly (sending me well-composed emails throughout the day from across the hall), and to set a proper table (the simple breakfast he'd arrayed on the kitchen island was fit for the leisurely elegance of a Sunday morning).

But this was not Sunday. It was a Wednesday, the middle of a workweek, nothing special. Even the newspaper was slim and unremarkable. Taking it to the kitchen, I handed it to Marson as I sat on a stool at the counter. At the far end of the island, Marson began his ritual of "cleaning" the paper:

After unrolling and unfolding it, he removed the creases by gently rolling and folding it in the opposite directions. Then he pulled a few stuffers, the want ads, and the sports section, setting them aside for recycling. Finally, he rearranged the remaining sections in the order he preferred for reading. Then he stepped over to the sink to wash his hands.

We kept an iPad in the kitchen. While sipping coffee, I checked for email. "Oops," I said.

Marson returned to the island, sitting on the stool next to mine. "What's wrong?" he asked.

"It's Clem Carter—again. A delay in the construction schedule—again." Marson and I were building a permanent home for ourselves; the loft had been a stop-gap solution to our immediate need for housing after we met. The new project, which we immodestly had dubbed "the perfect house," was proceeding more slowly than planned. No surprise. But lately, the delays encountered by Carter Construction seemed much more frequent—and more costly. This time, it was something about the custom steel-framed windows.

"The way this is going," I said, "it'll be a miracle if we're in by winter."

Marson grinned. "Meanwhile, we'll be stuck 'roughing it' right here." He placed a hand on my knee. "Don't stress over it, kiddo."

Kiddo, I thought. Being younger than Marson, I might have found his pet term for me condescending—and overly literal. But I knew him well enough to understand that his spontaneous use of the word carried not a hint of ageism. Or reverse ageism. Coming from him, it conveyed pure tenderness.

Placing my hand on his, I asked, "Know what I love about you?"

He cocked his head and arched one brow.

"Your practicality."

"Oh." His brow sagged.

Laughing, I told him, "*No.* I mean, you don't let things throw you. You're ... unflappable."

He shrugged. "Imperturbable."

"Right. But you're also sweet and caring. And intelligent. And very, *very* hot."

"That's better." He patted my inner thigh.

"Jesus"—I was instantly aroused—"I don't suppose we have time for ..."

He gave me a look. "We just got dressed." He reached over to straighten my tie. "And we have a full schedule at the office."

"Yeah," I said, hangdog, chomping a piece of toast. I checked my watch. "Mind if I tune in Chad Percy?"

We didn't usually watch morning TV—we didn't watch much at all—but one of the cable networks had begun airing daily cutaway segments from an out-and-proud gay commentator in Green Bay, of all places. He was associated with the university there, and his features ran the gamut from social issues to decorating and fashion. Flamboyant and fun, Chad Percy was just catching on nationally, but he'd already become something of a local cult hero. The largest city in central Wisconsin, Green Bay was about an hour's drive from Dumont.

"Fine by me," said Marson, reaching for the newspaper, "but not too loud, please. I'll be reading."

"Sure." I opened our cable app on the iPad, selected the news network, and propped up the screen just as a commercial was ending for some revolutionary prescription drug, which listed, as one of its many possible side effects, death.

Then bang, there was Chad Percy, jabbering at us from between the carafe of coffee and a pitcher of orange juice. "…disturbing reports that these incidents in Green Bay represent an uptick in anti-gay activity previously not encountered here…"

Marson mumbled, "How does he manage to look cheery while delivering *that*?"

I suggested, "Must be in his genes. I mean, come on, could he *be* any cuter? He's, like, total dollcakes."

Marson lowered the paper and took a closer look. "Not bad. But he's no Brody Norris."

Deflecting, I reminded my husband, "I thought you were trying to read."

Dollcakes told us, "And on a happier note—some marketing news I'm excited to share with you. File this one under 'branding.' After months of negotiation, development, and testing, I'm thrilled to announce that I've partnered with the legendary scentologists at Parfumerie Abraxas for the introduction of a new unisex fragrance you'll want to make your own."

Marson snorted. "Wonder what they'll call the stuff. 'Eau de Green Bay'?"

As if hearing Marson's query, Chad Percy responded, "And guess what we're calling it. 'Chad!' That's right—'Chad!'—with an exclamation point. Isn't it *fabulous*? And it's coming soon."

Marson turned to tell me, deadpan, "I can hardly wait."

Marson would never, I was certain, abandon his allegiance to Vétiver, the elegant, woody scent that had been introduced by Guerlain around the time he was born. I myself had never found much appeal in fragrances; from time to time I would try one, and they would invariably irritate my skin. But Marson came from a school of thought that considered a gentleman not presentable, not *dressed*, without a touch of fragrance. And on him, it was indeed the slightest touch—and it didn't smell the same on anyone else—and I loved it.

Sitting together at breakfast, he passed to me the front section of the *Register*, which he had finished. Dollcakes was still bubbling about Chad!, so I switched him off and began to skim the newspaper headlines.

"Oh, good," said Marson as he turned a page of the features section. "Glee has a column today."

He was referring to our dear friend Glee Savage, a local reporter who primarily covered the social scene and the arts. But she also wrote an occasional column titled "Inside Dumont," a personality profile of someone whom Glee wanted to introduce to the community. When I arrived in town from California some two years earlier, I was flattered when she ran such a column about me.

As Marson hunkered into his reading, I found a story concerning a conflict of interest on the local water board, but it was painfully arcane, and within a few minutes, my mind wandered. I focused instead on a golden triangle of buttered toast, trying to decide which jam would make the better pairing: gooseberry or apricot?

"I can't *believe* it," said Marson, lowering the paper.

"What?"

He handed me the page he'd been reading.

Inside Dumont

*Historic local parish welcomes
its first woman priest*

By Glee Savage

•

MAY 11, DUMONT, WI — The Episcopal Church in the United States approved the ordination of women as priests in 1976, but even today they are seldom encountered in some smaller or more rural dioceses. Dumont's historic St. Alban's parish is a case in point.

Founded in 1865 and funded largely by the area's timber gentry, St. Alban's soon established itself as the town's "society" church, enjoying a long period of prosperity and growth that lasted well into the twentieth century. However, like many of Dumont's mainline churches, St. Alban's has witnessed a slow change of tides over the past fifty years, with dwindling membership and resources. The school was closed a generation ago, and Sunday services often draw fewer than a hundred souls to the church's mahogany pews.

When the Rev. Charles Sterling, ninth and most recent rector of St. Alban's, announced his intended retirement to warmer climes late last year, some in the small parish feared the beginning of the end. But many in the struggling church have now embraced an opportunity for St. Alban's to renew and redefine itself with the arrival of the Rev. Joyce Hibbard.

"My path to the priesthood was anything but conventional," she said during a recent interview. "My initial training was in law, and I spent a dozen years practicing with a large firm in New York. But something was missing. It felt like such a dry pursuit. So I started a fashion business, which saw me through another dozen years. By then I was in my fifties—and still searching. This may sound cliché, but when I opened my heart, at last I heard the calling."

A calling from God?

She hesitated. Sitting in the tidy front parlor of the St. Alban's rectory, she reached to pour more tea for both of us. A Cartier watch adorned her wrist. A gold ring and bracelet matched the design of her earrings. She said, "Let's say it was a *spiritual* calling. My husband was shocked when I told him I intended to enter divinity school. Five years later, I'd earned two degrees; three years after that, I was ordained. And now, fresh into my sixties, I'm here to begin a new life as rector at St. Alban's."

When this reporter asked Mother Hibbard how the locals have reacted to a woman at the pulpit, she interrupted, patting my hand. "Please," she said, "we're friends now. Do call me Joyce." With a laugh, she added, "Mother Hibbard—it sounds like that dowdy old woman from the nursery rhyme."

Dowdy she is not. Stylish and worldly, the Rev. Joyce Hibbard fits none of the stereotypes one may associate with priests, not even the progressive Episcopal female variety. And the title "Mother" (used by many Episcopalians in place of "Father") does seem to stick in the throat, although that may stem more from its novelty in Dumont than from its aptness to her office.

With a firm background in both law and business, she brings a wealth of experience to the troubled parish that could indeed prove a blessing. She also brings her professional connections and doubtless a bulging Rolodex. Mother Hibbard's husband is the New York attorney Curtis Hibbard, who specializes in corporate governance.

At last month's institution ceremony, the new rector of St. Alban's told her flock...

As I lowered the paper, Marson repeated, "I can't believe it."

"What? Why?"

He explained, "This new priest at St. Alban's, I think I met her eons ago. She's married to a college friend of mine, Curt Hibbard. He and I stayed in touch for several years after school, and I went to visit him a few times in New York. I remember Joyce. She and Curt were…'dating.'" Marson enclosed the last word with air quotes.

"What does that mean?" I asked.

"Let's just say I suspect a marriage of convenience." Marson paused before adding, "I should know."

Indeed, Marson should know. He'd been married to a woman for some thirty-five years before I entered his life.

With a prim linen napkin, I wiped a smear of apricot jam from my fingers. Then I flashed Marson a grin and suggested the obvious: "Look up your old friend. Say hello. Get the dirt."

The offices of Miles & Norris, Architects, LLC, were located downtown on First Avenue, a few blocks from our loft. When the weather was pleasant, as it was that Wednesday morning, we could easily walk from home to work, but more often than not, we would drive at least one of our vehicles, since we were frequently taken away from our desks by meetings, client lunches, site visits, and such. That day, we rode together in Marson's whopping hunter-green Range Rover.

Business had been good—great, in fact. Three years earlier, Marson had scored a career-changing commission to design a local performing-arts center, funded largely by a wealthy widow, Mary Questman, whom we now counted as one of our closest friends. Questman Center proved to be an immediate hit, not only in Dumont but in the arts world at large, snagging a cover story in *ArchitecAmerica,* which brought Marson a good measure of later-life fame and the luxury of cherry-picking from an influx of proposals for high-profile future commissions.

We were now in the final construction phases of a new county museum located near Questman Center. Farther from home, we had a half-dozen public projects under way, including a university building in Appleton, a museum expansion in Chicago, and a civic center out in Oregon. Our office in Dumont had acquired additional space in an adjacent building, and our payroll had expanded to include a full-time accountant and two more design interns.

Later than morning, therefore, I was surprised to learn that Marson had taken a break from the grindstone to indulge in a bit of personal correspondence. A *ping* at the computer on my desk signaled an arriving email from Marson, across the hall, which he had sent to me as a blind copy.

From: Marson Miles, A.I.A.
To: Curtis Hibbard, Esq.

Isn't the Internet a remarkable invention, Curt? We haven't seen each other since that neolithic age preceding the magic of thermal faxes, but I noticed your name in this morning's local paper, and now, after a Google search that took all of five seconds, here I am, scratching at your in-box in New York. I hope this communication finds you happy and well.

So you and Joyce have been married lo these many years? This comes as something of a surprise, as my last recollection is that your affections were then focused on a ballet dancer. What was his name?

The far greater surprise was to learn that Joyce is now an Episcopal priest—and that she has set up shop here in Dumont! Though she always struck me as a wonderful woman, I never realized she was religiously prone.

Are you ever here, Curt? If so, we are long overdue to catch up. Back in college, I thought of you as my best friend. If you're inclined, let's pick up the conversation again before another thirty-odd years slip away.

Fondly,
Marson

Around one-thirty, when Marson and I returned to the office from lunch, we found our receptionist watching from the front window, opening the street door for us as we arrived. Wide-eyed, she told us in a stage whisper, "Mrs. *Questman* is here."

"How *nice*," said Marson. He turned to ask me, "Were you expecting her?"

"No." I couldn't imagine what she wanted.

Marson glanced around the small lobby, then leaned to our receptionist, whispering, "Where is she?"

She whispered back, "In the conference room. I gave her some water."

Marson gave a thumbs-up. "Good job, Gertie."

When we entered the conference room, Mary rose from her chair at the far end of the table, gushing, "*Marson*, love. *Brody*, sweets. I hope you don't mind my popping in without notice." She had brought her cat, an Abyssinian named Mister Puss, an exotic creature with flecked brown fur who resembled a wild predator from some faraway savanna, though he was no bigger than a trim-bodied house cat.

"Mind?" said Marson. "You know you're *always* welcome here— or in our home, or anywhere at all."

We gathered to exchange a round of smooches as Mister Puss wound his way around our feet, trailing a nylon leash that had a retraction device at the far end, housed in a plastic casing that clattered on the polished wooden floor.

"Now, now, Mister Puss," said Mary, "let's not make such a racket." She stooped to pick up the gadget and tried to reel him in toward her heel, but the cat would have none of it. He plopped down on his side as she dragged him across the slick floor to her jaunty yellow Ferragamo pumps. She wore them with a striking spring outfit of yellow and green and dashes of black—the woman knew how to dress.

But her choice of couture for the cat left something to be desired. The leash was attached not to a simple collar, but a vest of sorts, a synthetic harness covering much of his midsection, sporting a ridiculous pattern of paw prints and dancing mice. Mister Puss was a perfectly magnificent animal *au naturel*, but he looked miserable in this getup.

Mary unhooked the leash from the harness, explaining, "Mister Puss understands that he's not allowed out of the house on his own. He seems to prefer it that way."

"I don't blame him," said Marson. Most of Mary's acquaintances humored her with regard to her relationship with the cat, but Marson's tone carried no lilt of sarcasm.

She continued, "So I thought we'd try some leash training. Mixed results, obviously. But now and then, it's nice to take him out. Today, for instance—he wanted to come with me. He wanted to see Brody."

With a soft laugh, Marson repeated, "I don't blame him."

I pulled a chair out from the table and sat, patting my knee. "Here, Mister Puss."

He trotted over and hopped into my lap, purring.

Mary said, "He's excited about staying with you while I'm away.

I wasn't sure how he'd take the news—about my trip—but we had a talk last night, and everything's fine."

Mister Puss climbed my chest with his front paws and nuzzled my chin. His purr intensified as his snout worked its way up my cheek to my ear.

Help me.

"Mary," I said, "okay if I take off his harness? The door's closed; he can't get out."

"Of *course*, Brody. Do you need some help?"

"I think I can handle it." Mister Puss offered no resistance as I unfastened the vest and slid his front legs free from it. Eyeing me with an expression that looked for all the world like a grin of thanks, he stepped up to the tabletop, stretched his back, and bristled the fur that had been matted by the harness. Then he sat near my elbow and groomed.

Meanwhile, Marson had reseated Mary at the head of the table, then seated himself across from me. He asked Mary, "So you're ready for the trip?"

"Oh, *yes*. We had our monthly luncheon yesterday, and everyone is raring to go. All the arrangements are set. Now I just need to pack. Nine days till blastoff, and I'll need every minute of it." Pondering this, she added, "I know it's *only* Chicago, for *only* a week, but I haven't traveled in a while."

I said, "You'll have a wonderful time. And don't worry about you-know-who. The livestock will be well tended."

Mister Puss gave me a look.

"Of course," said Mary with a soft smile, "but I'm wondering if I could ask you boys *one* extra favor."

Marson and I exchanged a glance—not wary, but curious. He said, "Anything, Mary. What's on your mind?"

She heaved a little sigh, plopped her purse on the table, and extracted a blue envelope. Removing the contents, she explained,

"I got a letter yesterday from that new woman priest at St. Alban's. She wants to meet me, privately. And she practically *insisted* that I also attend some big, important parish meeting tomorrow night." Mary handed the letter to Marson, who read it. Mary added, "Mister Puss thinks she wants to put the squeeze on me."

I couldn't help laughing. "He may be on to something."

Mary tossed her hands. "I suppose I'll have to meet her *sometime*. I can't put it off *forever*. But I'd rather not meet with her alone. I'm afraid she might corner me into something stupid."

Mary was generous, easily the most philanthropic person I'd ever known well enough to call a friend. But it was hard to fault her for wanting to reserve the privilege of deciding, on her own, who would be the beneficiaries of her largess.

Passing the letter to me, Marson said to Mary, "Tell you what. Suppose I go to the parish meeting tomorrow night. I'll give some excuse why you can't be there, and I'll report back to you. And if Joyce Hibbard still wants to meet with you, I'll offer to sit in."

Mary's mood instantly brightened. "You're willing to *do* that, Marson?"

"It's the least I can do." He was referring to the fact that Mary's faith in him, when she insisted he be awarded the commission to design Questman Center for the Performing Arts, had been the turning point in his career, leading to recognition that had eluded him for more than thirty years.

"Actually," he added, "I've been meaning to say hello to Joyce. We used to know each other—long, long ago."

I passed the letter back to Mary, who returned it to her purse.

"What a delightful turn of events," she said.

Mister Puss purred.

Back at the loft that Wednesday evening, after dinner, Marson and I relaxed with a nightcap while catching up on some reading.

A couple of hours slipped by, and around eleven o'clock, Marson's phone vibrated. He opened an incoming email and sat reading it for a few minutes while I got up, took our empty snifters of cognac to the kitchen, and gave them a rinse.

"Take a look at this," he called to me from the front of the loft. The iPad on the kitchen island gave a *ping* with the arrival of the message he had forwarded to me.

From: Curtis Hibbard
To: Marson Miles

Hello there, Marson, old chum! I wondered when I'd hear from you, and it didn't take long. Yes, yes—all true. I have now been married to Joyce for more years than I was not. Time, as they say, marches on.

The days of my infatuation with Yevgeny (the dancer) are now but a distant memory, and a bittersweet one at that. While his body was an object of both lust and love, that pretty head of his harbored a propensity for betrayal. I knew it was over when he took up with a concert organist of some renown, a flamboyant showboat admired for the swift dexterity of not only his hands but also his feet. Yevgeny is now too old for leaping about in a pair of tights, though I hear the organist is still pumping away, which I hope brings them both great bliss. Ironically, in recent years, I have renewed my friendship with Yevgeny. Our *rapprochement* is strictly platonic, which no longer pains me, as he has lost the allure of youth.

It now occurs to me that you once met Fletcher (he of the talented feet). During your last visit to New York, well over thirty years ago, he gave an organ recital at St. John the Divine, and we all attended—you, me, Joyce, and Yevgeny.

At the time, I was "courting" Joyce, figuring the potential match could be good for business, but I was tangling the sheets, when circumstances allowed, with Yevgeny, who in turn, and unbeknownst to me, was doing the dirty fugue with Fletcher. At the time, I had assumed they were mere acquaintances from the performing-arts demimonde. Silly, gullible me!

Not to dwell on the treachery of organists—or ballet boys—but a more significant development was to emerge from that evening's recital at the cathedral. You see, Joyce and I were both in the process of establishing our respective law careers, and that was the night we discovered the majesty—and cachet—of Episcopalianism. You may not recall this, but seated in the surrounding rows that evening was a veritable who's who of Manhattan's upper crust, representing finance, law, publishing, politics, arts, charity, the works. *Jackie* was there. Need one say more?

This came as something of a revelation not only to me, with my humble Wisconsin roots and tepid Lutheran upbringing, but also to Joyce, a born and confirmed skeptic. That night, we found our spiritual home.

Our epiphany proved as rewarding to our social lives as it was to our ambitions. Overnight, we were "connected." Our practices were booming. It seemed the handwriting was on the wall, so we were married—by the presiding bishop, no less, in a side chapel with a few dozen friends, family members, and senior partners as witnesses. It was a lovely twilight ceremony. Couture all the way. Add a dash of liturgical pomp, with its incense and silver-tongued oration, and you've got a fairytale wedding.

Joyce often noted that the Episcopal Church felt more like a club than a religion, and that's how she justified her involvement, which was anything but faith-driven—though she can't admit that *now*, having teamed up for the hocus-pocus. But she needed to try a new gig, and I have never stood in her way, so here I am: Mother Hibbard's husband.

It brings to mind that old Cary Grant flick, *The Bishop's Wife*, doesn't it? There's plenty of material here for an updated, screwball sequel with a gender switcheroo. Meryl Streep could play Joyce (there's more than a passing resemblance). But whom, I wonder, would they cast in the role of *moi*?

The opening scene could be set in St. Alban's at Joyce's institution ceremony, with me seated in the front pew, having flown in that weekend for a conjugal visit at the parsonage. My thoughts would be narrated in voice-over as I pondered not my wife's investiture but the performance of the choir, which wasn't bad, and the studly young choirmaster, who was easy on the eyes. As you might guess, that's exactly what happened. *Cinéma vérité*.

I did attempt to see you, Marson. As soon as I realized Joyce would be moving to Dumont, of all places, I did a bit of research to determine if you were still located there—and I was pleased beyond measure to learn that this latter chapter of your architecture career has taken such a splendid turn. The performing-arts complex is magnificent, and I am bursting with pride to read of your many recent accolades. (Have you forgotten that I once offered to serve as your patron and help you establish a practice in New York? I was certain that your talent deserved a bigger canvas than Wisconsin, but you were determined to make a go of it there with Ted. What happened to him, by the way?) But I have digressed.

Once the date was set for Joyce's institution as rector—

and there was never any question that I was expected to attend—I decided to wait until a few days prior to the event, then phone your office, deliver the surprising news, and arrange to see you during my visit. But when I did phone, I learned that you were away for the week, in the remote stretches of Oregon, working on an important new commission.

So our timing was lousy last month, or at least mine was. I'm not sure when I will next make the westward trek to play husband at the parsonage, but there are bound to be future visits, probably sooner rather than later, and I'll be sure to give you ample notice.

All glibness aside, I must admit to being a tad concerned about Joyce's new career path. At first, I assumed she would be content to go back to school, get a degree or two, get ordained, then settle into some sort of administrative position within the church hierarchy. And for a while, that's what she did. She rattled around headquarters in New York and they put her in charge of planned giving—yes, she knows how to sniff out the money.

But she was back at a desk, back in business, back to doing the same sort of thing she'd always done, and she still had the itch to try something different. So they suggested a pastoral assignment in an ailing parish. Joyce snapped at it. She wanted a challenge.

Trust me: St. Alban's will be a challenge.

I assume you're familiar with the building, Marson. It's a charming little church, but in sad disrepair. The congregation is aging—and shrinking fast. The town's demographics offer little hope that a new generation will be bustin' down those crimson doors to fill those creaky pews. I told Joyce point-blank that St. Alban's business model is shaky at best, if not doomed. But she seems unfazed by the millstone she's taken on.

In her defense, she's a shrewd businesswoman, so if anyone can turn St. Alban's around, it's Joyce. My fear, however, is that her new mission has all the earmarks of an extremely expensive later-life hobby. To save the parish, she needs an angel (of the wealthy species, not the celestial), and I've already made it clear that I'm not looking to earn my wings. Sure, I'm willing to pop for a new boiler or whatnot, but that wouldn't begin to solve the problem. That church needs to be totally rebuilt—or razed and reimagined from the ground up, which may be cheaper—and I have zero inclination to buy the top spot on the donor list.

The irony, Marson, is that I *could* write that check. All my life, I have felt driven. I'm still working sixty hours a week, sometimes seventy, and while that's great for billings, it does take a certain toll. Back when we were in college, I had laser-focused dreams of success, all of them measured by material gain and ego. And those wishes have been granted. By any standard, I'm a lucky man. But now, here I am, beginning to entertain fantasies of retirement, of chucking it all, wondering what the hell I've done with my life.

Last week, I counted up: I serve on nineteen boards. I've had the same coveted box at the Met for twenty years. I flounce around in private jets to sign billion-dollar mergers. There are people to drive my car, fetch my laundry, and open my doors. But at the end of the day, I'm left wondering how and why I didn't measure up to a nelly old organist named Fletcher.

Joyce and I have always led independent lives, and now that her latest career whim has moved us a half-continent apart, I suspect we'll continue to function as the mutually supportive odd couple that was sanctified in that side chapel more than ten thousand evenings ago—but who's counting?

Forgive my self-sorry prattle, Marson. (Poor little rich boy. Just a bird in a gilded cage.) Your turn. Bring me up to date. I understand you are married?

Best regards,
Curtis Hibbard, Founding Partner
Hibbard Belding & Smith, LLP
New York • London • Berlin

CHAPTER

2

Thursday morning, I awoke earlier than usual—it was barely dawn—and I was surprised to discover that Marson was not there in bed with me. I rolled over, looking toward the bathroom; its door was open, only darkness within. I listened for activity downstairs, hearing nothing. But I smelled coffee.

Tentatively, I called into the stillness of the loft, "Marson?"

"Morning, kiddo," he said from downstairs. "Hope I didn't wake you."

"Is something wrong?"

"Not at all. Writing a reply to Curt Hibbard. Go back to sleep."

By now, though, I was wide awake. I got out of bed, slipped into a bathrobe of steely gray striped silk, and padded down the metal stairs barefoot.

Marson sat at the kitchen island, also in a robe, typing on the iPad with his mug of coffee at hand. The lights were on beneath the upper cupboards on the rear wall, glowing yellow, blending with the early daylight that filled the wall of windows facing the street. We exchanged a good-morning kiss while Marson typed. Then I poured myself some coffee and joined him at the island.

"There," he said, tapping to send his email. He turned the tablet to let me read it.

From: Marson Miles
To: Curtis Hibbard

Wow, Curt, I got far more than expected from you. This deserves some face time—and soon, I hope—but let me at least answer your question regarding my marital status. Sitting down? Yes, I have been married, for almost a year now, to the nephew of my ex-wife.

Perhaps I should back up and explain.

When you and I knew each other in college, the sexual revolution had just begun, and I think it's safe to say we were both struggling to understand ourselves in the context of an age that was still, nonetheless, closeted. All I knew for sure was that I was in love with Ted Norris, my roommate, who would later become my business partner. To my mind, I wasn't "gay." I wasn't lusting after everyone in pants—only Ted.

But Ted was straight as an arrow. He seemed to understand how I felt about him, though he never confronted me with it, and I think he even felt complimented. We bonded as lifelong friends and established our architecture firm, Miles & Norris, here in Dumont.

Around that time (around when you married Joyce), I married Ted's sister, Prucilla. In all honesty, I never found Prue loving or lovable, but if I couldn't love Ted, I figured I could at least marry into his family. By some perverse reasoning, that made me feel more *joined* to Ted.

Flash forward some thirty years. A couple of years ago, after Miles & Norris made such a splash with the opening of Questman Center, we found ourselves with more work than we could handle—and I'm talking big stuff—high-profile projects of artistic merit. We needed more staff, younger talent.

This is where Brody Norris enters the picture.

Brody is the son of Ted's (and Prucilla's) older sister in

California, Inez Norris, a single mother who gave Brody the Norris surname. Brody is also an architect, originally inspired by his uncle Ted. Brody had established a respected career in the LA area, but a failed marriage to another man left him looking for a change of scenery. So Ted suggested to his nephew that he might consider joining the Dumont firm, and Brody hopped on a plane.

When he arrived—you guessed it—pow, fireworks, head over heels, and it was mutual. I had slogged through an entire life feeling repressed and frustrated. Never again. Within a day of connecting with Brody, I announced to Prue that I was leaving her.

Yes, it was something of a small-town scandal.

But that was overshadowed a few months later when Ted's wife (his second, to be precise) died under circumstances that can only be described as bizarre. Amnesia. A past life. Witness protection. As you can imagine, this sent Ted into an emotional tailspin from which he has not yet fully recovered. He fled to an island where he could brood and heal, selling his interest in Miles & Norris to Brody and me. So the firm is still known as Miles & Norris.

But the *new* Norris is twenty-four years my junior. Enough said? More later.

Fondly,
Marson

When I finished reading, Marson said, "Hope you don't mind my bragging on you." With a sheepish expression, he added, "I still can't believe you're part of my life. And sometimes I can't help feeling that *I* got the better end of the bargain."

"Stop that," I whispered, kissing the tip of my index finger, then touching it to his lips. "That bargain works both ways. I've never felt cheated in the least. In fact—"

We were interrupted by a *ping* from the tablet, announcing an incoming email. Marson and I both looked at it, then laughed.

From: Curtis Hibbard
To: Marson Miles

Cradle robber. I'm *dying* to meet him.

Best regards,
Curtis Hibbard, Founding Partner
Hibbard Belding & Smith, LLP
New York • London • Berlin

Riding to St. Alban's that evening with Marson, I recalled the only other time I had visited the parish. The prior autumn, on a crisp morning, I had shuffled through fallen leaves to attend a funeral for a local doctor who had died under suspicious circumstances, which had gotten me involved in a murder investigation. But now it was spring, with its fresh beginnings and warmer days and later sunsets—and no hint whatever that I could be called upon once more to adapt the problem-solving skills of an architect to the headier conundrums of wrongful death.

Shortly before seven on that Thursday evening in May, the lingering sunshine angled golden through the arching elms and dappled the windshield of the Range Rover as we approached Dumont's historic downtown commons. From the driver's seat, Marson reached across the wide console to pat my leg. "It was sweet of you to come along tonight. I'm the one who volunteered for this."

I reminded him, "We're a team. Plus, it's for Mary." We not

only owed her a great deal—the successful trajectory of Miles &
Norris was due as much to her favoritism toward our firm as it was
to Marson's design talents—but we also loved her as a friend and
enjoyed being of help.

We drove past the town's original Carnegie library, a handsome
neoclassical limestone building, and circled the park to the opposite side, where St. Alban's steeple punctured the treetops. The
parish meeting had already filled the church parking lot to capacity, so we cruised ahead, parked at the curb, and walked back
a block.

Approaching the church, I thought it looked especially grim—a
reaction that was at least partly colored by my upbringing. Inez
Norris, a proudly single lesbian mom and community organizer,
had raised me as a "heathen" (her word). Therefore, even though
St. Alban's had a distinct architectural charm and historic significance, I couldn't help thinking of it as foreign turf, defined by
traditions in which I was not only untutored, but thoroughly un-
believing.

The prior October, when I attended the funeral, with every pew
packed shoulder to shoulder with mourners, I had paid little attention to the rites of Requiem being performed and, instead, had
focused on my physical surroundings, on the disrepair, the smoke
of candles and incense, the grime of ages, the leak-stained plaster,
and the warped floor that threatened to snap, plunging our hun-
dreds of hapless souls into a dank and dark forgotten cellar.

Granted, it was a frame of mind.

And truth be told, the windows were spectacular.

This evening, however, viewed from outdoors, the windows
were black against the building's dark interior, with the tips of
their gothic arches jagged and menacing, a procession of gashes in the exterior walls of weathered yellow brick. And the front
doors, painted a gleaming enamel that I have often described as

Episcopal red, were not flung wide and welcoming, but locked and bolted.

Marson said, "I assume the meeting's in the parish hall."

We joined a trickle of stragglers making their way alongside the church, walking back into the parish grounds, where a red brick elementary school, closed for many years, hulked next to a newer building, probably a gymnasium, that had been converted to its current use as an all-purpose church hall and meeting room. A crowd mingled inside the glass doors of its sterile, brightly lit lobby.

Marson and I stepped inside. The din of conversation had a nervous edge to it, as if everyone understood the gravity of the situation that had called them together—they would be weighing the future prospects for the very existence of their beloved parish. Old acquaintances met and greeted each other, but there was little joshing and no laughter.

"My God," said Marson, spotting a woman who stood greeting people at the entrance to the main hall, "it's *Joyce*." And he rushed me to her side.

She was just then disengaging from an elderly couple who took their leave to find seats. When she glanced over at us, she gave a polite smile, began to say something, then stopped short. With a gasp of recognition and a sparkle in her wide eyes, she asked, "*Marson?* Marson *Miles?*" And they fell into a hearty hug.

"Mother Hibbard!" said my husband. "What a remarkable co-incidence—of all people."

"*Stop* that." She smirked. Turning to me and offering her hand, she said, "I'm Joyce. And unless I'm mistaken, you must be ... Brody?"

I nodded. "Brody Norris. My pleasure, Joyce."

She eyed me up and down. "I've heard all about you."

Marson laughed. "Word travels fast—all the way from New York, I'll bet."

While Marson engaged in some quick catch-up with Joyce, I studied the woman, who had been accurately profiled by Glee Savage in Wednesday's local paper. Barely sixty, Joyce Hibbard was not only energetic, but *vital*. Her speech was quick and confident, exhibiting obvious intelligence. Consistent with her résumé in law and business, which had been detailed in the *Register*, she was a classic overachiever.

She also had a keen sense of fashion—which is saying something, for a priest. That evening she was dressed for business, in a gray skirt-and-jacket ensemble (it looked like Armani), set off with a priestly bib and Roman collar, not of black gabardine, but shocking mercurochrome silk. She dressed it up with a bit of gold bling, all of simple, tasteful design, nothing liturgical. And the finishing touch was the Cartier watch referenced in Glee's article—gold case and bracelet, diamond trim.

It was a warm evening, even more so in the crowded hall, and the stale air carried an olfactory stew of perfumes, colognes, and *eaux de toilette*. At close range, I winced at Joyce's fragrance, which was particularly pungent.

Marson was telling her, "So I'm afraid you're stuck with *me* tonight. Mary wanted to be here, but she had a commitment she couldn't break, at least not gracefully."

"Oh, dear. I had *so* hoped to get to know Mrs. Questman."

"And she's eager to meet *you*," Marson lied. "I'm here to 'take notes,' as it were. Sometime later, perhaps, we could all get together in a more social context. I'd be happy to introduce you."

"*Would* you, Marson? That would be lovely."

Marson said brightly, "I have an idea: I've been emailing with Curt, and he said he'll come out for a visit at some point, so maybe Brody and I could throw a little dinner party at our place, and we'll include Mary. It'll be a nice reunion for Curt and me after all these years; it'll also be a chance for you and Mary to connect."

"Perfect," said Joyce. Behind her thoughtful expression, I saw the gears turning.

"So," said Marson, "whenever Curt decides on his plans, just—"

Joyce interrupted, "As a matter of fact, I have an update. Curtis and I talked this afternoon, and it seems he suddenly misses me. He has some loose ends to tie up, but he wants to fly out here right away. He's arriving Sunday night."

Oh, brother. That same morning, Curtis Hibbard had sent Marson an email declaring he was *dying* to meet Marson's young husband—that would be me—and now Curtis was telling his wife that he was breathless to come visit her.

Marson's eye caught mine; his grin seconded my suspicion. Then he said to Joyce, "Let's see. Mary's planning a trip later next week, so we'll need to book our dinner fairly soon. Arbitrarily, how about... Tuesday?"

"Tuesday," agreed Joyce. "We're on."

Inside the parish hall, Marson and I got our bearings and looked for seats. Rows of gray metal folding chairs had been set up on either side of the doors, creating a wide center aisle where people milled and gabbed, making it difficult to distinguish which seats were available and which had been saved.

At the front of the room, a row of banquet tables was set up with about a dozen chairs facing the audience. Behind the table, which would seat the parish vestry, stood symmetrically placed staffs bearing the American flag and the Episcopal flag. Centered between them, on an otherwise bare wall of cement block, hung a small crucifix. Less than a foot high, it was so under-proportioned to the gaping space of the gym, it looked like an afterthought.

Typing on his phone, Marson said, "There. Checked with Mary. She's fine with Tuesday—not thrilled with it, but I promised to make the setup with Joyce as painless as possible."

"Well, good *evening*, gentlemen," said a voice from behind us.

We turned to find a tall, handsome man smiling at us—late twenties maybe, tousled flaxen hair, with a corn-fed hotness, arty to the max, a bit of a swish, and heavily perfumed. He looked familiar.

Then it clicked. "You're the choir director," I told him.

"Guilty," he said, flipping both hands. "David Lovell."

Marson and I greeted him, reintroducing ourselves, shaking hands. We had met him in this same hall at a reception following the funeral we'd attended in October. There wasn't much of a gay community in Dumont, so we had wondered if David's friendship might be worth nurturing. But life can be busy, and it never happened. David had recently sprung to mind, however, when Curtis Hibbard's lengthy email to Marson referred to "the studly young choirmaster, who was easy on the eyes."

"Know what?" I said, turning to Marson. "I think it might be a good idea to invite David to our little gathering on Tuesday night. Right now, it's dinner for five—might as well make it six."

"That's a *great* idea," said Marson. Turning to David, he explained that Mother Hibbard and her husband would be there, as well as Mary Questman. "Plus," he said, we'd like to get to know you."

"I'd *love* it," said David, all bubbly and adorable. When I asked how to reach him with details, he handed me his card, which listed contact information on the back. On the front side, a single elegant line: DAVID LOVELL, CHOIRMASTER.

The vestry members were drifting toward their table at the front of the room, so the crowd began to clear the aisle and take their seats.

Amid the jostling, I said hello to Thomas Simms, our dapper county sheriff, dressed impeccably, as always, in a dark business suit, immaculate white shirt, and a snappy striped-silk necktie.

With him were his wife, Gloria, and their son, Tommy, a second-grader who, I now recalled, sang in the St. Alban's choir. The Simmses were black—a distinct minority in Dumont. Sheriff Simms had once mentioned to me that they were the only black family at St. Alban's.

As we made our way across a crowded row of knees toward two empty seats at the far end, near the side wall, Marson paused to greet Dr. James Phelps, an old-time veterinarian who ran a one-man practice in a quaint, shingled office on the outskirts of town. Tonight he wore a corduroy sport coat with knotted-leather buttons and suede elbow patches. When I leaned to pat his shoulder and say hello, I got a whiff of the persnickety smell of his cherry pipe tobacco. Jim was Mary Questman's vet—or rather, Mister Puss's.

When we were at last seated and the babble of the crowd subsided, a metal chair clanged into position in the narrow space between me and the wall. And suddenly, there sat Glee Savage, hip to hip with me. "Room for one more, love?"

I told her wryly, "Seems so, yes."

She leaned across me to smooch Marson; I ducked as the wide brim of her hat grazed my hair. I smelled her scent, which she frequently switched. Her current selection was spicy, verging on bitter, reminding me of marijuana. I assumed it was patchouli.

Glee was the recognized fashionista of our timbered hinterland, having reported on all things cultural in the *Dumont Daily Register* for nearly four decades, so she rarely appeared in public without a big hat, big purse, big red lips, and big spike heels. Settling in, she snapped open the purse, removed a steno pad, and readied it on her lap, pen in hand.

Stupidly, I asked, "Working tonight?"

She gave me a look. "Let's hope they make this quick."

But something told me they wouldn't.

A gavel rapped.

Seated at the center of the front table was a bland-looking man in a drab business suit, not old, not young, maybe forty or so. An oblong brass placard identified him as BOB OLSON, SENIOR WARDEN. He stood, saying, "Let's start with a prayer."

Everyone stood as he began reciting, which the others picked up and recited with him. I didn't pray. Neither did Marson. Neither did Glee. She scribbled shorthand while leaning to tell me, "He's an accountant," which I presumed was meant to explain his dryness. She added, "Glad I'm not in *his* shoes," which I presumed was a reference to the financial plight of the ailing parish. Several people near us glanced in Glee's direction, as if to shush her, but if she noticed, she didn't let on.

Marson leaned over to tell both Glee and me, "Bob's a damned good money manager. St. Alban's is lucky to have him. In effect, the vestry's 'senior warden' is the board president."

"Amen." Bob Olson gestured for all to sit. A feisty toddler yelped. When his mother had reined him in, Bob continued, "Before we get down to the nitty-gritty of tonight's meeting, our rector would like to have a few words. Mother Hibbard?"

Joyce, seated next to Bob, arose from her chair and stepped around to the front of the table to address her flock at closer range. "My dear friends in Christ," she began, "during the short time that I have been entrusted with the care of your spiritual home ..."

I noticed at once that her manner of speech had changed. While gabbing in the lobby, her conversational tone was intelligent and proper, but now it was far more "elevated"—not only in the sense that public speaking requires a slower delivery, with greater projection, but more conspicuously, her tone had taken on an air of affectation. Her speech was now colored by a hint of British, as if she were an actor performing a role.

Marson noticed it, too. With a nudge of his elbow, he whispered to me, "Episcopalians—I think they're all anglophiles at heart."

"…so I seek your guidance tonight. As rector of St. Alban's, I am truly but a servant. I am here to serve your will—yours, and that of our esteemed vestry."

Glee turned to me. When I returned her gaze, she rolled her eyes.

To a smattering of applause, Joyce returned to her seat, next to Bob Olson.

Seated at Bob's other side was a prim little woman, identified by her placard as LILLIE MILLER, SECRETARY. Her stodgy, tweedy attire—dead wrong for a warm evening in May—made her appear frail and elderly, but her pleasant face and untroubled features suggested she was not that old, perhaps in her fifties. Bob asked her, "Could you read from the order of business, Lillie?"

She cleared her throat, lifted a printed page, and recited in a monotone: "May twelve. Special open session, parish vestry, St. Alban's Episcopal Church. The agenda contains a single item: Discussion and resolution of issues pertaining to the conditions of, and repair or replacement of, parish properties and structures. We note the presence of one invited speaker: Ms. Nia Butler, code-enforcement officer, City of Dumont."

"Very good," said Bob. "Officer Butler? I wonder if you could summarize for us the issues that bring us together tonight."

All heads turned toward the far end of the vestry table. In addition to Bob, Lillie Miller, and Mother Hibbard, another half-dozen vestry members fidgeted while clearing their throats and shuffling papers.

Nia Butler rose from her seat. A husky woman of color, thirty-something with a short-cropped Afro, she wore an olive twill uniform with an Eisenhower jacket that gave her the look of a motorcycle cop. White shirt, skinny black leather necktie. And incongruously, granny glasses. She strutted out from behind the table to face the assembly head on, feet spread, both thumbs hooked in her pockets.

Glee leaned to my ear. "In case you're wondering, sweets: yes, I do believe she's of the lesbian persuasion."

Someone behind us whispered through a hiss, "*Will* you shut up?"

We had caught the attention of Nia Butler, too, who glared at us from the front of the room. When at last she spoke, she did not mince words:

"You folks have one unholy *mess* on your hands here."

The upshot?

The abandoned school was a safety hazard that should probably be bulldozed, but because that building was not currently in use, the more immediate problem, which had to be addressed at once, was the church itself. Its state of structural disrepair had deteriorated greatly in recent years, and patchwork repairs would no longer cut it. Inspections revealed that the historic building was seriously out of compliance for public use. If remedial action was not undertaken quickly, the city would take steps to revoke the church's occupancy permit and perhaps even condemn it.

The assembled parishioners were thunderstruck. They'd known the old church needed work—it was halfway into its second century as home to their faith community—but they had not understood that St. Alban's was teetering on the verge of being *condemned*. It was beyond astonishing. It was unthinkable. So the meeting turned a bit raucous, at least for Episcopalians, who pride themselves more for their reserve than their zeal.

Amid the hubbub, a woman in the front row raised her hand. From the vestry table, Bob Olson said, "Yes, Angela?"

She stood. "I was wondering..."

Marson explained to me, "Angela is Bob's wife. Their daughter's name is Hailey."

Angela was pretty and blond, as was their daughter, who was maybe twelve or thirteen—not still a little girl, not yet a woman.

Angela was saying calmly, "…maybe if we could define our *options*, we'd be in a better position to decide how to move forward."

Perfectly reasonable, I thought.

"And I noticed," said Angela, "that Marson Miles is here tonight. I don't think he's a member of the parish, but he's an architect. Perhaps he could share some advice."

A murmur of interest rippled through the room as Bob looked about, asking, "Marson, are you here?"

My husband stood. "Here, Bob." Everyone looked in our direction.

With a weary smile, Bob said, "We've got a problem, Marson. If you were us, what would you do? What *can* we do?"

"First," said Marson, "I'd take Officer Butler at her word that the city inspections are correct in requiring drastic remedy—they know what they're doing. As for your options, there are only two. Both are costly, and both are disruptive. Option one: you can structurally restore and completely renovate the existing church. Or option two: you can raze—with a *z*, meaning demolish—raze the existing church and build something new, from a clean sheet. You'll need to study those options, compare the costs, and search your hearts for the right decision."

Joyce Hibbard asked Marson, "Do you think we should plan to move regular services out of the church?"

"Absolutely. As to when, that depends on how much leeway the city will allow. Meanwhile, tonight, I think you should organize into committees who will explore each option: Restore-and-renovate. Or raze-and-build." Marson sat.

A woman, the mother of the feisty toddler, shot to her feet and addressed the vestry without being recognized. "You *can't* be serious! How can you even *consider* the possibility of destroying that magnificent building?"

Bob Olson asked her, "Could you identify yourself, ma'am?"

Grudgingly, she told everyone, "I'm Kayla Weber Schmidt. No, I'm not a member of St. Alban's. But I *am* a member of both the Dumont Historical Society and the Wisconsin Preservationist League..."

Glee didn't bother whispering when she turned to tell me, "Look out for Kayla. She's a ballbuster."

Dark-haired and wiry, wearing a black jumpsuit, Kayla looked about thirty years old and spitting mad. She ignored her son, who wandered the center aisle, bumbled, and fell, whining. She ranted, "...and if you think for one second that we'll *allow* you to butcher a building of such historic significance, a designated landmark, a *protected* property—"

"Hold on," Bob said calmly. He asked anyone, "Does the church in fact have protected-landmark status?"

Joyce Hibbard shrugged. The other board members shrugged. Officer Nia Butler informed them, "No."

Kayla balled her fists. "You have *got* to be shitting me."

Bob said, "We've talked about it. Never got around to it. It sorta ties your hands."

"That's the *point!*" yelled Kayla.

Joyce stood, tugging the lapels of her jacket. "May I ask you to control yourself?"

A man rose from the far side of the hall and told the vestry members, "I've done plenty of repairs on that church, and it's a lost cause. Why, it's a miracle it's still standing. We need to start over—a 'clean sheet,' as Marson calls it."

Marson and I glanced at each other. It was Clem Carter of Carter Construction, the builder of our "perfect house." We hadn't

seen him earlier and were not aware he was a St. Alban's parishioner.

Turning to Kayla, Clem said, "Trust me, young lady—I know
what I'm talking about."

Kayla seethed at him. "Don't you dare 'young lady' *me*, Clem
Carter. It's more than obvious what *you're* up to. You see a nice, fat
construction project. You've got your greedy eye set on some easy
profits."

Clem shouted something as the crowd burst into conversation,
drowning him out. Kayla's little monster rolled on the floor, kick-
ing and shrieking in the throes of a full-bore tantrum. She shrilled
at him, "Jee-suss *Christ*, Aiden, give it a rest!" Marson buried his
face in his hands. Glee Savage snapped pictures with her phone.
Bob Olson pounded his gavel.

When an uneasy semblance of order had at last been restored,
Bob turned to the code-enforcement officer. "How long have we
got?" he asked her. "How long will the city give us to decide on
remedial action before you pull the church's occupancy permit?"

Nia Butler flipped through some papers in a manila folder. She
scrolled through something on her phone. Then she crossed her
arms. "End of the month," she said. "Tuesday, May thirty-first, just
shy of three weeks."

Bob gulped. "All right, then. Let's form our committees and set
some targets."

A sense of earnestness overtook the assembly as they got down
to business and moved forward with the work that needed to be
done. Volunteers eagerly signed up for various committees. Meetings were set, reports assigned, deadlines agreed to.

Mother Hibbard raised her arms and blessed the crowd with
words of benediction.

And then, in formally adjourning the meeting, Bob Olson reminded everyone, "We need to reach a difficult decision, and our

options are limited. There are only two: Restore-and-renovate. Or raze-and-build. I pledge my support for whichever direction the vestry and its committees select."

"A point of order, Mr. Olson?" said one of the vestry members, an older gentleman who had not previously spoken.

Bob turned to him. "Yes, Howard?"

"For the record, I think the minutes should reflect that, technically—realistically—we also have a third option."

No one, it seemed, wanted to ask about the third option.

But Howard said it anyway. "We could do nothing. Throw in the towel. Bring down the curtain and call it quits."

A dead silence came over the room.

St. Alban's had a church to redeem from its Gehenna of decay. On a brighter note, Marson and I had a dinner party to plan.

Being gay, we were good at this. Piece of cake. Marson was the consummate host, with an innate sense of timing and an eye for detail. We enjoyed entertaining at home, and our loft provided a setting of casual elegance with a touch of urban flair—no small feat in Dumont.

On Thursday evening, when Marson had first proposed the Tuesday dinner to Mother Hibbard, it was intended for five of us: Joyce and Curtis Hibbard, Marson and me, and Mary Questman. With such an intimate group, it would be a snap for Marson to do the cooking, for me to serve, and for both of us to clean up afterward. Only a few minutes later, however, we had added David Lovell, choirmaster, to the guest list.

Then, on Friday afternoon, Joyce phoned Marson to report an unexpected development: her husband, Curtis, had invited an old friend, Yevgeny, a ballet dancer (yes, *the* Yevgeny Krymov), to accompany Curtis on his visit to Wisconsin. Could we *possibly* include Yevgeny for dinner on Tuesday? Certainly, no problem at all, we'd be delighted.

On Saturday, Marson's predilection for symmetry and balance had kicked in, and he began perplexing over the challenge of setting a rectangular table for seven, with five men and two women. Although it would never be possible to achieve an even-numbered guest list with absolute boy-girl parity (not with two gay hosts), Marson wanted to smooth things out some by placing an additional rose among the thorns. So we invited our reporter pal, Glee Savage, who accepted with pleasure—not only had she become acquainted with Joyce Hibbard through the recent newspaper interview, but she had also been a close friend of Mary Questman for many years.

Which meant we would now be serving dinner for eight—no longer the easy-peasy evening that was first intended. We needed help. And we hadn't even *discussed* the menu yet.

Sunday morning, we popped over to First Avenue Bistro to beg the proprietor, Nancy Sanderson, to cater our dinner at home on Tuesday, and although it was short notice, she agreed. (Thank God. She was the town's only restaurateur who qualified as a true foodie.) She recommended a mixed grill for the main course as a sure way to please everyone, and we knew we were in good hands.

Later Sunday, Marson phoned Mary to let her know about the additions to the guest list. "Splendid," she said, "that'll make it all the easier for me to avoid that woman *priest*." Since the whole premise of the dinner party had been for Mary's benefit (meeting Mother Hibbard on neutral ground), Mary volunteered the services of her own housekeeper, Berta, to help with serving and cleanup. Marson had never much cared for Berta, whom he considered mouthy and impertinent, but some extra help wouldn't hurt, so he accepted the offer. "Oh!" said Mary as they were about to hang up. "I meant to ask: Would you mind *terribly* if I brought Mister Puss to the party? He'd *so* like to see you boys. And I made him promise he won't get underfoot."

Our homey little gathering had now grown from five, requiring no help, to ten, including a staff of two. Plus the cat.

Monday was nuts at the office, with constant calls to and from Nancy Sanderson regarding menu particulars and general logistics.

By Tuesday we were so stressed that neither of us bothered going into work. There were flowers to buy and arrange, wardrobe to press, silver and crystal to polish, toilets to scrub, music to select, a bar to be stocked, a table to set. And on and on.

That evening, we primped upstairs while Nancy and Berta fussed in the kitchen.

Gazing out over the edge of the mezzanine, I marveled that we had somehow managed to pull together a flawless setting for a lovely dinner at home among friends. The sun was setting in an amber sky beyond the front windows to the street. Between the two center windows, a three-foot section of brick wall rose from the floor to the twenty-foot ceiling, resembling a chimney; during our initial renovation of the space, Marson had designed a minimalist mantel and surround of feathered slate, resembling a fireplace—baldly artificial, yet wonderfully evocative. It contained several tiered rows of fluttering pillar candles, also fakes, but forgivably theatrical. Above the mantel hung a tall antique mirror. From the ceiling, a huge Mexican chandelier of punched tin hung squarely over the conversation area, casting playful starlight about the room. And directly beneath the railing where I stood, I peered down at the long black Parsons dining table, meticulously set for eight among a riotous arrangement of white flowers—tulips, roses, iris, anemones, lilac, alstroemerias, and several full-blown peonies the size of volleyballs.

"How do I look?"

I turned as Marson stepped out from the dressing room, looking especially handsome in a black mohair blazer and gray worsted slacks with a silvery silk shirt, open collar. He explained, "I decided to nix the tie."

"Good call." I was wearing a similar outfit, neutral colors, but with my sandy hair, I generally stuck to a warmer palette. I stepped over to kiss him and sniffed the touch of cologne on his neck. With a little groan, I said into his ear, "If we didn't have guests coming..."

"...and help in the kitchen," he reminded me. "Down, boy."

With an exaggerated whimper, I asked, "Maybe later?"

"Definitely later."

And I followed him down the spiral stairs.

Grrring.

The sputtering old twist bell at the loft's street door announced the arrival of the first of our guests. After two years of talking about replacing the bell with a modern, less grating update, I recognized that we never would.

Marson huddled in the kitchen with Berta and Nancy for some last-minute coaching while I answered the door.

There stood Glee Savage, dressed to the nines in a palette of jewel tones—emerald, sapphire, ruby—which coordinated nicely with her ancient fuchsia hatchback, parked at the curb. She whisked through the doorway bearing a wicker picnic hamper big enough to hold a baby.

"You shouldn't have," I said, leaning in for a big smooch, careful to avoid her glistening red lips.

"I did some baking this afternoon and got carried away with the cookies, so I decided to share the bounty. You can serve some with dessert—or tuck them all away for later."

Good idea, I thought. While Glee didn't fit anyone's notion of a Midwestern hausfrau—she was a professional woman, never married, with more interest in fashion than in domestic skills—she nonetheless could cook with the best of them. And she'd been mentored in the culinary arts only recently by none other than Mary Questman's housekeeper, Berta, who claimed that Glee "just took to it."

Berta had once confided to me that she and Mary Questman

sometimes enjoyed a little buzz from Berta's baked "treats," but I was reasonably confident our dinner guests would not be drugged that evening. Nancy Sanderson was in charge of the menu, which would include a fruit trifle for which she was renowned.

To the best of my knowledge, Glee Savage baked straight. I peeked inside the basket and saw what I hoped for—a generous supply of her signature cookies, peanut butter with chocolate chips and enormous whole cashews. These would not be shared tonight.

As I handed the basket off to Berta, Glee said, "Bert! I wasn't expecting you. They put you to work, huh?"

Berta gave Glee a wry look and trundled away with the cookies. She wore a crisp but homely gray maid's uniform and black service shoes.

Glee strolled to the middle of the main room, leaving a wake of her patchouli. *"Fabulous,"* she proclaimed, flinging her arms and twirling to take it all in. "And you boys make it look so *easy.*"

"You have no idea," I told her.

Marson had started some music—lively cocktail tunes, solo piano—and came over to greet Glee, who asked, "Well? Is the bar open?"

"Certainly, madam. This way, please." And he looped arms with her, walked her to the kitchen island, and popped a champagne cork.

"Nancy!" said Glee. "What's cookin'?"

Grrring.

Again, I played doorman. Swinging it wide, I found David Lovell at our stoop, standing tall and toothy, bearing an oblong box with the logo of a local florist. I shook his free hand and brought him in.

"My *gawd,*" he said, "this place is gorgeous. I've been *lusting* to see it."

I said, "We should have done this sooner—but glad you could

join us tonight." I took the box and looked inside. Long-stemmed red roses, well over a dozen. "This is far too generous, but thank you, David."

"Least I could do," he said, smiling, looking hunky in a smart silk suit of tight, modern cut—some youthful designer label, I wasn't sure which. He wore a heavy gold watch, maybe a Rolex, and drop-dead calfskin loafers that he had *not* found at the Target out by the highway. I'd had no idea that choirmastering was such a lucrative gig. And by all appearances, David was younger than thirty.

Marson came over to greet him, shaking hands. As they gabbed—David did a lot of talking with his hands, whipping the air—I noticed that he was again highly perfumed, as he had been at the parish meeting. Excusing myself, I said, "I think I'll put these in water."

In the kitchen, I dug out a cylindrical vase of clear glass and asked Glee to help me arrange David's flowers. As she worked on it between sips of champagne at the bar, I had a flash of inspiration and pulled a few of the red roses from the vase. I cut them short, then took them to the dining table, where I tucked them in among the profusion of white flowers, thinking they made a nice "hero element" in the composition—like drops of blood on a trail of snow.

Grrring.

This time, Marson answered the door, blurting, "My God, Curt—it's been at least thirty years. Welcome back to Wisconsin!"

"Ho-ho," said Curtis Hibbard, faking a laugh as he stepped inside. "Wis-*cahn*-sin. Your roots are showing, Marson."

Marson shrugged. "When in Rome…"

With a dubious chortle, Curtis straightened his tie, primped the knot. He wore a three-piece suit, deep blue, almost black. Spit-polished oxfords, black. Starched white shirt. Shaking Marson's hand, he said, "Good to see you again, old chum." He glanced about the loft, as if unsure what to make of it.

And then he spotted me.

Joyce Hibbard trailed in through the door as Curtis moved in my direction. Joyce was introducing Yevgeny Krymov to Marson as Curtis backed me up against the bar. He said, "Brody Norris, I presume. Curtis Hibbard. I've been *dying* to meet you." He offered his hand. I shook it. He held on to my hand with both of his, staring into my face like a cat sizing up a mouse. "I've heard so much about you," he said with breathy intensity, adding, "all of it completely true, I'm delighted to observe. And my God, those arrestingly green eyes. Astounding."

I noticed as he spoke that his tongue still carried the residual blue hue of mouthwash. His breath carried the freshly rinsed tang of mint. It mingled with the scent of his cologne, which was strong, spicy, and masculine, with a no-nonsense top note of citrus. I blinked the sting of the fragrance from those arrestingly green eyes of mine.

"Pleased to meet you, Curtis." I disengaged my hand from his as Marson, all smiles, approached with Joyce and Yevgeny. Introductions were made. Marson drifted off with Joyce and Curtis, approaching Glee Savage and David Lovell.

And then Yevgeny made *his* move on me. He wore a high-cut black bolero jacket, which showed off a stunning ass that could have bested the posterior of even the most sultry of fantasized matadors.

"I am so very pleased to meet you," he said, low and throaty. Although he had defected from Russia nearly forty years earlier, during the Cold War, he had not entirely lost his accent, and his speech carried the prim syntax of a nonnative speaker. He backed me up against the bar, as Curtis had, but stood even nearer to me—so close that one of his thighs pressed against mine.

Though retired from the stage, he still had the ropy musculature of a world-class dancer, and I was aroused by the feel of his powerful leg. With no whiff of cologne between us, I smelled only his musk and sweat. While Curtis Hibbard's come-on had left me, in a word, repulsed, Yevgeny's advance was having its intended effect.

"You have such *dah*-link eyes," he said with a smile I was tempted to kiss.

"Thank you," I said, sounding nervous as a schoolgirl. "I've been told that."

Since adolescence, I had found myself attracted to older, creative men. My previous husband, in California, was an architect, considerably older than I was. Ditto for Marson, my current love. While I was growing up, my lesbian mother had surrounded me with her circle of arty friends, including a buff ballet master, who taught me, when I was eight, to perform an energetic zapateado with him. And now, pressed against me in my own home was the legendary Yevgeny Krymov, age fifty-six (I'd Googled him). With his intense Muscovy stare, he seemed to be asking, Shall we dance?

Then his gaze shifted.

I tapped my nose, as if to remind him, We were talking about my eyes.

But he'd lost his focus. I glanced to the side, following his stare, and saw that he was watching Curtis Hibbard, who had pinned the comely David Lovell, ten years my junior, against the refrigerator. Yevgeny's eyes widened. "Excuse me," he said, moving off in their direction, on the hunt for fresher game.

Just when things were heating up, he'd dumped me like a day-old paskha.

Grrring.

With nothing better to do, I ambled from the bar to the door. When I opened it, my jilt-funk evaporated. "Mary," I said brightly, "and Mister Puss." The cat was in her arms, wearing the ridiculous paw-print harness, tangled with the nylon leash. I asked, "Are we ready for a party?"

Exchanging cheek kisses with me, Mary heaved a little sigh. "Brody love, I'm sorry to be late, but I've been putting it off till the last possible minute."

I checked my watch; it was half past the cocktail hour. "You'll be fine. You're among friends. Welcome."

Mary stepped inside and set the cat on the floor as I shut the door. She leaned to ask me, "Is *she* here—the priest?"

With a soft laugh, I said, "Over there. Don't fret. Marson will stand guard."

Resigned, Mary took a few steps into the room, holding the leash, but Mister Puss wouldn't cooperate, sliding a few inches on the polished concrete floor.

"Here," I said, "let me take care of him." I scooped the cat up into my arms.

Mary thanked me and stepped bravely into the fray.

Help me.

"My pleasure." I untangled the leash and unclipped it from the vest. Then I set Mister Puss on the floor and freed him from his bonds. He stretched, preening his fur as I set the offending paraphernalia on a console near the door.

When I picked him up again, he purred. We ventured into the gathering.

Music played. Ice rattled in glasses. Laughter punctuated the ebb and flow of conversation as Nancy Sanderson and Berta circulated through the living room, refreshing drinks and passing trays of delicate nibbles—brioche rounds with crème fraîche and caviar; carrot roulades with goat cheese; blini with quail eggs and tarragon.

Predictably, Mister Puss preferred the caviar to the eggs and was bewildered by the carrots. To be polite and tidy, I ate what he refused as we mingled. And I quickly discovered that the novelty of an exotic cat at a cocktail party never left our guests at a loss for words.

"He's *adorable*," said David Lovell, momentarily free from the competitive advances of Curtis and Yevgeny. He twiddled Mister Puss under the chin, eliciting a grateful purr. "Siamese?"

"Nope," I told him, "Abyssinian. Highly intelligent. Talkative, too."

Meow.

David laughed as Nancy stepped over to us with the tray of appetizers.

I told her, "Everything's wonderful, Nancy. Can't thank you enough for saving the evening—for *making* the evening." I helped myself to another bit of caviar, saving it for the cat.

"Glad you're pleased, Brody. Nice party." She offered a faint, courteous smile.

She seemed a little off that night. The food and the service could not have been better, but her mood seemed, for lack of a better word, strained. Which was understandable—Marson and I had felt stressed for days.

Marson had known Nancy for many years, as he was a long-standing patron of her restaurant. Although we both thought of her as a friend, we didn't have much connection beyond food and dining. A nice-looking woman in her fifties, she worked hard, kept her customers happy, and always had something pleasant to say.

David set his cocktail napkin, with an uneaten appetizer, on Nancy's tray. "I don't think I'll finish that, if you don't mind."

"No worries, David. No nuts." Her tone seemed oddly miffed.

"Not *that*," he explained with a chuckle. "Want to save myself for the main event. I'm sure it'll be wonderful."

With the slightest nod, she left us. I must have looked puzzled.

Free of the appetizer, David could now talk with both hands. "Nut allergy," he told me, aflutter. "But Nancy always looks out for me. She's a doll. And speaking of dolls, do you suppose I could hold this *magnificent* little creature?"

"Mister Puss," I said, "you have a new admirer. Let me introduce you to David Lovell." The cat gave me a wary look as I handed him over.

"Hello there, darlin," David said as he cradled the cat in his arms. "Aren't you a *special* boy?"

David apparently passed muster. Mister Puss purred loudly and climbed to David's shoulder, nuzzling his chin. Then the cat slid his snout up the side of David's face, working his way to David's ear.

Mister Puss sneezed.

"Whoops," said David. "Sorry, pussycat." Handing Mister Puss back to me, he explained. "I get carried away with fragrances sometimes—can't seem to smell it on myself. But I guess I overdid it."

"Not at all," I lied. "It's ... interesting."

"It's called 'Chad!' With an exclamation point. Isn't it *fabulous*?" And David moved off to mingle.

Purring, Mister Puss climbed to my ear.

He smells like a fruitcake.

Knowing that Mary Questman would not like to be stuck next to Joyce Hibbard at dinner, Marson and I decided to use place cards, assigning the women the "honor" of commanding opposite ends of the oblong table, which ran lengthwise between the kitchen and living room. Marson and I placed ourselves on the less desirable side of the table, facing the kitchen, with David Lovell seated between us. We assigned the better side, looking out toward the street windows, to Glee Savage and Curtis Hibbard, with Yevgeny between them. We all gabbed while enjoying Nancy's delightful vichyssoise, which provided a cool, refreshing start to our dinner on that warm evening.

Glee was saying to Yevgeny, next to her, "It's not often, Mr. Krymov, that we have someone of *your* stature visiting Dumont. It would be *such* an honor if you'd consent to an interview for our local paper."

"You flatter me, Miss Savage. I cannot imagine your people of Dumont have any interest in my story."

"Dumont," said Curtis wistfully from Yevgeny's other side. "Ho-ho. It's a long way from Stuttgart. Let alone Moscow."

Glee dared to touch Yevgeny's wrist, near her hand on the table. "Oh, *please?*" Begging wasn't Glee's style—at all—but she'd never found herself sitting beside a fabled dancer who'd been hailed by the *New York Times* as "artistic heir to the legacies of Nijinsky and Nureyev."

Yevgeny reconsidered, telling Glee, "Then, perhaps." He took her hand and held her fingers briefly before returning to his soup.

Seated directly across from Glee, I saw a vacant look in her eyes and feared she might collapse beneath the table.

At the end of the table, seated adjacent to both Glee and me, Mary said, "How delightful. It seems our sleepy little Dumont is finally growing up. We've already established the theater complex, and now we have the great honor of knowing Mr. Yevgeny, a true artist *par excellence.*"

"Hear, hear," said Marson.

"Mary," said Joyce Hibbard from the opposite end of the table, "it's no secret that *your* passion for the arts has been the catalyst for Dumont's cultural growth. From what I hear, the whole town is indebted to your sense of civic duty and philanthropy."

Here we go, I thought.

Nancy's mixed grill, the main course of our meal, consisted

of generous portions of beef tenderloin, chops of spring lamb, skewers of colossal shrimp, and hearty croquettes of fresh salmon. Nancy and Berta circled the table with trays, allowing each guest to choose any or all of the items. Then vegetables and sauces were passed while Marson played sommelier, pouring each guest's choice of red or white wine, or both.

The vichyssoise had been of no interest to Mister Puss, who perched halfway up the spiral staircase, where he could keep a bird's-eye view on everyone. But the arrival of the meat and fish triggered another reaction altogether, bringing him down the stairs at a trot. I recalled Mary assuring us that Mister Puss had promised not to get underfoot that night, and I was relieved to note that he was true to his word. Posing no threat of tripping Nancy or Berta as they served, he simply slipped under the table and stationed himself at the corner between Mary and me, where he could peep up at each of us. He knew his easy marks.

When everyone was settled, with the help retreated to the kitchen, Marson called them back briefly and toasted their efforts. Then our guests toasted Marson and me as their hosts. With the civilities attended to, everyone could then enjoy not only their dinner but also the pleasures of adult conversation.

I cut a small square from the rare center of my beef tenderloin and slipped it to Mister Puss, seated at my ankle. His purr didn't stop while devouring it, but intensified to a loud gurgle that resembled a miniature roar. Mary shot me a smile, then dangled to Mister Puss the plump end of a shrimp.

Joyce Hibbard was saying, "…and I understand that the Questman family practically *built* St. Alban's, so many years ago. What a marvelous heritage."

Mary reminded Joyce, "That was well over a century ago. I may be old, but I wasn't around."

Joyce tittered. "Well, I certainly didn't mean to imply *that*."

Mary took it a step further. "And although my late husband's family played some role in founding the parish, the Questmans alone didn't build the church. It was a community effort."

"Of course," agreed Joyce.

Marson stepped in. "It's no secret that St. Alban's now faces some tremendous challenges, as well as a major decision: repair the old church, or build a new one." As he spoke, he leaned to his side to offer a scrap of something to the cat.

Mister Puss shot to Marson's chair. When he finished, he moved to Joyce, who also fed the cat a morsel.

She was saying, "...with a bit of divine guidance and with prayerful deliberation, I have faith that the St. Alban's family is up to these challenges. As Philippians tells us: In Christ, all things are possible."

"Ho-ho," said Curtis Hibbard. "You're laying it on a bit thick, aren't you, Poopsie?"

Mister Puss sauntered over to Curtis, but no food was offered, so the cat settled under his chair.

Joyce set down her fork and turned to her husband. "I know you've questioned my calling to the priesthood, and to a degree, I understand your skepticism." She told the rest of the table, "But faith is a journey. We often face unexpected and mysterious turns along the path to enlightenment."

Quack.

Joyce's eyes shot back to her husband. "Really, Curtis, there's no need to be rude."

He sputtered, "Poopsie, I...I would *never...*"

Mister Puss emerged from beneath Curtis's chair and traipsed around the table to Mary, who invited the cat up to her lap.

Somberly, Joyce said to Mary, "St. Alban's now finds itself at a crossroads."

The cat finished eating a wad of shrimp from Mary's fingers

and, purring, stretched his snout to nuzzle her chin—then her ear.

Joyce continued, "And the sad reality is that the future of our historic parish will depend upon the availability of funding. At times such as these, therefore—"

Mary blurted a jolly laugh.

Taken aback, Joyce asked, "Is it something I said?"

"*No,*" said Mary, still laughing, "it's something Mister Puss keeps telling me."

A sudden stillness fell over the table. Marson, Glee, and I were well aware of the special rapport between Mary and Mister Puss, but the others were newbies to this.

Tentatively, Joyce asked, "Your cat... *tells* you things?"

"Yes, Joyce, he does. When it comes to St Alban's, he's told me more than once, and I quote: 'Hold on to your wallet.'"

Dead silence. Then Curtis cleared his throat. "Your cat may have a point."

Mary held Joyce's gaze with a steady stare that tethered them across the length of the table. She asked the priest, "Know what else Mister Puss told me? It changed my life when he told me, and I quote: 'God is a myth.'"

Joyce closed her eyes. I recalled what Curtis had written in his long email: that his wife could no longer admit her own skepticism, having teamed up for the hocus-pocus.

Yevgeny turned to Mary. "I agree with cat, dear lady. God is Santa Claus for adults—old man in sky brings shiny gifts, or lumps of coal. Bah. Is crazy."

I figured that Yevgeny must have acquired that analogy during his Soviet school days. My proudly heathen mother had taught me a similar parallelism.

Curtis had been eyeing David Lovell across the table; for all I knew, they were playing footsie. Curtis said, "What does the talented young choirmaster think about this?"

David hadn't spoken much since we'd sat down to dinner, so all heads turned in his direction. Like a deer in the headlights, he said, "I'm afraid I don't know. I believe in the traditions. I believe in the *idea* of God, the *idea* of religion. But most of all, I like the music." He told Mother Hibbard, "Sorry if that seems lame. Or unworthy."

She dismissed his concern with a soft smile and the slightest shake of her head.

"Fortunately," David explained, "I don't need to work, but I love what I do. And it sure beats the hassles with my brother, Geoff—who's been threatening a visit."

"Really?" said Curtis, tantalized. "I didn't realize there was more than one of *you.*"

"Trust me. We're nothing alike."

Joyce said to David, "The organ. With all the upheaval that's ahead for us, do you think the organ can be saved? Is it *worth* saving?"

"Absolutely. It's a three-manual Möller, built in Maryland in the early 1900s. St. Alban's didn't scrimp on that one; it even has a celesta, *fabulous* for Christmas. It could use some restoration—cleaning, tuning, releathering the motorized bellows—but with a little TLC, it should be all set for another hundred years."

We learned that since the sudden retirement of St. Alban's previous rector, the doddering Rev. Charles Sterling, the parish had also lost its longtime organist, the equally doddering Arthur Wimbly, who had fled with Father Sterling to Montserrat, where they had set up house together. Meanwhile, David Lovell, choir-master, had been pinch-hitting as organist as well. He explained, "Organ is *not* my forte, and the situation is less than ideal, but as a stopgap, it's fine. And I must admit, it's a thrill to take command of the 'king of instruments' and make that sucker sing."

I said, "Aren't they amazing? Pipe organs—these mechanical

behemoths, so majestic, with a history stretching back for centuries."

Marson said, "I never knew you had such a passion for them."

"Back in college, I had a roommate one year who was a music major, an organist. So sometimes, I'd go along with him when he practiced, just to listen. Then, when he gave recitals, he'd ask me to help out—turning pages, pulling stops, and so on."

Yevgeny asked David, "You are familiar with Fletcher Zaan?"

"Well, *sure*," said David. "One of the all-time greats."

"Perhaps I introduce you sometime. Or perhaps not." He winked.

Curtis explained, "Yevgeny and Fletcher have been doing the dirty fugue for many years now—I hear he's clever with his feet. It's a long, sordid story."

"Gosh," said David, wide-eyed.

Curtis continued, "And since your forte is not organs, but singing, I assume you're familiar with Renée Fleming."

David gasped so deeply, I thought he might swoon. "I have *all* of her recordings, but I've never seen her perform. Don't tell me you *know* her!"

"Afraid not," said Curtis, examining his manicured fingernails. "But I *do* have tickets to a special concert at Carnegie Hall that's being billed as 'an historic event.'"

David gasped again.

Flapping his hands, he asked, "The *Beethoven*? The Ninth. The 'Choral.' Featuring a massive chorus assembled for one night only. With that *stratospheric* roster of soloists—ranging from bass René Pape to soprano Renée Fleming. Oh, my *gawd*. In my dreams."

Curtis pounced: "Would you like to go with me?"

David fell back in his chair, trying to catch his breath.

Yevgeny turned to Curtis. "That was supposed to be *my* ticket."

Curtis flicked an imaginary speck of lint from his lapel. "So

I'm an Indian giver." He told David, "It's a week from Sunday, the twenty-ninth."

David reminded him, "But I *work* on Sundays."

"Sunday *mornings*," said Curtis. "I'll book you on a noon flight, have a car meet you at JFK, and get you back to the penthouse in plenty of time to freshen up before the eight-o'clock curtain. Stay a few days, if you like. You can use our guest room and I'll show you the town."

"Curtis!" said his wife, seething. "Must you be so damn obvious? I've cut you a lot of slack over the years, but I have a right to a modicum of respect here in Dumont. Think of my *position*."

"We'll talk about it, Poopsie. But not here, not now." Curtis then winked at David, as if to say, Pack your bags.

The table was quiet as Berta and Nancy cleared the main course in anticipation of the fruit trifle. Mary appeared to be deep in thought. She hadn't said a word since before the flap over Renée Fleming, which she didn't even seem to notice.

"Joyce?" she said pensively. We all looked in her direction. Mister Puss sat in her lap, purring, as she stroked the nape of his neck.

"Yes, Mary?"

"Earlier, I didn't mean to cut you off—with my beliefs, or *lack* of them. As you know, in recent years, I've taken great pleasure in making a *difference* in our lovely little town. I'm also well aware that St. Alban's has long been a force of good here, regardless of how I may feel about faith issues per se. And I know that you're facing difficult times with the parish. So what I'm trying to say is: I might be persuaded to consider your needs, but only if Marson deems the project to have sufficient *artistic* merit. I'm far more interested in your aesthetic impact on the downtown commons than I am in your mission. Fair enough?"

Joyce Hibbard's mouth twitched, as if trying to suppress a grin.

Curtis turned to his wife with a sly smile, as if to say, Reel her in, Poopsie.

Joyce said, "Of *course*, Mary. That's more than fair. And woman to woman, I must say that I appreciate your candor." She turned to Marson, seated next to her. "Well? Are you willing to—shall we say—intercede in this matter?"

My husband replied, "For Mary, certainly. I'd be happy to give her my honest assessment of the project's merits. But first things first—you'll need to reach a decision on which direction to take. Restore and repair? Or build from scratch?"

"Exactly," said Joyce. "If you have some time tomorrow, maybe you could come over to the rectory. We could dig into some files together, then walk through the property and maybe start talking some numbers. Is one-thirty good for you?"

"Perfect," said Marson.

"Perfect," said Joyce. "I'm feeling better already. Progress!"

"Perfect," agreed Mary. Offhandedly, she added, "But it goes without saying that Mister Puss will have the final word on the matter."

The cat looked up from Mary's lap, lavishing his mistress with an adoring gaze. Then his head slowly turned, riveting Mother Hibbard with a cold stare that wiped the grin off her face.

As the meal concluded, our guests were lavish with their thanks and compliments, even offering Nancy Sanderson and Berta a round of applause for a job well done.

Glee Savage was first to leave, as she had an early appointment on Wednesday.

Yevgeny was next. Although he had arrived with the Hibbards, he was not staying with them at the rectory and decided to get some exercise, walking to the Manor House, a posh bed-and-breakfast that had been converted from one of the mansions built by the town's early elite, a few blocks away on Prairie Street. Watching him leave, I couldn't help wondering, Why is he here? It seemed odd that he would venture to Dumont merely to keep Curtis company; they could see each other anytime in New York. In addition to this point of curiosity, I also felt an unmistakable twinge of attraction—Yevgeny was one hot man.

Mary was fussing with Mister Puss, getting him into his harness and leash, while Joyce and Curtis Hibbard lingered near the door. Marson and Curtis engaged in some backslapping and reminiscing, happy to reconnect after so many years, but as far as I was concerned, the sooner Curtis left, the better.

Mary toddled over with Mister Puss cradled in one arm; he refused, as before, to be walked in that hideous vest. Mary had warmed some to Joyce Hibbard—not much, but a little—so she offered a hug in parting, with the cat as a buffer. Mary said, "Oh, my. I *do* like your perfume, Joyce. What is it?"

I thought it was overpowering. I'd had the same reaction the night I met Joyce at the parish meeting.

She explained, "During my years in the fashion industry, I developed a line of cosmetics, as well as this fragrance. It's discontinued now, but I've always liked it, so I keep a personal stash for my own use."

"Ho-ho," said Curtis. "I call it her 'secret sauce.'"

I was getting annoyed by that fake laugh of his. He could leave now.

And he did, along with Joyce, Mary, and Mister Puss, who retreated into the night.

David Lovell had hung behind. "Guys," he said, hands aflutter, "I *cannot* thank you enough for asking me here tonight. The place is gorgeous, the meal was fabulous, and you two are *the* best. Plus—" He paused for a deep breath, eyes closed.

"Let me guess," said Marson. "Renée Fleming?"

David squealed. No words were necessary.

When David arrived, he had greeted us with handshakes. Now though, standing at the door, it was time for hugs. David wasn't shy about it. He wrapped his arms around Marson and gave him a tight squeeze. Then it was my turn. As I leaned into David's embrace, cheek to cheek, I noted that Mister Puss had hit the nail on the head.

David did indeed smell like a fruitcake.

Wednesday, the long streak of bright, lusty May weather was broken by a day that turned gray and muggy, threatening rain. Marson and I had no lunch appointments, so we decided to walk from the office to First Avenue Bistro. Because it was nearby and consistently good, the Bistro had become our default lunch destination when we had no other plans. Plus, we wanted to thank Nancy Sanderson again for stepping in on such short notice to take culinary command of the prior evening's dinner party, which everyone had agreed was splendid.

"I was happy to do it," she said as Marson and I were finishing lunch. With a soft laugh, she leaned low to confide to us, "You two know how to *entertain*. Most of my customers don't have a clue." She gave us a wink and moved to chat with another table.

I said to Marson, "She seems in good spirits today. Last night—a little moody."

Marson reminded me, "We were *all* a bit stressed. But all's well that ends well."

When we left the restaurant and stepped out to the street, I checked my watch. "You're about due at St. Alban's. Mind if I tag along?"

"I was about to make that exact suggestion. This appointment has the markings of a dreary afternoon."

"Uh-huh. And misery loves company, right?"

"In *your* company," he said, "I could never be miserable." As corny as he sounded, I knew he meant it; I felt the same way about him.

But in truth, I questioned my own motives for wanting to tag along. Certainly, I enjoyed the company of my husband—anywhere, anytime. Equally, I was intrigued by the dilemma faced by Mother Hibbard and her parish, and I wondered how they might resolve it. At another level—and this is what made me uncomfortable—I had been nagged through the night by thoughts of Yevgeny Krymov, by the sense memory of his muscular leg pressed against mine, and while I knew he was forbidden fruit, I was intrigued by the notion that he might be hanging around St. Alban's with Mother Hibbard's husband. Shame on me. But underlying all of these considerations, there was something else. There was something in the air. Literally.

During the time we were at lunch, the iffy weather had worsened. The muggy air had grown sultry. And it smelled. It was not the whiff of approaching rain—not exactly, though that was a fair bet. Rather, the stagnant air hung heavy with the dross of stale breath. The sky seemed to sag and wheeze, bloated by a troubled atmosphere of foreboding and heat.

As we walked along First Avenue, headed toward the parklike setting of the commons, I took off my sport coat and carried it, draped over an arm.

Marson left his on.

Joyce Hibbard greeted us at the rectory door and showed us inside. Standing in the front hall, she said, "I wasn't expecting both of you, but it's wonderful you're here, Brody. Three heads are better than one, considering the challenges ahead ..."

I wasn't really listening while I scoped out the surroundings. It was a dark old house, dignified but in no sense lavish—lots of wood paneling, stained and waxed, with carved ornamentation along the cornice and below the chair rail. The light fixtures were all fitted with glass tinted a cloudy amber, either by design or by the yellowing passage of many years. All was quiet, the sort of environs in which a grandfather clock might be heard ticking in another room, but no, there was no such clock. I glanced into what appeared to be the main parlor; if I was thinking I might spot Curtis and Yevgeny together in there, reading poetry or playing cribbage or sipping an afternoon espresso, I was wrong.

"Please," said Joyce, "come into my office," and she led us through a carved pair of sliding doors.

Her office was brighter than the rest of the house, without the antique heaviness. Her sleek Apple computer and minimalist Breuer desk chairs—chrome and black leather—stood in striking contrast to the rectory's stuffy liturgical ambience. I noticed a small side office through a doorway in a wall of bookcases, where a woman worked at a desk. When she peeped out at us, I recognized Lillie Miller, the parish secretary, who had sat at the vestry table during the prior week's open meeting.

Joyce seated herself behind her desk as Marson and I settled into a pair of chairs facing her. She jogged a stack of file folders on the glass desktop, preparing to speak.

But then Lillie stepped into the room, carrying her purse, her keys, a folding umbrella, and a tidy canvas tote bag stuffed with this and that. "Excuse me, Mother Hibbard—good afternoon, gentlemen—I need to dash out on a few errands, and I also have my practice session with David. I'll be gone for an hour or so, two at most, unless you need me for anything." She sounded a bit dotty, but earnest.

Joyce said, "That's fine, Lillie. And you'll stop at the post office?"

"Oops. Yes, of course." She skittered back into her office, then returned, stuffing a few envelopes into her tote. With a bob of her head, she turned to leave.

Curiosity got the better of me. I asked, "Practice with David? You're in the choir?"

With a shy laugh, she explained, "Heavens no, sir. I couldn't carry a tune if my *life* depended on it. Our organist retired, and David's filling in for him, but with some of the more involved pieces, he can't handle both the choir *and* the organ, so he asked me to help out. I'm not much good at it, but I couldn't say no—not to *David*. So he arranges simple accompaniments, then helps me practice, and we sort of muddle through."

Joyce assured her, "You do a beautiful job. And we're all grateful for the effort you put into it."

Blushing, Lillie stepped out of the office and left the rectory through the front door.

Joyce waited until the lock clicked shut in the hall. Through a grossly pained expression, she told us, "She's a terrible organist. Truly *lousy*." Then Joyce's countenance brightened. "But thanks to the deadline imposed by the city, after two more Sundays we won't be hearing that wretched organ for a while."

Despite Joyce's attempt to find a silver lining in the city's ultimatum, it was scant consolation for the looming crisis faced by the parish, so we got to work.

Joyce reviewed for us the history and condition of each of the parish buildings—church, rectory, school, and the newer gymnasium building now used as the parish hall. She unrolled in front of us a detailed plat map of the parish grounds, showing setbacks and easements, as well as the precise location of existing buildings. She opened her files to show us tax records, property assessments, operating budgets, dwindling membership rolls, and the yearly progression of expenses to cover maintenance and repairs, which was daunting.

After nearly an hour of focusing on mind-numbing minutiae,

Marson stepped back for the bigger picture, telling Joyce, "Any way you slice it, by the end of this month, your existing church is off-limits. Fortunately, you can start holding services in the parish hall. So at least you're not thrown out on the street or stuck in a tent. But obviously, you need and want a permanent solution, preferably one that's handsome and inspiring, not just 'up to code.' And realistically, there are only two possibilities."

Joyce nodded. "Thoroughly restore the old church. Or build a new one—either on the footprint of the old church or elsewhere on the parish property."

"Luckily," I said, "you have some flexibility if you decide to build." Tapping the plat map on the desk, I pointed out, "You have a lot of land here, and if the school comes down, you'll have even more."

Joyce agreed, "Space isn't the issue. The issue is money."

"Right," said Marson. "And considering only the cost issue, I think your two options are essentially a wash. Historical restoration, done right, is expensive, but at least you'd already *have* a building, so you're not starting from scratch. On the other hand, to my way of thinking, it's far more satisfying to spend funds designing and building correctly from the outset—from a clean sheet—rather than throwing good money at fixing old problems. Others will disagree. So in this case, it's not a matter of dollars, but philosophy."

"Okay," she said, "philosophy aside, since the expenses are likely similar—how much? In very round figures."

Dazed by the question, Marson replied, "Without a *lot* more input—without establishing the basic parameters of the project—it's impossible to say."

She reminded him, "Whichever way we go, we already have the land."

"Right," said Marson, "good point. Which ought to leave you

on the hook for something in the neighborhood of..." Marson twirled a hand, eyes to the ceiling.

Then he ballparked the millions.

Mother Hibbard winced. "God help us," she muttered.

Through the office windows, the afternoon sky had darkened.

Round figures can be sobering, especially in the round millions. Mother Hibbard suggested, "Shall we get a bit of air? Let's take a tour of the grounds." She reached for a large ring of keys.

Saying nothing, Marson and I followed her out of the office, through the entry hall, and out the front door of the rectory.

The air was still. The grounds were quiet. Even the birds were hushed, not bothering to sing for rain; they must have sensed the inevitable. Our shoes crunched the path of pea gravel as we rounded the side of the rectory and skirted the abandoned playground next to the red brick school building. A set of rusted swings hung rigidly vertical, like brittle fossils from some distant culture, long vanished and forgotten.

Joyce told us, "I can show you inside the school, but I'm warning you—it's a fright."

I stopped in my tracks and cocked my head, away from the school, wondering aloud, "What's that?"

"What, kiddo?" asked Marson.

"That sound. Do you hear it?"

Joyce's features wrinkled. "That *is* odd. A siren somewhere?"

Now Marson heard it. "Strange. It's more like ... like *bagpipes* or something."

Walking in the general direction of the eerie sound, which intensified, we found ourselves nearing the church from its ungainly rear wall.

Joyce's keys rattled as we hustled along the side of the building, moving toward the street. The row of arched Tiffany windows had their bottom ventilator panels flopped open, from which we could hear the sustained, discordant bray of the organ; we also saw smoke and sniffed the piercing licorice smell of myrrh.

"*Jesus,*" said Joyce as we scuttled around to the front of the church, facing the commons.

I led the charge up the worn limestone steps to the crimson doors, asking Joyce over my shoulder, "Do we need the key?"

"It shouldn't be locked."

But it was.

We fumbled at the door, got it open, then dashed through the vestibule, through the inside doors, and into the yawning space of the nave.

Joyce, Marson, and I froze, gaping in disbelief as we took it all in.

The air was thick with incense and gray with its smoke, which clouded the windows and assaulted my lungs. The bitter smell reminded me of Glee Savage's patchouli, but far more intense and stinging. The source was shockingly obvious: halfway down the center aisle, the red carpet runner had begun to burn where an ornate brass thurible—the censer with a lid and chains, normally swung during worship services—now lay tossed aside, spewing glowing coals and a grainy mound of myrrh, frankincense, and God knows what else.

Marson asked Joyce about fire extinguishers, she pointed to one, and they both ran off to fetch it.

All the more shocking, however, was the sight and sound of David Lovell, up near the sanctuary, collapsed at the bench of the hundred-year-old Möller organ, splayed facedown on the keys of its three manuals. Rank upon rank of towering pipes joined voices to blare a hideous, nasal shriek.

"David!" I shouted, running to the console, fearing he would not respond.

My pace slowed as I neared. I could see that he had vomited, adding another layer of stench to the noxious scene. The top of the console was cluttered with stacks of sheet music, a bag of chips, plate of cookies, bottle of water, David's phone and keys, a notebook, pencils. I reached beneath David's chin, trying to find a pulse, but I could not. So I tried to lift him upright on the bench, but his limp body would not cooperate. Sliding on the polished wood, his full weight dropped to the pedalboard.

Abruptly, David's freakish farewell recital modulated from the upper registers to the lowest of lows. The full complement of huge bass pipes disgorged a continuous groan and rumble. David's bluish face seemed to stare up at me, though his eyes had swollen shut; his puffy lips were ringed with hives. As I attempted to tug him from the pedalboard, one of his knees lodged into the crescendo pedal.

The whole building rattled. My stomach shook as I tried to turn off the bellows pump, but virtually no two pipe organs are identical, so I couldn't find the switch among the dizzying rows of stop knobs. Although St. Alban's organ was indeed an antique keyboard instrument, its console more closely resembled the cockpit of a B-52, leaving me clueless.

And then, it blew.

With a final, thunderous gasp, the beast fell silent, spewing from its majestic row of façade pipes a shower of dust and grit, the accumulated grime of a century of hallelujahs.

Joyce screamed. With a clang, Marson tossed aside the spent fire extinguisher and rushed to my side. The pile of coals and incense hissed, smothered by a pool of foam. Outside, the rain had started, pelting hard against the barnlike roof of the old church. The organ's blower still ran, flapping the leather scraps of the bellows.

Hunched in one of the pews, Joyce phoned nine-one-one.

Slumping on the edge of the organ bench, I phoned the sheriff's office and asked to speak to Thomas Simms.

While I waited, the first few drips began to leak from the rotten rafters.

"Thomas," I said, "this is weird as hell. I think you'd better get over here."

PART TWO

Mother Hibbard's Secret Sauce

Mary Questman hadn't heard about it. She'd spent a quiet evening at home on Wednesday, reading, as the rain continued into the night. So she was unprepared for the news on Thursday morning.

She awoke as usual, sometime before seven, with Mister Puss sharing her pillow, nesting against her hair. The curtains at one of the bedroom windows were not fully closed, admitting a shaft of sunlight that angled across the foot of her bed. How nice, she thought. The storm had passed.

Getting out of bed, taking care not to disturb Mister Puss—but he stirred—she shrugged into her housecoat and stepped into her slippers, then headed downstairs. By the time she reached the bottom tread, the cat was at her feet. "Good morning, Your Majesty." Proceeding into the kitchen, she asked, "Are we hungry?"

Of course he was. Mary started the coffeemaker, fed Mister Puss, and popped out to the back porch to fetch the paper. Waiting for the coffee, she sat at the table, opened the *Dumont Daily Register*, and gasped as she lifted the front page.

Tragedy at St. Alban's

Choir director dies in bizarre incident involving fire damage to church

Compiled from *Register* staff reports

•

MAY 19, DUMONT, WI — The parish family of Dumont's historic St. Alban's Episcopal Church is in mourning today, following yesterday's death of choir director David Lovell, 28, whose lifeless body was found at the console of the church organ while a fire began to spread from a toppled incense burner in the center aisle of the nave.

The scene was discovered by the Rev. Joyce Hibbard, newly installed rector of St. Alban's, in the company of Marson Miles and Brody Norris, local architects who are advising the parish regarding restoration issues that have plagued the old church. Dumont's code-compliance department has threatened to condemn the building if a suitable remediation plan is not arrived at by May 31.

City fire, medical, and police crews responded to the scene yesterday at approximately 2:45 P.M. Also summoned were the Dumont County sheriff, Thomas Simms, and medical examiner, Dr. Heather Vance.

When asked by a reporter to characterize the incident, Sheriff Simms responded, "It's suspicious, to say the least. We're working on the assumption that the fire must have been related to the death of Mr. Lovell, but at this point, we have no idea why or how. And the cause of the victim's death is still a mystery, but we have a theory. We're just getting started."

Due to the fire and impending investigation, the church is now closed indefinitely. Regular services will be held in the parish hall, adjacent to the vacant school building, until further notice.

What's wrong?

Mary lowered the paper to find Mister Puss sitting on the table. She said, "I'm stunned. Remember the young choir director, David, from the dinner party?"

He smelled like a fruitcake.

Mary frowned. "Perhaps. But now, he's dead. And they're not

sure why. It was terrible."

Sorry.

"That's more like it."

Mister Puss padded over to Mary and gently butted his head against her shoulder, purring, as if to offer apologies and condolences.

In these quiet moments, Mary still marveled that such a creature had simply walked into her life a year ago, unannounced and unexpected, creating a bond that defied all rational explanation. The vet had *tried* to explain it. Dr. Phelps had assured her that Mister Puss could not possibly speak to her, that she was lapsing into an occasional mental loop with the cat, similar to déjà vu. She was using him to clarify her own thinking, said the vet. The voice she was hearing was her own, said the vet. The cat was incapable of telling her things she did not already know, said the vet.

But hearing is believing, concluded Mary.

After breakfast, Mary and Mister Puss went back upstairs to the bedroom. Mary made the bed—though a woman of privilege, she always made her own bed promptly after breakfast—then bathed and dressed for the day.

While she checked the mirror, primping her hair, Mister Puss lay sprawled in the middle of the taut chenille bedspread, luxuriating in a blast of May sunshine. His ruddy coat gleamed.

On the settee opposite the bed, two suitcases were packed but not yet closed. Two other bags sat on the floor, also packed but not closed. The trip with her book club would begin tomorrow. And to Mary's surprise, Mister Puss was only too willing to spend the week in Brody's care—they had discussed it. Often.

But now, considering what had happened at St. Alban's, considering that Sheriff Simms had deemed David Lovell's death "suspicious," Mary had to wonder if Brody might possibly be drawn into the investigation. It had happened before. And if that were to happen, would he regret having agreed to look after Mister Puss? The cat, after all, could be *quite* the handful. Should she cancel the trip?

Out in the hall, the stairs creaked. "Morning, Mary."

"Come on in, Berta," Mary called to her housekeeper, who'd arrived for her duties.

"Lordy," said Berta, entering the bedroom, "ain't it awful, what happened at St. Alban's?"

Mary gave her head a woeful shake. "I barely knew David—met him Tuesday night—but he seemed like such a *nice* young man."

"Flighty, but friendly enough. Before he left, he came into the kitchen to thank me and Nancy. Loved the meal."

Mary shuddered. "Finding him dead like that. In church. At the organ."

Under her breath, Berta said, "Sheriff Simms called it 'suspicious.'"

"Yes, I noticed." Mary tossed her hands. "To think that something so ... *sinister* could happen here in Dumont. It's dreadful."

Berta gave her a soft smile. "Well, don't let your imagination get carried away. Fretting does no good. Who knows? Coulda had a stroke or something. When your time's up, your time's up."

Mary wasn't buying it.

"Oh," said Berta, "mail's here already." Fishing something from her apron, she added coyly, "I *know* how you've been looking forward to this." She handed Mary a note-size blue envelope, then retreated into the bathroom to tidy, scrub, and spritz.

Mary rolled her eyes. The envelope was from St. Alban's rectory, postmarked yesterday. Opening it, she sat at her dressing table to read the handwritten letter.

Dearest Mary,

What an absolute delight it was to meet you last night at Marson and Brody's home. Thank you so much for taking time out of your busy schedule to spend the evening with us.

Now that "the ice is broken," so to speak, I hope we may get to know each other far better. I was greatly heartened by your openness to the possibility of playing some role in resolving the issues now facing our parish, which has been your family's spiritual home for so many, many years.

If you'll forgive me for a wee touch of vanity (not one of the seven deadly sins, thank God!), I was bursting with pride (oops, there's one!) when you noticed and complimented the perfume I was wearing last night. As you know, my signature fragrance is out of production and in short supply, but I am sending you a bottle of it—under separate cover, which should arrive soon.

I hope you will enjoy it, dear Mary.

Yours in Christ,
The Rev. Joyce Hibbard, Rector
St. Alban's Episcopal Church

Just what I need, thought Mary. Mother Hibbard's "secret sauce," her husband had called it. Though Mary had complimented the scent, she had found it so-so. Not bad. But it could never replace her beloved L'Air du Temps.

Mary returned the letter to the blue envelope and set it on her dressing table, propped against the Lalique perfume flacon with its frosty, kissing doves. The letter, thought Mary, had surely been written yesterday morning, before tragedy struck. With its effusive style, the chatty note could not have been composed by a woman whose thoughts were muddied by sudden death.

In the mirror, Mary saw the bed behind her, where Mister Puss snoozed, oblivious to the intrigue that had clouded such a lovely sunny morning in May.

I slept later than usual on Thursday morning; so did Marson. Our harrowing experience the prior afternoon at St. Alban's had left us rattled and jittery all evening, then unable to sleep after climbing the spiral stairs to the bed on the mezzanine of our loft. Well after midnight, we at last drifted off, but Marson's rest was surely no less fitful than mine.

Sometime after eight, the intense sunshine pouring in through the skylights could no longer be ignored, so we got up, put ourselves together, left a message at the office that we were running late, and then settled in the kitchen with coffee and the morning paper. As expected, the story of David's death was headline news in the *Dumont Daily Register*, including a reference to "Marson Miles and Brody Norris, local architects."

"Whataya know," I told my husband. "We made the front page."

"We also made the features section," he said, passing it to me. "Glee's column, page three. It's datelined today, but it must've been written yesterday, early." I turned to it:

Inside Dumont

*Timely tidbits: Roundup of newsy notes
from one drop-dead dinner party*

By Glee Savage

•

MAY 19, DUMONT, WI — Your intrepid social reporter had the

great honor and delight to attend a marvelous dinner party on Tuesday evening, hosted at home by architects Marson Miles and Brody Norris in their First Avenue loft. When this dashing duo decides to entertain, the results never disappoint. Tuesday's soirée delivered not only star-studded company, sparkling conversation, and superb cuisine, but also several pages of newsworthy notes.

Ready for some gossip? Space is limited, so here we go.

1. This reporter was awed to find herself seated next to none other than Yevgeny Krymov, the world-renowned ballet dancer who made his way from Moscow to New York by means of a risky gambit in Stuttgart at the height of the Cold War. Recently retired from the stage, he is now visiting Dumont for reasons not yet known to this scribe. But watch this space. Mr. Krymov has hinted he may sit down for an interview, which I hope to share with you soon.

2. On the architectural front, Messrs. Miles and Norris, who are married, report that progress on their new home, being built on the outskirts of town, has been stalled by unforeseen delays. Having studied the plans and visited the construction site, this writer can assure you that the new residence, while of modest scale, will have lasting and recognized design significance. Look for an extensive photo feature upon completion of the project.

3. Further, the new Dumont County Museum, designed by Marson Miles and already well documented in this column, is nearing completion on schedule, adjacent to Questman Center for the Performing Arts. Looking ahead, the county library system has begun discussions with Brody Norris for the design of a new main library, to be located on the same cultural campus.

4. On the social scene, you'll need to act fast if…

I set aside the paper, saying, "I didn't see her taking notes. Did you?"

"No," said Marson, "but there's no stopping Glee when she sniffs a story. At least she didn't write about Joyce Hibbard putting the hammer on Mary." Sitting with me at the kitchen island, he was fiddling with our iPad. "How do you watch TV on this?"

"Here." I took the gadget from him and logged in to our cable account. "News?"

"Please," he said. "I wonder if they're covering the St. Alban's story in Green Bay. I mean, it's *weird*."

I found the channel and propped up the tablet against the carafe of coffee. The newscast was on, but they weren't talking about suspicious death. Rather, Chad Percy was doing his segment, talking up his new fragrance. Dollcakes was saying, "... and we call it 'Chad!' That's right, with an exclamation point..."

I switched it off just as the phone rang.

Marson answered our land line. "Well, good morning, Mary. Yes, it was ghastly. But we're all right, a little shaken, no harm done. Wish we could say the same for David Lovell, poor guy." He paused while Mary spoke at length about something. Then he said, "He's sitting right here, Mary. Let me pass the phone."

I took it. "Mary? Good morning. What can I do for you?"

"Brody love," she said, sounding winded, "after reading what happened yesterday—and you were there—and Sheriff Simms was there—and that *poor* David Lovell is dead—and Thomas called it 'suspicious'—and Mister Puss is planning to stay with you—and I'm wondering if it might not be too *much*."

"Wh...*what*?" I said, trying to sort it out. Marson was grinning at me.

"I mean, I'm wondering if I should cancel my trip—so you won't have to look after Mister Puss—so you can concentrate on the investigation."

I laughed. "Mary, don't be silly. It's sweet of you to be concerned, but do *not* cancel your trip. You're going to have a ball. Mister Puss will be a *great* house guest. And I will *not* be getting involved with the investigation. Why would I?"

She reminded me flatly, "It's happened before."

Marson's grin grew wider.

I told Mary, "Now, I want you to bring Mister Puss over this evening, exactly as planned, okay? Marson and I are looking forward to the patter of little feet."

Marson held a hand to his mouth, got up from the island, and stepped away.

"You're *sure* it won't be an imposition?" asked Mary.

I heard the beep of a call-waiting alert and checked the readout. I told Mary, "Don't give it another thought. See you tonight, love."

When Mary said good-bye and rang off, I answered the other call.

"Hello, Thomas."

Marson stifled his laugh, but I could barely hear the sheriff.

Sheriff Thomas Simms invited me to his office, on the pretext that he needed more information regarding my discovery of David Lovell's body yesterday—but I found it curious that he made no mention of including either Joyce Hibbard or Marson, who had entered St. Alban's with me, witnessing everything I had witnessed. I also found it curious that he intended to invite the medical examiner, Heather Vance, to join us. He suggested eleven o'clock.

Leaving the loft, I drove to our Miles & Norris offices and then caught up at my desk for a couple of hours. Shortly before eleven, I walked to the sheriff's headquarters, which was only a few blocks away, adjacent to the county courthouse.

When I arrived outside Simms's office, a deputy said, "He's expecting you." She opened the door, then closed it behind me. Both

Simms and Dr. Vance stood to greet me as I entered.

"*Brody*," said Simms in his mellow baritone through a broad smile as he reached to shake my hand, "thanks for coming in on such short notice." He looked dapper as ever. His attire never varied much—always a dark, beautifully tailored business suit with a crisp white shirt and jazzy silk tie. But the neckties themselves varied greatly. Today's featured bold stripes of white, silver, and chrome yellow.

Heather gave me a hug. "We keep meeting under terrible circumstances, but it's always a pleasure." It was an accurate observation. The medical examiner and I were on a hugging, first-name basis because this was not the first time we had met in the context of untimely death.

Having spent most of my life in California, I hadn't known much about medical examiners in Wisconsin, but I had come to learn that the office was independent of any police agency or hospital. I also knew they were responsible for investigating "reportable" deaths—and I had a strong hunch that David Lovell's bizarre demise, with the suspicious circumstances surrounding it, fell squarely into that category.

When I had first met Dumont's medical examiner, I was expecting someone older, more wizened, and less vibrant, but Heather Vance was blond and pretty, surprisingly young, thirty or so. Today she looked sharp and lively in a chipper skirt and jacket of cerulean blue.

"Have a seat," said Simms as he stepped behind his desk and sat. Heather and I took chairs facing him. He told me, "I asked Heather to stop by and summarize her initial findings. I thought you might want to hear this, too, Brody."

"Sure," I said, though I was confused. Had Mary Questman— and Marson—been right? Had they foreseen that I would be drawn into another investigation?

Heather set a folder on the front edge of Simms's desk and

opened it, drawing out a raft of odd-sized notes, forms, and reports. Jogging them on her knees, she explained, "It's not yet twenty-four hours since we were first called to the scene, so this is *very* preliminary, but I think we already have a sense of direction. First, the time of death could have been no more than a few minutes before the time the victim was found, as reported by Brody."

I said, "I was the first to hear the odd sound of the organ—while we were over by the school, near the playground. We weren't even sure what it *was*, so we went to find the source, which led us to the church. By the time we got the door unlocked, went inside, and found David, I'm guessing three or four minutes had passed. Maybe five."

Heather nodded. "That would be perfectly consistent with the temperature, lack of lividity, and other factors pertaining to the corpse."

I said, "His face appeared bluish to me. Isn't that livor mortis?"

"Easily confused, but I'm fairly sure the bluish flesh was a symptom of cyanosis—which develops quickly from lack of oxygen. Essentially, David choked to death."

Envisioning the scene, I suggested, "And struggling for air, seated at the organ, helpless and paralyzed, he finally lost consciousness, collapsing on the keyboards. Intended or not, the wailing of the organ was like a siren—a last and futile cry for help."

"Phew," said Simms, tugging his collar to ease his breathing. "What do you think choked him? He wasn't strangled, was he?"

"No, definitely not," said Heather. "There were no signs of struggle or abrasion of the neck. I think he choked because of something he ate. Any guesses?"

I took a stab: "Nuts?"

"It's a strong theory. He was allergic to nuts, and his allergy was widely known."

"Yeah," said Simms, thinking aloud. "Even I knew that. Tommy's in the choir—my son—and there were parties and potlucks, and David always warned about his nut allergy. Everybody knew about it."

I said, "I knew it, too. He mentioned it to me the night before he died. He had dinner with us."

Heather said, "So here's my working theory: David ate nuts, or something with nuts *in* it, and he went into anaphylactic shock. In rare instances, the reaction can be sudden and severe—even lethal. Symptoms include David's observed vomiting, swelling, and hives. Swelling of the throat, clogged with vomit, could easily asphyxiate a victim. We'll perform a postmortem. The stomach contents will be analyzed, as will the vomit and the food that was present—potato chips and a plate of cookies, which appeared to be homemade macaroons."

Simms asked if David carried an EpiPen, an injectable antidote to anaphylaxis.

"We didn't find one," said Heather. "But the bottom line is this: I'm fairly confident that our testing will conclude that the *cause* of death was anaphylactic shock and the *mechanism* of death was asphyxiation. We'll know soon enough. But that still leaves the *manner* of death. And that's up to you guys."

Simms pondered aloud, "Manner of death: natural, accidental, suicide, or homicide."

But I was still stuck on Heather's declaration, "That's up to you guys."

Throughout the meeting, I noticed that neither Thomas Simms nor Heather Vance was asking me anything at all regarding what I had witnessed the prior afternoon—which had been the pretext for inviting me to the meeting—and instead, they were opening their files to me and drawing me into their confidence.

When we had finished, Thomas stepped to the door with us and thanked Heather as she left. He then turned to ask me, "Can you stay a minute?"

I returned to my chair. Simms followed and sat next to me, in the chair Heather had occupied, rather than behind his desk. Whatever he had to say, evidently, was more personal than official. He angled his chair toward me and scooched it a few inches closer.

"Tommy is taking this *real* hard," he said. "He's seven years old, and he's never had to deal with the death of someone he knew—and liked."

I recalled watching an encounter between Tommy Simms and David Lovell the prior October, after the funeral I'd attended at St. Alban's. Tommy beamed with pride stemming from his participation in the choir; Gloria Simms told the choirmaster how much her son loved singing and always looked forward to rehearsals; David patted Tommy's shoulder and said he had a strong voice with perfect pitch and timing. I now realized, with a measure of shame, that David had been far more than a pretty-boy musician who wore too much perfume—he was a teacher and friend who'd made a profound difference in the lives of those he fostered with his talents. As a cruel addendum to his sudden death, dozens of other innocent lives had been robbed of his mentoring and affection.

"I'm so sorry, Thomas."

Simms shook his head. "It's a 'life lesson,' as they say. Someday, sooner or later, everyone learns the reality of death—when it's suddenly no longer an abstraction. But it's hard to watch a kid go through it."

"Is there anything I can do to help?"

Simms grinned.

I asked, "What?"

"You have a way with this, Brody. You have disciplined problem-solving instincts and great recall. Plus, the victim was gay, so you may have insights that would otherwise escape me. In short: I'm wondering if you'd be willing to supply this investigation with some friendly assistance."

And there it was. Mary Questman was right. So was Marson. I was a sidekick again.

Hearing no protest from me, Simms continued, "So, then: manner of death. Any thoughts?"

I nodded. "I'd rule out that it was a *natural* death because David was young and vigorous, apparently healthy; the postmortem should clarify that quickly. I'd also rule out suicide because the whole setup was too goofy, and besides, I know from our dinner, the night before David died, that he was jazzed about the prospect of hearing Renée Fleming perform in New York, an opportunity he would *never* miss. Which leaves only two other options: David's death was either an accident or a homicide."

"Exactly my thoughts," said Simms. "David could have accidentally eaten something with nuts in it. Or someone could have intentionally slipped it to him, knowing of his allergy, resulting in his death—which would be homicide."

I raised a finger. "One more thought. What about the incense and the fire? The strangeness of that detail suggests that whatever happened was not an accident, but 'staged,' either to make a point or purely to create confusion."

Simms raised a finger. "One *more* thought. Yesterday you told us that when you arrived at the front door to the church, Joyce Hibbard thought it would not be locked, but it was. That sounds like deliberate tampering. Combine that with the incense fire, and the whole scenario looks more and more like—say it with me—"

We said it together: "Murder."

Murder always has a motive. Neither Simms nor I had known David Lovell well enough to fathom a guess as to why someone might want him dead, so we simply needed to start digging and then weigh the possibilities.

Simms had already checked with the parish office that morning and, through its employment files, identified David's brother, Geoff Lovell, as next of kin. The listed contact number was Geoff's mobile phone, and when the sheriff's office reached him, he was visiting Dumont. He agreed to meet with Simms later that afternoon, and Simms invited me to sit in.

After lunch (after enduring some good-natured ribbing from Marson, calling me Sherlock), I returned to the county complex, as requested.

As before, the deputy outside the sheriff's office told me, "He's expecting you." She took me in, but the office was empty, and she led me through another door that opened into the conference room where, the prior fall, Simms and I had explored the details of another untimely death.

The room had a high ceiling with tall windows and venetian blinds that were tilted to admit abundant sunlight but no view; there was nothing to see outside other than a brick wall of the jail. Opposite the windows was a wall of wooden bookcases, brown and varnished, containing cockeyed binders of whatnot. The space was sort of pleasant, in an old-timey, comfy kind of way, bearing no resemblance to the sterile, fluorescent interrogation rooms depicted on cop shows.

Simms brightened when he saw me and waved me in; the deputy left. Someone else—I assumed it was a police stenographer—was setting up a few feet away from the oblong conference table. Simms sat at the head of the table, arranging a stack of file folders. Behind him, I noticed a darker rectangle on the faded surface of the green wall where there had previously hung an old oil portrait, cracked and yellowed by the passing of years, depicting a man with a horse and something that looked like a monkey. The painting had always baffled me. Now I was baffled by its absence.

I pulled out a chair along the side of the table and sat near Simms. Unzipping a small leather portfolio containing a notepad and pen, I said, "At dinner on Tuesday, David mentioned something that caught my attention and piqued my curiosity."

Simms arched his brows. "Let's have it."

"David dropped two details in passing conversation. He said he didn't 'need to work.' And he mentioned 'the hassles with my brother.' He added, 'We're nothing alike.'"

"Hmmm," said Simms, "something to do with money, and something to do with family friction." Dryly, he noted, "That's always promising."

The deputy opened the door. Simms and I stood as she admitted a young man, presumably Geoff Lovell, who was followed into the conference room by a young woman and a large dog. I could tell from the sheriff's expression that he was not expecting this. As the deputy bowed out, Simms and I stepped over to greet Geoff and the tagalongs.

Geoff looked several years younger than David, but the fraternal resemblance was obvious—to a degree. While they shared a strikingly similar build and features, Geoff had none of his older brother's polish and style (I mean, let's face it, he was straight). More to the point, Geoff seemed a little rough around the edges, with grungy clothes and neglected grooming. I noticed chewed, dirty nails and wondered if he smoked. Whatever I smelled, it wasn't his brother's perfume habit.

He vaguely introduced us to his companions, named Cindy and Spark.

The girl was petite and looked a few years younger than Geoff. Her bedraggled appearance matched that of her boyfriend, and her eyes had a vacant look, making me wonder if there was a drug problem. She sported a full-sleeve tattoo on her right arm, depicting a whirl of Japanese calligraphy and manga characters. All the ink was jet black, matching her hair, worn in a messy shoulder-length pageboy.

The big, leggy dog resembled a pony next to the girl. Of indeterminate breed with a shaggy brown coat, the poor pooch looked underfed and unhealthy. It wore an indigo paisley bandana instead of a collar.

Simms invited everyone to sit. Geoff and the girl took chairs on the side of the table opposite me. The dog settled on the floor between them.

Simms recited a few preliminaries while opening a folder, then offered Geoff condolences on the death of his brother, assuring him that the sheriff's office was committed to sorting out the tragedy. Nothing was said about my presence, other than the fact that I was the person who had found David dead the day before.

"For the record," said Simms, "let me nail down some personal information." He established that Geoff Lovell was twenty-three years old and had been living in Madison with his girlfriend since completing college a year ago. He had a degree in history, was not continuing with grad school, and was not employed.

Simms said to the girl, "And I'm afraid I didn't get your last name."

"Kavanaugh," she said and confirmed the spelling.

Simms asked, "And is it Cindy or Cynthia?"

The dog barked.

Wearily, the girl explained to Simms, as if he were stupid, "Cindy's the dog. I'm Spark."

Simms and I exchanged a bewildered look.

"Yeah," said Spark Kavanaugh, "my parents are weird." She further explained that she was twenty years old, majoring in communications, and had wrapped up the final exams of her sophomore year the week before. "So Geoff thought it would be a good time to drive up and see his brother."

"Where are you guys staying?"

Geoff said, "Pine Creek Suites, out by the highway."

"'*Suites*,'" said Spark derisively. "It's a motel, a dump."

She was right. There wasn't a pine or a creek within sight of the place. Only asphalt.

Geoff added, "But they take dogs. And it's cheap."

"Okay," said Simms, "this gets a little touchy, but I understand there may have been some friction between you and your brother. If that's the case, why the visit?"

"It's a long story."

Simms said, "I have nothing better to do. Tell me about it."

"Well, for starters, Dave's five years older, first born, got Dad's name, the 'junior' thing. Me? I always felt like—not exactly an accident—but more like an afterthought. And Mom used to joke that she always wanted a girl. And then Dave turned out gay. So in a crazy way, she sorta got the wish that I didn't deliver."

"How'd your dad feel about all that?"

"Hell, *he* didn't care. Too busy making money. Sure, he was a jock, real macho—always said it was good for business—and I think he *liked* being 'the man in the family,' so, no, it didn't bother him that Dave went gay."

Simms asked Geoff, "And *you're* not a jock?"

Dryly, he reminded the sheriff, "I have a history degree."

"How did your father make his money?"

"The way I hear it, he grew up in Green Bay and was sort of a jock hero in high school. Then he met my mom, who went to college in Appleton, and that's where they settled when they got married. He went into real estate and did great with it, trading on his jock-hero thing—people just seemed to like doing business with him. Then, by the time Dave and I were growing up, he quit real estate and started an investment company in order to make what he called '*real* money.' It worked—I'll hand him that. But it all ended three years ago. You may know about this. Dad and Mom were both killed in a car accident. Driving back from dinner at this country place they liked. Hit a tree. I guess he was drunk."

Simms nodded. "Now that you mention it, I do remember that. And you're right—he was drunk."

"Like father, like son," said Geoff. "I didn't take after him as an athlete, but I did inherit his weakness for, shall we say, bad habits."

Gently, Simms said, "Explain."

"Well, I drink, sure—sometimes too much—who doesn't? And I've also done a little too much experimenting with drugs, a college thing, but that is *over* now—I swear it, Sheriff. Trouble is, along the way, I had a few scrapes with the police, including a robbery. Dad had to bail me out of jail so I could get back to classes. That was less than a year before he died."

Simms turned to me. "Brody, tell Geoff what his brother said the night before he died."

I hesitated. "Geoff, this is awkward. David had dinner with us Tuesday night, and at one point, he said, 'I don't need to work, but I love what I do. And it sure beats the hassles with my brother—who's been threatening a visit.'" I added, "Sorry if that seems harsh. What was he talking about?"

Geoff took a deep breath, then exhaled noisily. "It's all related. After Dad got me out of jail, his attitude toward me changed—totally. I was now 'the bad one.' I was the immature ne'er-do-well who couldn't be trusted. He threatened to disown me. A few months later, he was dead. He didn't disown me, thank God, but he had time to tinker with his estate plan. As survivors of both Dad *and* Mom, Dave and I were the only heirs. But my inheritance was put in a trust, with Dave as trustee, until I turn thirty—after I've had a chance to 'do some growing up,' the will said. The trust made available enough money for me to finish college, but basically left me on my own after that, with a measly 'allowance' to be paid at Dave's discretion. Did I hassle him about it? Sure I did."

Simms asked, "And in the event of David's death...?"

"Huh?"

"David was trustee of your portion of the inheritance. What did the will stipulate would happen in the event of David's death?"

"Beats me," said Geoff. "Never thought about it. I'm probably screwed."

Spark groaned, looking sick. Cindy the dog whimpered.

But I highly doubted that Geoff had been screwed by his brother's death. To the contrary, I thought there was a good chance the entire estate would now pass to the only surviving son. Had that not occurred to Geoff? Or was he playing dumb?

Simms asked him, "Who was the lawyer, the estate planner who set this up? You need to look into this. And frankly, so do I."

"Umm," said Geoff, whirling a hand, "Stan something—Stanley Burton? He has a law firm in Appleton."

Both Simms and I made note of the name.

"So *anyway*," said Geoff, "that's why Dave always thought I was hassling him, that's why Spark and I are visiting Dumont, and that's why I met Dave at the church yesterday—to talk money."

Simms looked no less stunned than I felt.

I said to Geoff, "You met with David? Yesterday? At St. Alban's?"

Simms added calmly, "Tell us about that meeting."

"Dave knew why I was coming to Dumont, and when I texted him yesterday to let him know I was here, he didn't want to see me, as usual. He knew I'd be asking for a bigger monthly allowance—I think they call it a stipend—or at least an advance. But I told him I wouldn't leave town till we had a chance to talk, so he told me to come to the church anytime after lunch, when he'd be practicing at the organ. He said the church was unlocked during the day, so I could just walk in. And that's what I did. It was maybe one-fifteen."

Simms asked, "Did you go alone? Or was Spark with you?"

She answered, "I felt like crap. I was in bed at the motel."

Geoff continued, "So I was alone with Dave. We had our discussion—it went the way it always did—he said his hands were tied, there was nothing he could do. According to him, the terms of the stipend are spelled out in the will. As trustee, he could only approve the monthly payments or not; he was *not* able to change the amount or the schedule. To be honest, I believed him, but I figured it never hurt to do a little begging—I mean, *he* was loaded."

"So," asked Simms, "how did you wrap it up?"

"We didn't, not exactly. You see, we were interrupted. This older gal walked in, all in a tizzy about her lesson or something, or errands she needed to run—"

I interrupted, asking, "Was it Lillie Miller, the parish secretary?"

"Yeah," said Geoff, "that's it—her name was Lillie. I *think* she said she needed to take something to the post office, so she left Dave a plate of cookies and said she'd be back as soon as possible. When she was gone, Dave told me about this setup they have, where Lillie plays some of the organ pieces, but she's not very good, and he tries to coach or whatever. I wasn't really listening. I was worried about money and I needed his help and I guess I started to cry. So he took out his wallet and gave me what he had on him—about a hundred bucks, which doesn't go far—and he said he'd send me a personal check the next day, and asked where to send it, and I said I'd pick it up. Then I left. And now he's dead."

The girlfriend said, "Geoff, I'm gonna be sick. Can we get outta here?"

Simms said, "Soon, Miss Kavanaugh. Geoff, everyone was fond of your brother. At St. Alban's, everyone loved David like part of the family. My little boy is in the choir and thought the world of him, so we're all sharing a measure of your loss. We're trying to figure out exactly what happened to him, and one possibility we need to consider is that his death might not have been an accident. So I'm wondering: Do you know if David had any enemies?"

Geoff seemed dazed by the implication of the question. "Ene-

mies? Dave? The golden boy? You said it yourself, Sheriff: everyone *loved* Dave." Geoff added, "Sometimes, to a fault."

A scene flashed through my mind: at Tuesday's dinner, Curtis
Hibbard and Yevgeny Krymov had tussled for David's affections
like predators fighting over meat. Then Curtis offered David a
New York fling featuring Renée Fleming, pissing off both Joyce
Hibbard and Yevgeny.

Simms asked Geoff, "People sometimes loved David to a fault?
How so?"

"Well"—Geoff squirmed—"the old gal at the church, Lillie.
Like I said, she seemed ditzed out. When she left, Dave told me
about their lessons, but he also said he was worried about her. He
thought she was coming *on* to him, which freaked him. I mean,
she's old enough to be his mother, plus, he's *gay*. Everyone knew
that."

"*Geoff*," whined Spark, "I need to leave. Let's *go*."

Geoff asked Simms, "Okay if we split?"

"Uh, sure. You'll be in town awhile, right? I've got your number;
here's my card. I'll keep you informed, and you do the same."

Geoff pocketed the card. "Sure, Sheriff. Fine."

Everyone got up and headed toward the door. The girl clutched
her stomach. The dog limped.

"Geoff," I said, checking my wallet and slipping him a hundred,
"I hope that'll help. Try to take care of them."

Looking astonished, he shook my hand. "Thanks, guy."

When Simms had seen them out through his office, he returned
to the conference room, dismissed the stenographer, and closed
the door.

I was standing near the widow, peering through the slats of the
blinds, staring at the brick wall of the jail as I pondered what we'd
heard from David Lovell's brother.

Simms sat on the edge of the conference table, glancing over his notes. As if thinking aloud, he said, "So Geoff was *there*. And Lillie Miller was *there*."

I turned to him. "And Lillie may have felt the sting of a woman scorned."

Simms stood. "What the hell was *that* about? That's nuts."

I reminded him, "There's an uncharitable term for straight women who get obsessed with gay men."

Mulling this, Simms suggested, "I bet Lillie would like you. I bet she'd trust you—and maybe even open up to you."

"If you want, I can pay her a visit. But the underlying issue is delicate, to say the least. The conversation might be easier if I take along a sympathetic woman."

Simms nodded. "Maybe Heather Vance?"

"Just what I was thinking. And she'd provide a good pretext for the visit—questions about the macaroons."

Simms returned to his chair at the head of the table, sat, and phoned the medical examiner.

Waiting for him to button down our plan, I studied the bare wall behind him and the ghosted shadow of the missing painting. The man with the horse and the odd creature that looked like a monkey—where had they gone?

At home that Thursday night, Marson and I concocted an easy meal from the trove of elegant leftovers remaining from Tuesday's dinner party. Seated at the kitchen island with a good bottle of pinot noir, we noshed on warm beef, lamb, and shrimp that Marson had arranged in a free-form salad of chilled greens and tabbouleh, sauced with his masterful vinaigrette. I set aside a generous slab of beef tenderloin for our four-footed house guest, who would arrive that evening.

While we ate, I updated Marson on the day's developments with

Sheriff Simms. While cleaning up afterward, Marson engaged in a fresh round of playful razzing, addressing me as Sherlock.

When it started wearing thin, I asked with a smile, "Enough of that, okay?"

He took me in his arms. "Sure, kiddo. Sorry."

"That's better." We kissed. "*Way* better."

We had no sooner cleaned the countertops and switched on the dishwasher when—*grrring*—His Majesty's retinue arrived at the loft's street door.

Marson broke stride to fluff a few throw pillows on his way to open the door. I hung back, watching from the kitchen as he admitted Mister Puss in Mary Questman's arms, followed by Berta, overburdened with the cat's whatnot. Marson bowed deeply until they had filed past, then closed the door behind them as I crossed the room to welcome our guests.

Mary set Mister Puss on the floor. He wore his garish paw-print harness, dragging behind him the nylon leash and its clunky retractor. When I hunkered down to greet him, he jumped into my arms. Sounding befuddled, Mary said, "In spite of his *obvious* intelligence, Mister Puss still hasn't picked up the concept of walking on a leash." With a twitter of laughter, she added, "It's easier to carry him."

The cat purred as I freed him from his reviled getup and returned him to the floor. He gratefully circled my feet, leaning into my shins, and then light-footed his way across the living room, checking out his accommodations. With an effortless, fluid hop, he settled atop the back of a loveseat, where he could keep an eye on all of us.

Berta schlepped the litter box, litter, cat carrier, bowls, food, brushes, and toy collection to the back hall of the kitchen. Mary hunched over a list with us, reviewing dos and don'ts, feeding schedule, and emergency numbers. Marson recited assurance after assurance that the cat was no trouble and would be in good hands. I exhorted Mary to have a fabulous trip, to indulge in the many literary splendors of the week-long festival, and to bask in Chicago's magnificent architecture. And finally, amid a flurry of kisses and hugs with us—and sweet good-byes with the cat—Mary disappeared into the night, followed by Berta, who pulled the door closed behind them.

The loft seemed suddenly, eerily quiet.

"Well, now," said Marson to Mister Puss, "it's 'just us.' Alone at last."

The cat hopped down from the loveseat and followed Marson into the kitchen, who rummaged in the refrigerator, asking me over his shoulder, "Do we have something to serve our little guest as an amuse-bouche?"

"Foil packet. Bottom shelf." I joined them.

"Aha," said Marson, opening the foil, shutting the fridge.

Mister Puss caught the scent and broke into a loud, pleading purr. He paced between us, nearly dancing, then focused on Marson, circling my husband's legs as he cut up the meat. The kitty dishes left behind by Berta would never do, not for Marson, so he chose a couple of small Art Deco bowls—Puiforcat—to serve as our guest's temporary dinnerware. He filled one of the bowls with a fistful of the diced tenderloin, rinsed his hands, and then set the bowl on the floor. Mister Puss was on it at once, partaking of his bounty with evident rapture.

"A nice Côtes du Rhône would be perfect with that," said Marson.

He was joking—at least I hoped he was, since he had not yet fully grasped that Mister Puss had acquired some distinctly human habits.

When the welcoming meal was finished and the kitchen was again spiffed (Marson could not otherwise relax), we settled into our evening at home. Marson got comfortable with a book in the main room. Mister Puss did a bit of exploring, then curled on the cushion of the loveseat where Marson sat reading.

With our guest contentedly acclimated and accounted for, I decided to clock a bit of office time, so I sat at the computer desk we had hidden behind folding doors along a side wall of the dining area. My workday had been impinged upon by the meetings with Thomas Simms, and I needed to revise my notes for the library proposal, which would soon be due for consideration by the county board.

After a couple of hours, Marson set down his book, got up, and stretched. "I think I've had it. I'm heading upstairs."

"Will I bother you if I work a while longer?"

"Not at all." Stepping over to where I sat, he leaned to give me a kiss. "Night, kiddo." He crossed the room and started up the spiral stairs, then looked back from the third or fourth step. "And good night to *you*, Mister Puss."

When Marson disappeared on the mezzanine, I returned my attention to the computer and finished typing a thought that had been interrupted. Moments later, I felt Mister Puss nuzzle my ankles. Pushing my chair back, I patted my knee, and the cat jumped into my lap.

His back arched beneath my touch as I stroked his spine, asking, "Are you finding everything you need?"

He purred. He stretched his snout to my chin. Then his face slid up my cheek toward my ear. The purr thundered. The voice was small but distinct.

You need a break.

"You may be right," I answered. I couldn't help wondering whether I had actually heard the cat's words or had only imagined them to suit my frame of mind.

You could use a drink.

I asked Mister Puss, "Now, why didn't *I* think of that?" So I closed the file I was working on, did a quick check for email, and turned off the computer.

I carried Mister Puss to the kitchen and set him on the counter (Marson would never know). The cat watched my every move as I poured a paltry slug of superb cognac into a large snifter. I swirled it close to his face; his golden eyes followed the wave of amber as it sloshed around the inner rim of crystal. When I tilted the mouth of the glass to his nose, it wrinkled.

Not a good year.

Aha, I thought. His wisecrack proved not only that he knew nothing about cognac (always an undated, graded blend), but also that he was not echoing my own thoughts (and therefore speaking for himself). Or was I needlessly splitting hairs?

I shut off a few lights. Carrying the cat in one hand and the cognac in the other, I moved to the living room and set both on the low table. I slipped off my shoes and curled into the corner of the adjacent sofa, drawing one foot up to the cushion, beneath my other knee.

When I reached for the snifter, Mister Puss hopped from the table to my lap. He purred as I sipped the liquor and let it linger in my mouth. Time seemed to drift and stall. Then he climbed to my shoulder and settled atop the sofa's upholstered back with his paws touching my neck. I felt the soft fur of his chin reach my ear as the purring intensified. Another sip of cognac. I set down the glass. Eyelids heavy.

Beneath the rumble of the purr, other sounds arose, as if from a distant past. A forgotten time of ancient dynasties. Gods and goddesses. Sacred temple perfume. As if slipping into a trance...

I drifted off...

Friday morning, I arrived at the office earlier than usual, needing to get some work done because the day would again be interrupted by duties that were more investigative than architectural. Sheriff Simms had arranged for Dr. Heather Vance, the county medical examiner, to accompany me on a visit to Lillie Miller, the St. Alban's parish secretary, which was a part-time position. Since we preferred not to interview Lillie while she was on the job, logistics made it sensible for Heather to pick me up at work and drive together to Lillie's home. Heather said she would come for me promptly at ten, and I said I'd be waiting outside our First Avenue offices.

The day was warm, so I carried my sport coat and stood under the awning that spanned the front of our building, which faced the morning sun. My phone vibrated with a text from Heather—she was two blocks away. By the time I returned the phone to my pocket, she pulled up to the curb in a snazzy German convertible, bright red, top down.

"Morning, handsome," she said, waving me into the car.

I thumped the door closed and buckled up. "Nice wheels," I told her. "It's not quite what I imagined, given your line of work."

"What'd you expect me to drive—a hearse?"

We both laughed as she lurched from the curb and gunned it.

Though I had never seen where Lillie Miller lived, I knew from the address that it was a neighborhood of more modest homes on the far side of town, away from the highway as well as the town commons. Heather and I chatted while she drove.

She said, "Yesterday on the phone, Thomas was fairly vague when he asked if I'd go with you today. While I often play a role in police investigations, I've never interrogated a murder suspect."

I detected a note of facetious overstatement in her words: our meeting with Lillie was not an "interrogation," but an informal conversation, and at this early stage, Lillie herself was not a "suspect," merely a person of interest. However, I wondered aloud, "Was it, in fact, murder?"

Heather said, "Don't know yet. The macaroons are being tested for the presence of nuts. If they test positive, then it's up to you and Thomas to decide what that implies. For whatever it's worth—and this is utterly unscientific—I thought the macaroons had an almond smell." With a laugh, she added, "Then again, that's often the smell attributed to cyanide."

I must have looked aghast.

"Sorry," she said. "Gallows humor—it's a hazard of the trade." As we turned onto Lillie's street, Heather asked, "Now, what's this 'matter of delicacy' that Thomas mentioned on the phone?"

"Can you pull over for a minute? We're almost there." After Heather braked the car and we sat idling at the curb, I explained, "Simms and I interviewed Geoff Lovell, David's brother. He saw Lillie give the plate of cookies to David. After she left, David said that Lillie had developed a romantic obsession with him."

"But"—Heather sputtered—"but the *age* difference. And everyone *knew* that David was gay."

"Exactly."

"*Ohhh…*"

I reminded her, "But this is all secondhand, and there's a lot we don't know. For instance, Geoff could've invented the story. If not, David could've been mistaken about Lillie's interest in him.

If not, we don't know if Lillie had ever made overt advances. If so, we don't know if David had explicitly rebuked her. And finally, if David did snub Lillie, we don't know if she felt the rage of a woman scorned."

"Sounds like 'he said, she said.'"

"Except," I noted, "*he's* no longer around to give us his side of the story."

Heather drummed her fingers on the steering wheel. "I see what you mean—a matter of delicacy."

Lillie Miller lived alone in a spare but neat little house on Lamoureaux Lane, named after a long-ago logger who had helped build the early encampment of Dumont, back when the deer and the antelope played. Today, though, the bleak and faded neighborhood, once a working-class subdivision of middling, affordable housing, had morphed into a tenuous refuge for other precarious species—the old and lonely, the widows and pensioners, the renters and couch-surfers and clerks.

Heather's sleek red roadster looked rudely out of place, as if mocking those who might scrimp for bus fare. Instinctively, Heather parked a few doors down from Lillie, where the car would not be seen—at least by Lillie.

Approaching the house, I shrugged into my jacket as we followed a narrow walkway that bisected two rectangles of weedy lawn. A row of purple petunias planted along the foundation of the porch tried to perk things up, but I found the color sad. The weathered gray floorboards creaked as we approached the door. Heather rang the bell.

And we waited. I checked my watch: ten-fifteen, right on time. Heather rang the bell again. Another half minute passed, and then Lillie opened the door. "Oh," she said through the screen of the storm door, looking surprised, "you made it after all."

"I'm sorry?" said Heather. "Are we late?"

Lillie's brow furrowed in thought. "Weren't you coming at nine-fifteen?"

Heather and I glanced at each other. I said, "My apologies, Lillie. There must've been a mix-up. May we come in?"

"Please do," she said, swinging the outer door. "How rude of me."

Entering, we stepped directly into the cramped living room. Lillie had already met me in Mother Hibbard's office on Tuesday afternoon, but not by name, so I introduced myself. And although Heather had phoned Lillie to set up today's meeting, I extended the courtesy of introducing them as well. Heather hugged Lillie. Then Lillie hugged me. She wore a strong fragrance, which I found odd in the middle of the morning, but I reminded myself that she was welcoming guests into her home. Her scent was rich and assertive, with notes of something exotic, perhaps Far Eastern.

"Please make yourselves comfortable," said Lillie, stepping farther into the room with us. Heather and I settled on a lumpy brown sofa pinned with white lace doilies. Lillie sat in a spindle-back maple dining chair, turned out from a tiny table for two. I noticed a small crucifix hanging above the table. And the entire space was infused not only with Lillie's perfume but also with the aroma of something baking, something sweet and distinctive. Unless I was mistaken, it involved coconut.

Lillie said, "I hope you'll forgive the way I look."

I thought she looked fine—a bit too prim, as usual, but nicely dressed and perfectly groomed.

She explained, "I've been crying. I still can't believe what happened—to David."

"Oh, *Lillie*," said Heather, moving from the sofa to hunker near Lillie, grasping her hands, "I'm sorry for your loss. I'm afraid I didn't know David, but I've heard he was deeply loved by many friends."

"Yes"—Lillie sniffled—"he was deeply loved. Thank you, Dr. Vance."

"Now, now. You *must* call me Heather."

"Thank you, Heather."

Rising from her crouch, Heather straightened her skirt and returned to sit next to me on the sofa.

Lillie sat looking quietly at us, as if studying us. She blinked away a tear as the trace of a smile turned her lips. She said, "The two of you make such a *lovely* couple."

While Lillie was off by a mile, I could understand why she might perceive us as a couple—we were both in our thirties, both young professionals approaching middle age, both sharing a certain sense of style that probably did look good together. I told Lillie, "That's a sweet thing to say, but we don't want to give you the wrong impression. You see, I'm gay."

"Oh, I know *that*," said Lillie. "You're married to that other architect, Mr. Miles."

Heather said, "And I'm pretty much wed to my work these days."

Lillie chuckled. "I suppose I should've said: the two of you *would* make a lovely couple. Don't you agree, Heather, that most gay men are just *perfect* gentlemen?"

Awkwardly, Heather replied, "Well, *this* one is." She patted my arm.

I had worried that the underlying purpose of today's conversation would be difficult to broach, requiring great delicacy, but Lillie had flung the door open, so I stepped right in, asking her, "Your friendship with David was special, wasn't it?"

She didn't flinch. "It certainly was. I thought of him as more than a friend—more like a soul mate. Losing him, it's like part of my *heart* was torn away." Pain gripped the features of her pallid face. Her fingers blanched as she clenched her hands.

I offered condolences before asking, "Did David consider you a soul mate as well?"

She stiffened. "No. I don't believe he did."

"How could you tell?"

"A woman *knows*, Brody. A woman always knows when a man wants his distance."

"Did he tell you that?"

"Of course not." Lillie flashed me a telling grin. "David was a perfect gentleman."

I gave Heather an inconspicuous nudge with my elbow. The next question needed to be asked by a woman.

Heather picked up the cue. "Lillie," she said, "I know how it is to fall for a gay guy—it happened to me once, back in college. I was lucky. I learned my lesson. Neither of us got hurt, and we're still friends—well, Christmas cards and such. So I know about those 'special friendships.' There's a lasting and difficult bond: *she* wants but fears closure, while *he* feels flattered but sympathetic. Not easy, but better than nothing. Does this sound familiar?"

Lillie closed her eyes and gently folded her hands in her lap, taking a few deep breaths. When she opened her eyes, they seemed clear and bright.

"When I was young," she began, "fresh out of high school, I married a boy because he got me pregnant—not a match made in heaven, and we both knew it. A few months later, he ran off. A few months after that, my baby died in childbirth. I was devastated— about my baby boy—but I felt nothing but relief that my husband was gone. Never tried to find him. He was *no* gentleman. So after a while, I divorced him in absentia on grounds of abandonment. And that was that."

Heather said, "I had no idea…"

"Why would you?" asked Lillie. "So at least I have the slim comfort of not being, in common parlance, a 'spinster'—I was married, and I had a son."

I felt compelled to ask, "What was your son's name?"

"Harrison. Not very original—Harrison Ford was on a roll back then."

I said, "That was around the same period when I was born. I went to school with a couple of Harrisons."

"Kids at school, I thought they'd call him Harry... but he never..."

After a respectful silence, Heather reminded her, "We were talking about 'special friendships.' With gay men?"

"Ah! We were." Lillie rattled her head. "Everything's crazy lately. The whole world's confused. Or is it just me?"

I assumed her question was rhetorical. In any event, I didn't answer.

She continued, "I have a younger brother who has a large family in Green Bay, four kids, all grown now. But when the kids were young—this was a few years after Harry died—I helped out a lot because their mother worked. So I was sort of their nanny as well as their Aunt Lillie. And they're all wonderful kids. But the youngest was special, always the perfect little gentleman." Lillie smiled at the memory.

My eyes slid toward Heather, who glanced toward me as well.

Lillie continued, "Being the youngest of four, Davie—that's his name—he didn't grow up having the same burdens of expectation from his parents. The older kids, they were all supposed to *perform*, to *measure up*, as if their parents needed to prove something. Which is all well and good. But by the time Davie came along, the pressure was off, and as he grew into a young man, he could be *himself*, so to speak."

Heather mused, "Something tells me Davie turned out gay."

"He did. He came out in high school, which seemed pretty amazing at the time. But now, I understand, kids come to grips with this even younger."

"Some do, yes," I assured her.

"Davie was always my favorite of the four. I shouldn't say that, but it's true. And when the time came for him to tell his secret, he shared it *first* with me. To this day, we have a 'special friendship.'"

It did not escape me—and I assumed it had not escaped Heather—that Lillie's pet nephew had the same first name as David Lovell. Finding this more than a little troubling, I asked Lillie outright, "Did you have the same feelings for your nephew as you had for David Lovell?"

"Well, *no,*" she said, horrified. "Davie was a *child.* And I'm his *aunt.*"

Heather said, "To be clear about this, Lillie—how, exactly, would you describe your feelings for David Lovell?"

More calmly than I expected, Lillie explained, "David Lovell wasn't a child; he was a man. I wasn't his aunt; I'm a woman. He was a perfect gentleman, and I was desperate to know his love."

"But he was gay," said Heather.

"Love conquers all," said Lillie.

"Oy," said I.

Coconut was in the air, smelling toasty and sweet, drifting from the kitchen.

Heather asked Lillie, "Are you baking macaroons?"

Lillie nodded. "Don't you love them? Ever since I was a little girl, I've considered them a *special* treat. Growing up in Wisconsin—plenty of pines, no palm trees—coconut always seemed exotic. Still does."

"Do you make them often?"

"Whenever my fancy strikes. This morning, when I thought you'd missed our meeting, I figured: put the time to use. So I made a batch. It's pretty simple."

I said, "I believe you took some to David on Wednesday—at the church—correct?"

"I did." She smiled. "David *loved* my macaroons, so I always brought a fresh batch to our lessons."

Heather said, "So he'd eaten your macaroons before."

"Heavens, yes. Many times. Wednesday, when I pulled the covered dish out of my tote bag, he ate a couple on the spot." She laughed, recalling, "I wondered if there'd be any left by the time I got back."

I asked, "Why did you leave?"

"I had office mail to take to the post office. There's usually nothing urgent, but that day there was a large payment on an insurance policy—property and liability. Mother Hibbard asked me to send it by registered mail. I wanted to make sure it would go out with the afternoon dispatch, so I took care of it before my lesson. By the time I got back to the church, well … you know what happened."

I thought, That's easily checked, the story about sending registered mail.

I said, "David's brother, Geoff Lovell, told us he went to the church that afternoon to talk to David. He said he was there when you brought the cookies. Did you see him?

Lillie paused. "There *was* someone there, yes, but I didn't pay much attention. During the day, people come and go—the church is open."

Ding.

Lillie stood. "The macaroons are ready. Care to try them?"

Silly question. After sitting there smelling them for some twenty minutes, on the verge of drooling, I felt ready to pounce—and I thought of Mister Puss reacting to a whiff of beef tenderloin, purring, pacing, nearly dancing at my feet. I told Lillie, "*Sure.*"

Leading us into the kitchen, she said, "You're supposed to let'm cool awhile, but why wait? Just blow on'm."

Lillie's little kitchen was tidy and efficient, a galley with steel cabinets that I assumed had a white factory finish, originally, but had subsequently been brush painted by various occupants of the house. They were now a light pink—chipped and forlornly outdated.

Heather and I needed to huddle at the far end of the galley, by the refrigerator, while Lillie bent down to open the oven door. Over her shoulder, she asked Heather, "Could you get some saucers from the cupboard? Napkins are in the drawer below."

Heather leaned and whispered to me, "Look for nuts."

We quietly opened and closed as many cabinets as we could reach, rattling a few dishes as Lillie slid the cookies from the baking sheet to a wire rack that clattered on the sink's porcelain drainboard. "There," she said, turning to us as we handed her the saucers and passed the napkins around, "these are looking splendid. Careful, though—still steaming hot."

We stood in a tight circle, blowing on the sticky cookies we pronged in our fingers, nibbling at the golden, crusty outer shreds of coconut, cooing at the utter decadence of the combined taste and texture and aroma. The distinctive scent conjured in my mind the warmth and breezes of a beach in Hawaii.

Heather told Lillie, "These are flat-out delicious. Are there nuts in them?"

Lillie shook her head, licked her fingers. "No nuts in macaroons."

"I didn't think so," said Heather. "Only reason I ask is, we're trying to figure out exactly what happened to David, and we wonder if maybe he ate some nuts."

Lillie set down her saucer. "No, I'm sure that wasn't the case. You see, he was highly allergic to nuts—*everyone* knew that."

"That's what I've been hearing."

I said, "Lillie, your macaroons are *the* best. Could I possibly take a couple home to share with my husband?"

We were sent on our way with a round of hugs and a wad of

warm cookies wrapped in waxed paper. Walking from the house to the car, I passed the cookies to Heather, suggesting, "Compare them to the macaroons you took from the church."

"Got it." She dropped the bundle into her purse. "So? What do you think?"

"I think she wears too much perfume."

Heather laughed. "Yeah, I noticed that. It's Shalimar—I'd know it anywhere. My mom always wore it. Still does. She calls it 'the perfume of temptation.'"

"Scary thought." But I was mulling another thought, scarier still, regarding Lillie's repeated forgetfulness:

On Wednesday afternoon, Lillie had to be reminded to take the mail from Mother Hibbard's office. This morning, she forgot the correct time of our meeting and then drifted off-topic several times during our conversation. And yesterday, Geoff Lovell described her as 'ditzed out' when he'd seen her in the church. All of this made me wonder if Lillie could have forgotten that her macaroon recipe never included nuts. More important, could she have forgotten that David Lovell was allergic to nuts?

And finally, the scariest thought of all: What if Lillie could *not* forget David's snub of her advances—and deliberately killed him?

Sitting in the passenger seat of Marson's Range Rover seemed like an embarrassment of spaciousness—compared to the passenger seat of Heather Vance's roadster, in which there was so little room for my feet, I needed to pull my knees up to my chest. After my morning meeting with Lillie Miller, Marson had driven me to a lunch meeting with clients in an industrial park out near the highway, and on our way back into town, I spotted one of those big-box pet stores in a strip mall. I asked my husband, "Mind if we stop here?"

"Whatever for?" he asked with feigned innocence.

Once inside, Marson browsed the pet dishes, dismissing all of them as "hideous," while I headed down another aisle in search of a more suitable harness for Mister Puss.

There were plenty resembling the gaudy fabric vest that Mary Questman had been foisting on her cat—with no success at all. What I had in mind, however, was something much simpler, more classic, and above all, more complementary to Mister Puss's regal Abyssinian manliness. (Yes, I was perhaps overthinking this.) Fingering through a rack of unpromising choices sized for small dogs and cats, I was growing discouraged when, aha, hiding behind a particularly ugly specimen that was padded with synthetic plush lining and upholstered in reflective hazard-orange nylon—*there it was!* I lifted the display hanger reverently from the rack, as if finding the needle in the haystack, the Holy Grail. Consisting solely of thin strips of tanned leather with brass buckles and fittings, it reminded me of a horse's bridle.

Finding a matching leash proved far easier than finding the harness itself. There were many basic leashes—hand loop at one end, clip at the other. I chose one in tanned leather with brass rivets, about three or four feet long.

By then, Marson had collected an armload of treats and toys. After checking out, we returned to his SUV and headed back to town.

We were planning to visit the construction site of our new house that afternoon, but it was still early—Clem Carter, our contractor, wasn't expecting us until two—so we decided to go home first and look in on our guest. That morning was the first time Mister Puss had been left alone at the loft.

As we entered through the back door, the loft was quiet, save for the hum of the refrigerator. I called, "Mister Puss?"

We set our purchases on the kitchen island and walked into the main space. Looking for the cat, I spied him on the top step of the spiral staircase, yawning.

Marson laughed. "He seems to have settled in. Bet he found the sunny spot on the bed, under the skylight." Marson had a habit of making the bed with military precision, tucking the covers taut, but he didn't seem at all bothered by the notion that a cat had whiled away the morning sprawled in the center of the duvet.

"Begging His Majesty's pardon," I said, "but we come bearing gifts."

Mister Puss shook himself awake, then trotted down the stairs.

Marson said, "I wonder if this stuff really works." He opened a small plastic canister of catnip, took a goodly pinch of it, and grinding it between his fingers, let it fall to the concrete floor at the base of the stairs.

Mister Puss approached it with interest, giving it a close sniff.

He sneezed. Then he rolled in it.

I said to Marson, "Easy. We just got him awake." I scooped up the cat and whisked the herbal debris from his snout. He was purring loudly as I grabbed the bag containing the new harness and leash. I singsonged to him, "I think you're going to *like* this."

Stepping into the living room, I sat on the low table and set the cat next to me. I slid the contents of the bag onto the table, telling Mister Puss, "If you can learn to use this, we can take you out and show you off." The purring stopped.

Marson chuckled. "Good luck with *that*." And he headed upstairs to freshen up.

I lifted the cat's chin with my fingertips and looked into his eyes. "I know you don't like the harness Mary got for you, and I don't blame you. It's not your style at all. But I found something that'll be quite handsome on you. Shall we give it a try?" I rubbed behind his ears and stroked his back. He was purring again, though it was soft and tentative.

"That's better," I said. "Trust me, if you don't like it, it's gone. Now, stand up—all fours." He complied while I examined the harness, figuring out what went where. Then I got him into it and buckled him up. "Very nice," I said, setting him on the floor. "*Very* nice."

He stepped around—strutted, in fact—twisting his neck to get a look at himself.

"Here, I'll show you." I picked him up and took him to the mirror by the front door. He leaned toward his reflection as we neared, purring. I could tell he liked it. "So," I asked, "how's that?"

Kinky!

"Don't go there."

Kitten with a whip!

"Stop that." I took him back to the low table, explaining, "Now, the *point* of all this is the leash." I waited for a comeback.

Set my people free.

I plowed ahead. "The leash allows us to go outdoors together. It keeps *you* out of harm's way, and it keeps *me* from worrying. I clip this to your harness"—I did so—"and then, when I walk, you walk alongside me. Don't pull ahead, straining the leash; let it hang limp and walk near my feet. And most important: If I stop, you stop. Got it?"

Piece of cake.

"Good. Let's try it." With leash in hand, I plopped the cat to the floor and began walking toward the kitchen. To my immense relief, I did not need to drag him to get him moving, as Mary had tried to do. Rather, he did exactly as I had instructed, walking at my heel. Rounding the dining table several times, I tried speeding up and slowing down, which Mister Puss mimicked exactly. And when I stopped, he heeled and sat.

I leaned down to give him a vigorous rub. "That was freaking *fab*-ulous," I told him as he erupted into a loud, rolling purr.

"All right," I commanded, "again." And I walked him throughout the loft, tracing a figure eight around the kitchen and living room—faster, slower, stopping—several times. He didn't miss a single cue.

Returning from the mezzanine, Marson had stopped halfway down the spiral stairs, where he was watching us, quietly amazed.

"Well, I'll be damned," he muttered.

Our visit to the building site that afternoon was an ideal trial outing to check Mister Puss's newly acquired leash skills in the wild. While I was confident he would perform as expected when we arrived at the site, I wasn't sure what to expect during the ride in the Range Rover, so I put him in the cat carrier—in case he got freaked by the drive.

He was in the backseat, in the carrier, in his harness, with the leash strung through the cage door. Up front in the passenger seat, I held the other end of the leash, which I thought might give the cat a sense of connection and security. Marson glanced over while driving. "How's he doing back there?"

I checked. "Fine." Mister Puss sat comfortably in the kennel, nose to the grate. His eyes were wide and alert, showing no agitation or concern, as if taking in the scenery. I asked Marson, "Okay if I try letting him out?"

"Entirely up to you," he said. "Keep a grip on that leash, though." The SUV had begun to lurch and wobble along the bumpier paving of the country road.

Reaching back, I twiddled the cat's nose through the grate, asking, "Care to join us up here in first class?" He purred loudly enough to be heard over the engine noise. So I unlatched and opened the cage door.

Mister Puss sat stone still for a while, then walked halfway out, with his front paws on the edge of the seat. I patted the console, beckoning him forward. Emerging fully from the carrier, he stepped from the seat to the console, where he perched, taking everything in. The overhead foliage whizzed past the windshield as we were propelled through a tunnel of green.

I had shortened the leash as Mister Puss advanced. When a rut in the road challenged his balance, he quickly recovered before hopping over to my lap, where he curled up and closed his eyes.

"Look at that," I told Marson. "Instant catnap."

"I don't blame him. I'd *love* to nap in your lap."

"Save that thought for later." I winked.

Our destination was only a couple of minutes away, but I thought I should check in with Sheriff Simms, so I fished the phone from my pocket and placed a call.

"Hey, Brody," he said. "I heard from Heather Vance. Sounds like you had a real heart-to-heart with Lillie."

"We did indeed." I told him about Lillie's misplaced affections for David Lovell. I told him about Lillie's macaroons, about the samples I gave to Heather for comparison to the cookies taken from the church. And I told him about the insurance premium Lillie sent by registered mail—right around the time David died. I asked, "Is there any way to verify that, Thomas?"

"Probably," he said. "We'll look into it."

"Meanwhile, Marson and I are on our way to check on the new house and talk to Clem Carter. We've been having too many delays."

"Yeah," said Thomas, "I read about that. Hope you have a productive talk."

"Thanks, but I'm planning to probe a bit deeper."

Marson gave me a quizzical look.

"A bit deeper about what?" asked Thomas.

"About the confrontation Clem had with that preservationist—Kayla somebody—at the parish meeting last week. Clem got all wound up. We've dealt with him a lot, and I've never seen that side of him."

"Kayla sure knew how to punch his buttons," agreed Simms. "Interesting."

The tract of land where Marson had challenged me to design "the perfect house" was originally owned by Mary Questman's family, a remnant of the vast holdings they acquired during the heyday of their timber empire.

The site was lightly wooded with birches where it opened to a prairie, which was now held in trust by a conservancy. A stream ran through a craggy ravine, forming a playful waterfall of perhaps twenty feet where some Ice Age mischief had cleaved upper and lower plateaus. When Marson had first taken me there, my heart skipped a beat, and I knew how Frank Lloyd Wright must have felt on his first visit to Bear Run in Pennsylvania. The similarity of the two settings was arresting, and I quickly formed a mental image of the vista that would be enjoyed from a house perched on the upper plateau—a prairie view that would never change, preserved for posterity.

When Mary first showed Marson the land, she told him she'd been tendered many offers for it over the years, but she'd never felt right about parting with it. Later, however, after I had entered Marson's life, he approached Mary with an idea—our perfect house—and she was all in. She sold him the land for a song. They sealed the deal then and there. As a deposit, she took whatever cash Marson had in his pocket.

Now, as Marson and I approached the building site out near the edge of town, our dreams for the perfect house, once merely a concept, were becoming a physical reality—in steel, glass, and concrete—above that isolated stream in a grove of birches. When Marson first saw my design for the house, he had called it "a faceted jewel in the woods." For the time being, however, the scene was dominated by a huge sign with burly black lettering against an eyeball-searing background of cadmium yellow: CARTER CONSTRUCTION.

We pulled the SUV into a clearing where various builders' trucks were parked at slapdash angles—the project may have been behind schedule, but it was good to see plenty of activity today. Getting out of the vehicle, I set Mister Puss down on the gravel, and he looked about, seeming far more interested in the birds than in the house taking shape over the waterfall.

Marson joined me, and we began to trudge with the cat up an embankment toward the building. I noticed Clem Carter standing on the upper level of the house, engaged with another man in what appeared to be a heated conversation. At the bottom of the driveway, Nia Butler, Dumont's code-enforcement officer, stood beside an SUV that bore the city emblem on its door. She was facing away from us, talking on her phone.

"Uh-oh," said Marson. As we walked in her direction, he called, "Officer Butler?"

When she turned to us, her eyes bugged. "Sweet Jesus, what the hell is *that*?"

I realized she was transfixed by Mister Puss, who did indeed resemble a leashed cougar, although a very small one. "It's a *cat*," I explained with a laugh. "A house cat."

She put away her phone and walked over to us. "It's a *kitty*?" She hunkered down for a closer look, lifting her granny glasses and twiddling her fingers, which the cat sniffed, purring. "How'd you teach a cat to walk on a leash?"

"He just sorta took to it."

"My, my." She stood.

Sounding anxious, Marson asked, "Officer Butler, is there—"

"Mr. Miles," she interrupted sternly, "unless I'm mistaken, we are *all*, the three of us here, 'members of the tribe,' so to speak." Her lips curled into a wry smile. "Marson. Call me Nia. And I've been wanting to meet your husband. Brody, correct?"

I introduced myself, adding, "And the little guy is Mister Puss. We're looking after him; he's Mary Questman's cat."

"Nia," said Marson, "while it's always a pleasure, I can't help feeling concerned running into you *here*."

She raised both palms in a soothing gesture. "I came along for the ride. I saw that teaser from Glee Savage in yesterday's paper, so I was curious to get a look at the house—and I must say, it is looking *real* fine. Congratulations, boys. But Hudson has some issues, I guess, and he needed to talk to Clem."

I asked, "Who's Hudson?"

Marson said, "He's the city's building inspector."

Nia explained, "Hudson's in charge during construction. After it's occupied, my turn."

"Those distinctions aside," said Marson, "this is *not* looking good." He directed our attention to the top deck of the house, where Hudson stood with a roll of blueprints tucked under one arm while dashing notes on a clipboard, yelling something at Clem Carter, who was also yelling, looking so red-faced—even from a distance—I feared he might have a stroke.

Nia was apathetic. "Boys will be boys. They'll work it out."

I wasn't so sure. Hudson was now trudging down the embankment, looking pissed. He made a beeline for his SUV, hopped in, slammed the door, started the engine, and honked.

Nia leaned in our direction to stage-whisper, "Gotta go," then made a dash for the SUV as Hudson flung the passenger door open from inside. Nia hoisted herself up over the running board, pulled the door closed, and off they roared, spraying gravel.

From the upper deck, Clem had spotted us. He pointed to the garage—which was not yet finished but served as a temporary construction office—indicating we should meet him there.

Marson asked Clem, "What the devil was *that* all about?"

Clem was sweating and still agitated as we seated ourselves on folding chairs around a long folding table, one of several in the garage that were stacked with plans, schedules, invoices, and all manner of paperwork, none of it having any apparent order. Tools were strewn about in disarray—try finding that angle grinder when you need it. Mister Puss sniffed at the bare cement floor and sneezed. It had been poured only recently and still had the dusty smell of lime and damp sand. Clem blotted his neck and forehead with a rumpled handkerchief before answering Marson's question.

"It was nothing," he said. "A miscommunication."

Marson persisted: "About what?"

"Materials. Specs. 'Unauthorized changes,' according to Hudson. The jerk."

I knew Clem was married, but I'd never met his wife, and I

didn't think they had kids. He was in his fifties with an impressive build that had begun to turn paunchy. His reddish hair, still thick and full, was streaked with silver—and today, it was matted with sweat.

"What sort of changes?" asked Marson. He reminded Clem, "Brody's the designer. And this will be our *home*. But we're behind schedule and over budget. I've heard complaints that subs aren't getting paid. And now the city inspector is finding 'issues' with the work."

"Okay, okay, I get it. You have a right to be concerned, but no need to be worried. Honest." Clem tried to be accommodating and detailed for us the issues raised by Hudson, as well as the various reasons the project had fallen behind schedule—a long winter, supplier problems, undependable subcontractors, and finally, bad luck.

However, there was more to it, I was sure. "Clem," I said, "this is awkward, but we need to get it in the open. It's no secret that you're overextended with that spec house on the west side."

He'd begun a project two years prior, during a boom, building a fat-ass house in a new development, tricking it out with "features" intended to appeal to some unknown but status-seeking buyer. The boom, however, had passed. The market for houses like that had dried up. And not to be snobby, but the design was pure crap. I couldn't imagine that he'd find a buyer at *any* price, let alone a price that would cover what he had in it—and the meter was still running on the loans, with most of his resources tied up.

"Yeah …," he said slowly, "that's a problem." He stood and pulled himself together. "But look. That's *my* problem, and it won't be yours. This house of yours, it's by *far* the best project I've ever built. Swear to God, it's an honor to be part of it. I will *not* let you down; you'll be in by winter. And the problem on the west side? Someone, or something, is bound to come along and turn things around."

Feeling better, having cleared the air, we all shook hands and parted with smiles. Clem Carter went back to work with his crew. Marson, Mister Puss, and I climbed into the Range Rover and headed back to town.

But I had to wonder: What was Clem banking on to "turn things around"? Why the optimism that something would save him from the bad investment he'd made?

At the parish meeting a week earlier, Clem had argued strongly in favor of building a new St. Alban's, rather than restoring the old church. As a member of the parish, he could have a leg up in snagging a plump, lucrative construction contract.

And only two days ago, when David Lovell died at the organ in the church, his swan song had been accompanied by a mysterious incense fire in the center aisle. Had that fire spread, the option of restoration would have gone—literally as well as figuratively—up in smoke.

CHAPTER

8

Joyce Hibbard had been on my mind. A complex and accomplished woman, she also struck me as adrift and, for lack of a kinder word, compromised.

She was adrift on her career path, which had made such radical swings—from law, to the fashion industry, and much later in life, to the priesthood. This was not the reasoned evolution of a calling. Rather, this was the thrashing of frustration.

And she was compromised—emotionally, perhaps even ethically—by the enormity of two life-defining choices she had willfully made. She had joined with a gay man in a marriage of convenience because they calculated it would advance their careers. And now, as her husband phrased it, she had "teamed up for the hocus-pocus" of the priesthood, not because she truly believed what she preached, but because she was in the mood for a challenge.

It was not my place to judge Joyce, let alone to censure her. As far as I knew, she had not *hurt* anyone with these deceptions, and it might even be said that her instincts were laudable. Nonetheless, I was unable to shake the disquieting notion that she was acting out a lifelong charade and—at a fundamental level—could not be trusted.

She was also at the nexus of an odd and fragile triangle with her husband, Curtis Hibbard, and his erstwhile lover, Yevgeny Krymov—a triangle that might have become a quadrangle, had David Lovell lived. Which suggested a tantalizing stew of possibilities regarding David's untimely demise.

On Saturday, therefore, when Marson asked me if I wanted to join him and Mother Hibbard for lunch, I didn't hesitate to tag along. They were meeting at First Avenue Bistro to compare notes regarding the status of St. Alban's fix-or-build dilemma. Only ten days remained for the parish to reach a decision; otherwise, the city would make the decision for them and condemn the old church building.

We decided to walk from the loft to the restaurant, and I regretted that we would not be able to strut along First Avenue with Mister Puss. He had been quite the elegant little gentleman during our prior day's outing to the construction site, but we'd be pushing our luck if we thought Nancy Sanderson would allow a cat, however well behaved, inside the Bistro.

Because lunch would be crowded on a Saturday, Marson wanted to beat the rush and had asked Joyce to meet him a few minutes before noon. When we arrived, Joyce was already there, and Nancy had seated her at our favorite corner table, between the fireplace and the front windows, where we could keep an eye on the entire room as well as activity on the street. The noontide bustle of Dumont's main drag was hardly cosmopolitan, but it offered a lively note of connection to the outside world.

Joyce stood as we approached the table. "*Brody*. What a nice surprise. Lovely of you to join us." She leaned forward for a smooch, accompanied by a strong whiff of her secret sauce.

The restaurant was already getting crowded, and as the three of us were settling at our table, I noticed a family arrive—parents and their adolescent daughter—who looked familiar. "Oh," said Joyce, "it's the Olsons." And she was up again, greeting Bob Olson, the senior warden of St. Alban's parish vestry. He ushered over his wife, Angela, and their pretty daughter, Hailey, whom I remembered from the parish meeting, now nine days past.

Angela was saying, "Hailey isn't doing so well—the shock of

David's death. I guess we're *all* in shock. What an awful tragedy."

Bob held his arm around their daughter, who hung her head. Bob said, "Hailey was in the choir, and right now—Saturday noon—this is when they always practiced for Sunday services. So we're here for a nice lunch instead. We could all use a little boost."

Joyce cooed something about God. Marson and I offered words of commiseration and assured the girl there would be happier times ahead. As we sat again and they moved off to their table, Bob glanced back to thank us with a discreet thumbs-up.

And then, Glee Savage arrived.

We were on our feet again with a round of greetings, which was considerably more upbeat than our encounter with the Olsons. Even with David's death barely three days ago, there was an aspect of Glee's exuberant spirit that simply would not be tamed. "So," she said, beading me with a grin beneath the floppy brim of her big flowered hat, "have you figured it out?" She'd seemingly gotten word that I was on the investigation.

"Not yet, doll." But I assured her, "I'm working on it."

"It's a dreary business, I'm sure. And speaking of dreary business, guess who *I'm* meeting for an interview." She didn't look happy about it, so I assumed she hadn't finally snagged the sit-down with Yevgeny.

I told her, "I'm afraid to guess."

Marson said, "I'll pass."

Mother Hibbard shrugged.

Glee slumped. "It's that *horrid* Kayla Weber Schmidt. After her performance at the St. Alban's meeting, I thought there might be some newsworthy conflict brewing with the preservationist faction—"

"God help us," intoned Mother Hibbard.

"—so I mentioned it to my editor. Then *he* turned around—the son of a bitch—and assigned the story to *me*." Glee tossed her hands;

her beads rattled. "Guess that'll teach me to keep my trap shut."

"Not gonna happen," said Marson.

"I hope to God she doesn't bring that brat. Say a little prayer for me, Joyce."

Joyce wagged her hand in a mock blessing, and Glee trudged off to her table.

Once more, we sat.

Nancy Sanderson came over to welcome us and recite a few specials.

"The quiche sounds divine," said Joyce.

Nancy beamed. "I'm sure you'll enjoy it. It's one of my favorites."

Joyce said, "David Lovell told me that as well—he loved it."

The cheery expression drained from Nancy's face.

"Nancy," I said, "did David Lovell dine here often?"

"Often enough."

"And you said something at our dinner party about David's nut allergy."

"Maybe." Defensively, she added, "Everyone knew about that."

Surprised by her tone, I tried changing the topic. "This may sound like a strange question, but I had a conversation with someone yesterday who said there are no nuts in macaroons, which I hadn't known. Since you're the expert, maybe you could tell me: Is that true? No nuts in macaroons?"

She brightened again. "Correct, no nuts in American macaroons. You could *add* them, sure, but the standard recipes don't call for nuts. Why do you ask?"

The possible connection between macaroons and David's death was not yet known outside the investigation. I told Nancy, "Just curious."

She continued, "On the other hand, French *macarons* are often made with almonds—and usually no coconut. The two cookies are entirely different." With a laugh, she added, "To be honest, I've never understood why they share such similar names."

"Hngh," said Marson. "Interesting."

Dispensing with the cookie chat, we ordered lunch.

Then Marson and Joyce got down to business. He asked her, "The committees you appointed at the parish meeting—any reports yet?"

"Nothing in writing," said Joyce, "but lots of talk. They seem to be leaning toward the build-from-scratch option. After what happened in the church Wednesday—with all the additional damage—I think the choice has become a foregone conclusion."

Marson nodded. "Nearly *anything* can be fixed—if you throw enough effort and money at it. But what do you end up with? An old, problematic building."

Others would disagree. And I noticed that one of them had just walked through the door. Kayla Weber Schmidt made her way through the room to meet Glee, whose prayer had been answered—Kayla's bratty toddler was not in tow.

Our conversation continued through lunch. Joyce confirmed that the parish hall was now set up for regular services, which could no longer be held in the church, starting tomorrow. "But we won't have a choir, of course."

I felt compelled to add, "You won't have an organ, either."

Joyce set down her fork and looked to the ceiling. "I wonder if *that* can be fixed."

Marson repeated, "Anything can be fixed."

Joyce's gaze moved from the ceiling to the window. Squinting, she said, "Is that *Curtis*—across the street?"

We turned to look just as Curtis Hibbard and another man walked out of view.

"Why, yes," said Marson, "that was Curt. Who was that with him?"

Looking perplexed, Joyce told us, "No idea. He *told* me he

was driving to Appleton with Yevgeny. They were going to visit someone on the dance faculty at the conservatory. But that wasn't Yevgeny—and they obviously aren't in Appleton."

Marson said, "Plans must've changed. Too bad we didn't know. Curt could have joined us."

Oh, please, I thought. I'm trying to eat.

Joyce returned her attention to her quiche. "You might want to mark your calendars: we're planning a funeral of sorts for David on Thursday, early afternoon. It'll be a simple memorial, rather than a full-blown Requiem, since we don't know when or if the body will be released by the medical examiner. And David apparently has no family other than his brother, Geoff. I spoke to him—he's indifferent about the arrangements—claims he has no funds. Which is fine. David was part of *our* family, St. Alban's, and we want to do this for him."

Nice. Although I had approached today's lunch with the attitude that Joyce could not be trusted, this glimpse into the sincerity of her pastoral instincts was heartening. While I had not previously been inclined to share with Joyce that I'd been recruited by Sheriff Simms to assist with the investigation, Glee Savage had spilled those beans upon her arrival, so I now had nothing to lose by questioning Joyce about an issue that had perplexed me.

"On Wednesday," I said, "when the three of us rushed to the church, you told me on the front steps that the door should be open, but we found that it was locked. Fortunately, you had your keys. Since then, I've been tussling with a couple of questions."

Joyce said, "What would you like to know? If I can help, I will."

"First, when we approached the church from the back and realized something was wrong, we went past the back door and ran all the way around to the front. Why didn't we go in through the back?"

"Because the back door—to the sacristy—is always locked. I

had the key, but thought we'd get in quicker from the front."

I asked, "When someone leaves through the sacristy door, they always lock it?"

"It locks by itself."

"Okay, got it. Now the front door: It's usually unlocked during the day?"

Joyce nodded. "It may seem impossibly trusting—in this day and age—but Father Sterling, who preceded me, had upheld that tradition during his many years here. He thought the church should be open and welcoming. And as far as I know, it was never a problem. Being the new rector, I didn't want to be thought of as 'the woman who locked the church.' In retrospect, I probably should have."

"And yet," I said, "we found the front doors locked on Wednesday. Since they're usually left open, I assume they don't lock by themselves."

"Correct. From the outside, it takes a key to lock or unlock them—and it can be a hassle, as you saw—big doors, old hardware. So the front doors have always been locked at night from inside. It's much easier. You throw the bolt, no key required."

Mulling this, I said, "In other words, without a key, you could lock yourself in and then leave through the sacristy, which locks itself."

Marson joined the conversation. "Which means: anyone could have done it."

"Yes," said Joyce. "Afraid so."

"But," I noted, "whoever locked the doors is almost certainly the same person who set the incense fire. Which probably required at least a passing knowledge of where things were kept—the thurible, the incense, the coal."

Joyce said, "Possibly. It's all kept in the sacristy, but not hidden or locked away."

I asked, "Could I get a list of everyone who has 'backstage access,' so to speak?"

"Sure. I'll have Lillie put that together for you."

Across the room, at Glee's table, Kayla Weber Schmidt was getting noisy, drawing disapproving glances from Nancy Sanderson and most of the other patrons. Thumping her hand on the table, Kayla told Glee, "But it's *not* just a matter of economics—there's a piece of the town's *heritage* at stake!"

"Oh, dear," said Marson, sotto voce. "Glee's got her hands full."

"That Kayla," Joyce harrumphed. "She's a viper."

I had wanted to broach with Joyce the topic of her marriage and to explore any jealousy or resentment she might feel, stemming from her husband's wandering eye for men and his brazen disregard for Episcopal propriety. But we were at lunch, in public, amid genteel surroundings on a balmy May afternoon. So I was at a loss to find a tactful way to question her regarding issues that were intensely personal, doubtless painful, and—in the final analysis—none of my damn business.

When our meal was finished and the check was paid, I noticed Glee and Kayla also wrapping up their lunch meeting. Kayla stood, said something in parting, and left. Glee remained at the table with a cup of coffee, jotting notes.

Marson pushed back his chair, and the three of us stood. I said good-bye to Joyce, then told Marson, "I think I'll hang around and schmooze with Glee."

"Sure, kiddo. I'm going to check in at the office. See ya later at home." He leaned to give me a peck, then escorted Joyce out the door.

The lunch crowd had thinned, and I wound my way through the empty tables toward the back of the dining room, where Glee sat alone, focused on her notes.

"Hey, doll," I said, "can I intrude?"

She looked up with a smile. "Please *do*. I could use some friend-ly company after an hour with Kayla—what a churl."

"Joyce Hibbard called her a viper," I said as I sat.

"Viper," Glee repeated with a glint in her eye. Then she made note of it.

"You are *not* going to print that."

"Well, I won't attribute it."

I hardly needed to ask, but did anyway: "How'd it go?"

"Unpleasant. Sometimes, though, that's the price of a good sto-ry. I'll have to discuss this with our editor—liabilities, defamation, and such. It's a delicate balance—gossip and journalism."

"What are you *talking* about?"

Glee set down her pen. "As you know, I don't normally report hard news—I'm society and arts, which I try to keep glib and en-tertaining. Then there's *Kayla*. Yes, she's a devoted preservationist, and the county historical society is definitely within my realm. *But*. She's so whacking opinionated, everything she says comes across as strident and irrational and, more to the point, slander-ous." Glee raised her coffee cup, holding it near her chin, thinking. The rim was smeared red with her lip prints.

I asked, "For example?"

Setting down her cup, she leaned over it and lowered her voice to tell me, "Clem Carter."

That got my attention.

Glee continued, "It was largely the same pissing match that Kayla started with him at the parish meeting—she accused him of having a vested financial interest in seeing the old church de-stroyed so he can step in as builder of the new one."

I had to admit, "To a degree, there's some logic to that."

"Except"—Glee leaned closer—"today Kayla took it a giant step further. And the *language*. Referring to Clem with vulgarities

I'm not inclined to repeat, let alone print, she *accused* him of setting the incense fire and, by implication, killing David."

"Whoa." I sat back in my chair. "That's a leap. How'd she back it up?"

Glee flipped her hands. "Instinct. She says it's obvious; she just *knows*."

"Instinct"—I snorted—"more like insane."

"*Tell* me. I can't imagine what Tyler sees in her." Archly, Glee added, "If I were he, I'd flee."

"Who?"

"Tyler Schmidt is Kayla's husband. Their little terror is Aiden Weber Schmidt; he must be the four-year-old glue that keeps them together. They live in an old farmhouse—'historic,' I'm sure—out on Perkins Road. Tyler is a few years younger than Kayla, kinda quiet, the perpetual-student type. But he's also an artist and, from what I've seen, pretty good. Works in metal, welding, abstract. Big studio in a barn near the farmhouse."

"More coffee?" asked Nancy Sanderson, appearing at the table with a carafe.

"No, thanks," said Glee, "I need to be going soon. But could you box up a dozen of your *madeleines* for me to take home? They're *absolument parfait*—and one day I'll get the hang of baking them myself."

"Sure, Glee. I'll have it at the register whenever you're ready."

Watching as Nancy stepped away, I said to Glee, "It's strange. Nancy is such a great gal—friendly and nurturing, salt of the earth. Same with David Lovell—I didn't get to know him very well, but it seems everyone flat-out *loved* the guy. And yet ..."

"And yet," Glee suggested, leaning low over the table, "you've noticed some 'frostiness' from Nancy regarding David?"

"*Yes*, precisely. At the dinner party at the loft, Nancy's attitude toward David was chilly. And here today, she went all ice-queen at the mere mention of his name. What's that all about?"

Glee glanced over her shoulder. She then told me, "I happen to have a few insights. It's a long story—goes way back—but this isn't the time or the place."

I whipped out my phone and checked my calendar. "How about Tuesday? Lunch at the club. My treat—but I want the dirt."

"Deal." She stood.

I stood. We moved together to the gleaming display case of to-go items adjacent to the checkout counter. Nancy gabbed with Glee while ringing up the *madeleines*. I browsed the goodies that glistened beneath the curved glass.

My gaze was instantly drawn to a tempting mound of macaroons, all golden brown and gooey and bristling with toasted coconut. Next to them sat a selection of prim, smooth French *macarons* in assorted pastels with a variety of delicate fillings.

Then, moving to the cash register, I noticed a small display of tiny bottles containing gourmet specialty oils and extracts. When I leaned in for a closer look, my eye stalled on one of the labels: PURE ALMOND EXTRACT.

Sunday morning, Marson and I relaxed in the living room of the loft, sharing sections of the *Dumont Daily Register* and dropping finished pages to the floor for Mister Puss's amusement. He would slide beneath them as they landed, then shred them as he escaped, pouncing into the mess he'd created. The front section carried an updated story regarding the investigation of David Lovell's death, but skimming it, I found there was nothing reported that I didn't already know, so I dangled the sheet to catch Mister Puss's attention. He leapt, snatching it from my fingers and tumbling with it to the floor.

Marson gathered up some of the shreds and took them to the trash in the kitchen when he went to get more coffee. While he was there, the iPad on the center island *pinged* with an incoming email, which he sat down to read. A few minutes later, he brought the tablet to the living room. Handing it to me, he said, "Take a look."

From: Curtis Hibbard
To: Marson Miles

Marson, old chum, my precious Poopsie has been in a bit of a dither regarding the financial challenges now facing St. Alban's. When she sought my advice last night, I adroitly sidestepped the issue, ho-ho, and suggested she take up the matter with her bishop, who is paid to deal with such unpleasantries. I thought the attached correspondence might be of interest to you.

On another matter, I do hope to see you (and your charming young man) again soon, while I am still here in Dumont. Perhaps dinner?

Best regards,
Curtis Hibbard, Founding Partner
Hibbard Belding & Smith, LLP
New York • London • Berlin

Following is a copy of Poopsie's message to her bishop.

From: The Rev. Joyce Hibbard
To: The Rt. Rev. Stuart P. Wiggins

Dear Bishop Wiggins,

Barely two months after being entrusted to serve St. Alban's as rector, I have been confounded by a situation that could prove of great significance to the future of the parish. Attempting to sort out this dilemma, I have sought direction from my pastoral training and from fervent prayer, but without success. So I turn to you, Bishop, in hopes that you might guide me with the wisdom of your good counsel.

As you know, St. Alban's is a historic parish that has suffered through many years of declining membership. As a result, the physical properties of the parish have fallen into varying stages of disrepair and neglect. The church itself is the most stirring and enduring symbol of St. Alban's former greatness, but it, too, has reached a point where serious action is needed, and soon. (It may already have come to your attention that, earlier this week, our beloved choirmaster died, and was possibly murdered, on the premises. As if that weren't sufficient frosting on the cake, a minor fire inflicted further damage to the building.)

Amid lengthy discussion, soul-searching, and prayer, our parish vestry is now considering whether the current building should be replaced with a new structure that better reflects the purpose and aspirations of a Christian community entering the third millennium. The decision seems imminent, and I support it. The difficulty, of course, is funding.

Our great hope in this regard rests in the potential generosity of Mrs. Mary Questman, a widow (childless) of considerable means whose family has a long history as parishioners at St. Alban's. Given your tenure in the diocese, Bishop, do you perhaps know her?

The predicament I now face is that Mary seems to be suffering a crisis of faith. I would offer to pray with her— to gently nudge her back into the loving embrace of the Church—but Mary's doubts do not stem from within. Rather, she has fallen under the influence (and I hesitate to write these words) of her cat, with which she imagines to communicate. She told me matter-of-factly that the cat informed her that "God is a myth." You will wonder, perhaps, if she might have been joking. I can only assure you that her manner of delivery lacked any hint of mirth.

Mary cannot be more than ten or twelve years my senior, so it troubles me to realize that the mind is so fragile at our age, that dementia is so indiscriminate, that it can strike such a good and kindly soul without warning.

None of this, however, negates the possibility that Mary could be swayed to step forward as a major donor, though the cat does present obvious complications, having warned her, and I quote, "Hold on to your wallet." If I am unable to appeal to Mary's faith, would it be ethical to appeal instead to her vanity? Her ego? Perhaps she would find it gratifying to serve as honorary chair of the St. Alban's pledge drive.

Any thoughts you can offer will be most gratefully received.

Yours in Christ,
The Rev. Joyce Hibbard, Rector
St. Alban's Episcopal Church, Dumont

Following is the bishop's response to Poopsie.

From: The Rt. Rev. Stuart P. Wiggins
To: The Rev. Joyce Hibbard

Dear Mother Hibbard,
Sweeten the deal. Make her an offer she can't refuse.

Yours in Christ,
The Rt. Rev. Stuart P. Wiggins, Bishop
Episcopal Diocese of Central Wisconsin

I was perplexed by the undertones of Curtis Hibbard's email. What had motivated him to share this communication with Marson? Was the whole thing merely a pretext for setting up another social rendezvous that would include *me*, described as Marson's "young man"? And what were we to make of Joyce Hibbard's approach to her bishop? Her suggestion, coupled with his response, amounted to collusion—a disturbing exploration of schemes to invade Mary Questman's wallet.

Mister Puss, who had warned of such conniving, now rode in my car as I drove toward the edge of town on Perkins Road.

Earlier that Sunday, I had made an appointment to meet Kayla

Weber Schmidt's husband, Tyler Schmidt, the metal artist, who would be working in his welding studio that afternoon. I'd had no difficulty finding him on the Internet, so I texted that Glee Savage had spoken highly of his art, which was true. I also mentioned that, as an architect, I might find use for one of his pieces in a current design project, a half-truth at best. He told me to drop by anytime after two.

Tooling along Perkins Road, I watched for various landmarks described by Tyler, who'd warned me that the farm could be difficult to find. Passing the intersection of a quiet county highway as I left the city limits, I felt confident of my bearings. Up ahead, I saw a sign for a secluded picnic area Tyler had mentioned, and checking my watch, I decided to pull in for a few minutes, since it was not yet two o'clock.

The picnic area was a tiny county park, designed to take advantage of the view from the shore of a small body of water, Meteor Lake, which was not much bigger than a pond, but perfectly round, the imprint of a celestial intruder from eons past. That long-ago cataclysm was belied by today's tranquil setting. Though it was an ideal Sunday afternoon for a picnic, no one else was present as I rolled into the gravel parking lot. Where were they? Had they been misguided by the patchwork of rural byways? Though seeking serenity, were they now lost and late and wandering?

Well into my third year of living in Dumont, I had never even heard of Meteor Lake. But there it was—blue and placid, deep and cold—the focus of an improbable landscape framed by my windshield.

Mister Puss began to purr as I clipped the leash to his harness and opened the car door. Jumping to the ground, he followed at my heel as I strolled past the weathered wooden tables and continued through the lush May grass to the shore. The tendriled branches of a willow moved in the breeze, rippling the surface of the water. High in a birch, a hidden bird chattered and pecked, drawing the cat's radar gaze. I heard the lowing of a cow at some distance, across the lake and beyond a berm that was crested with the shining barbs of a wire fence.

Reaching down, I picked up Mister Puss and cradled him like a baby in my arms. "What do you think?" I asked him. "A little slice of heaven?"

He looked up at me, purring, squinting into the sun.

Back on the road, a few minutes past two, I spotted the coun-try mailbox stenciled WEBER SCHMIDT. The historic farm, like Meteor Lake, was hidden from view. A bank of maples with a lower hedge of wild honeysuckle, resplendent with starry white blooms, screened the homestead from the street, allowing a mere glimpse of an opening where the driveway entered beneath a nat-ural arch of the trees.

Driving in slowly, I saw the house to the right and the barn to the left. From the tone of Glee's description, I expected the house to resemble a dilapidated pioneer shack, but instead, it exhibited some serious design integrity—an artful blending of neoclassical and Greek Revival motifs—which had been meticulously re-stored. The barn, of course, was far more utilitarian, and because its original purpose was now nil—the land was no longer being farmed—the hulking space had been sensitively updated and re-purposed as the studio of a working artist.

I hung a left.

A pickup truck was parked near a side door to the studio. I parked behind it and got out of the car, telling Mister Puss, "There might be dogs. Pay attention." His eyes swept the surroundings on high alert. Somewhere beyond the buildings, from a neighbor-ing parcel, I heard a cow and wondered if it was the same one I'd heard from the other side of the lake.

The door had no bell or buzzer or any kind of sign, so I rapped on the window pane, but there was no response. The cat looked up at me. I shrugged, then opened the door and stepped inside, calling, "Hello?"

"In here," replied a muffled voice from the space beyond the small room where I stood, which seemed like a mudroom or an indoor porch. From the connecting doorway, I heard a steady hiss, a radio playing hard rock—softly, which seemed odd—and the squawk of a child. But no dogs.

With Mister Puss in tow, I walked through the doorway and into the wide-open interior of the barn proper. "Tyler? It's Brody Norris."

The radio clicked off. From behind a partial wall hung with tools and whatnot, Tyler Schmidt stepped toward me, removing a welder's mask. From the other side of the wall, a toddler sprang forward and clung to his father's overalls as they neared.

"Hi there, Brody," said Tyler with a smile, setting aside the mask and offering his hand, which I shook. It was heavy, callused, and manly, despite Tyler's lean frame, fair complexion, and younger years; I had learned from his website that he was twenty-five.

"Hey!" he said, eyeing Mister Puss. "Who's this? What a beautiful cat."

"*Kitty!*" said the child, squatting for a closer look.

"This is Mister Puss. I'm looking after him for Mary Questman," I explained. "And who's *this* little guy?" I was well aware that he was the same monstrous four-year-old who'd thrown a tantrum at the parish meeting.

"This is Aiden," said his dad. "Aiden? Stand up and say hello to Mr. Norris."

The boy refused, focused solely on Mister Puss, whom he approached on hands and knees. "*Kitty!*"

Mister Puss backed off. The boy screamed.

Tyler pulled Aiden up off the floor, wrapped his arms around the boy's shoulders, and gently rocked him, calming him. "Kayla's working with a bunch of volunteers all afternoon, so I have a 'helper.'" Tyler winked at me.

While I hadn't planned on the kid being there, any annoyance I might have felt was outweighed by relief, knowing that Tyler's wife, the abrasive preservationist, would not appear.

Tyler said, "Let me show you around." Taking his boy by the hand, he led me, with Mister Puss following on his leash, around the partial wall and into Tyler's work area.

Having been an architecture student in college, I had known many artists-in-training and had frequently spent time in the disarray and seeming mayhem of their studios, so I felt that I was entering not only familiar territory but also sacred ground—this was where Tyler's creativity flourished, where he made magic out of nothing but ideas and vision and brute strength and fire. A welder's torch hissed, standing at the ready to rearrange molecules of iron, sending off a wisp of white smoke that bore the broiled atoms of unknown elements, reminding me of an acrid incense. Mister Puss sneezed.

And the offspring of Tyler's artistry stood all around us. Towering totems of steel—and stone and bolts and thick, rusted cable—had sprung from the depths of his imagination and now rose like giant, eyeless sentinels keeping watch over nothing. And everything.

I was speechless. Glee had described Tyler's work as "pretty good." While even faint praise from Glee qualified as a ringing endorsement, I felt she had sold him short. Tyler's phantasmic metal abstracts, some of them twelve feet high, had a timeless, visceral appeal in a singular style that defied categorizing. What's more, they had obvious potential as inflection points to modern architecture—I could think of several such projects currently in the works, including a "perfect house" being built over a waterfall.

"Tyler," I said, "we need to talk."

We got comfortable in a corner of the studio that might be described as Tyler's lounge—or man cave—a retreat from the actual work of producing his art, where he could think, relax, refresh. The coffeemaker was gurgling. The boom box, silent. Mister Puss snoozed in my lap as I sat in an old stuffed chair, talking to Tyler across a low makeshift tabletop supported by five-gallon paint buckets. Little Aiden scrounged around the periphery of the space, exploring scraps of metal, lumber, and abandoned tools. "Careful," Tyler admonished the boy.

When we had finished discussing my enthusiasm for the totems and what it might cost to acquire one, maybe two, we drifted into more personal topics. I said, "My husband and I are living in a downtown loft—an old haberdashery on First Avenue. It's exciting to find a new use for buildings that would otherwise be shuttered and forgotten. But then, *you* know all about that, living here with Kayla."

"That's, uh, putting it mildly. She has passion, I'll give her that. It's her life."

I noted, "And your life, your passion, is out here—with your art."

"Right." He paused. "We have an understanding. We love each other. We have a kid—he's challenged and challenging, and sure, we love him, too. But love and passion aren't necessarily the same thing."

"They're not," I agreed. "It's nice if they align, but it doesn't always happen."

Mister Puss stretched, stood, and hopped down from my lap. He wandered behind my chair, still tethered by the leash I held.

Tyler continued, "So Kayla does *her* thing, and I do mine. And basically, she makes *this* possible." He gestured broadly toward the whole setup in his studio. "She's five years older, with a steady career. From the start, we sorta joked that she's my 'patron.' She likes to call the shots."

This came as no surprise to me. What surprised me was that he readily acknowledged it. I ventured to ask, "Because Kayla is so passionate about historic preservation, I'm wondering how she's been affected by the debate at St. Alban's. Does she ever talk about it?"

"Well, she can't *stop* talking about Clem Carter. In *our* household, he's affectionately known as Bulldozer Boy, plus a few expletives that—"

The heavy sound of metal sliding was followed by a crash and clang behind my chair that shot through the cement floor. Mister Puss screeched a death yowl that brought me to my feet as he tried to escape, practically yanking the leash from my hand, but my grip held tight, as did the clip on his harness. Aiden was bawling, then screamed as his father shot over to him and lifted him from some harmless rubble. But Mister Puss was still sprawled and clawing at the cement, mere inches from where a six-foot I-beam had chipped the floor and raised a cloud of dust.

When I lifted the cat in my arms, he had a wild look in his eyes, and his heart was beating so fast I truly feared that something vital would burst inside him.

"I need to get help," I told Tyler as I rushed toward the door with the cat.

Aiden was still screaming.

"Brody, I'm sorry," yelled Tyler. "Let me know if—"

But I was already dashing through the mudroom and out the door, crunching across the gravel to my car.

In the quiet of the closed car, I sat with Mister Puss in my lap, stroking him gently, whispering worried words, soothing him. His frantic pulse eased. Soon, he was purring. I pulled him up to my chest, as if burping a baby. With a soft laugh, I told him, "I think we *both* had an awful scare."

I'm fine.

"Hope so. But I want to get you in to see Dr. Phelps first thing in the morning."

I chipped a nail. I'm fine.

I pulled out my phone, started the car, and drove out onto Perkins Road, heading back toward Dumont on that unsettling Sunday afternoon. Glancing at the phone, I punched the vet's number. At the tone, I left a long message. Mister Puss clung near my ear, purring.

Put down the damn phone and drive.

10

On Monday morning, I awoke at daybreak, eager to have Mister Puss checked out by Dr. Phelps, but it was far too early; the veterinary office wouldn't open till nine.

Although I put zero credence in the old 'nine lives' adage, I had to marvel that Mister Puss seemed none the worse for Sunday's brush with death, which still left me pondering, with a measure of guilt, whether the leash had saved him from being crushed—or had restrained him from his instincts to flee. While a different adage assured me that all's well that ends well, I knew that if the leash had been six inches longer, I would be grieving this morning rather than sitting in my kitchen petting the cat and enjoying coffee with my husband.

"Well, well," said Marson, passing me a section of the paper, "Glee got her interview with Yevgeny."

"What a minx," I said, looking at her column. "She gave no hint of it Saturday."

Inside Dumont

Yevgeny Krymov still tight-lipped about surprise visit to Dumont

By Glee Savage

•

MAY 23, DUMONT, WI — Only four days ago, dear readers, I shared with you some tantalizing news regarding Yevgeny

Krymov. A living legend whose fame extends far beyond the rarefied world of ballet, he had not only arrived unexpectedly in Dumont but had also hinted he might grant us an interview. I am delighted to report that a last-minute change in his schedule allowed me to sit down with him for a relaxed conversation on Saturday evening, during which he proved to be every bit as charming as he is talented.

Your nosy culture-hound first inquired about the reasons for Mr. Krymov's visit. What could *possibly* bring him to Dumont?

He replied, "Miss Savage, your reputation precedes you, even in Big Apple. I had been longing to make your acquaintance. When Curtis Hibbard, my old friend, invited me to visit his wife at church job, I say, '*Oki doki!*' And here I am."

Finding this explanation dubious, though flattering, I pointed out that he had already been in Dumont for six days.

He said, "But only tonight, we sit down for talk at last."

Sensing that further probing of the nature of his visit would be futile, I shifted the topic to his illustrious career. Going back to the days of his defection...

I tossed the paper aside; the cat pounced on it. "Well, that was a big nothing. I wonder why Yevgeny is being so secretive."

Marson asked, "At lunch with Joyce, what was she saying about him?"

"She said Curtis had planned on driving Yevgeny to Appleton—something about the conservatory—but they apparently never went. In Glee's column, she mentions a 'last-minute change' in Yevgeny's schedule that freed up his Saturday evening. At least *that* part makes sense."

But little else made sense. While chauffeuring Mister Puss toward the vet's office on the outskirts of town, I wondered not so much about the purpose of Yevgeny's visit, but rather, about the tangle of emotions he may have felt regarding David Lovell.

At our dinner party, Yevgeny had lusted after David at first sight, instantly losing interest in *me*, preferring to spar with Curtis Hibbard for the choirmaster's affections. By the end of the meal, however, the dynamics had changed. Curtis had used a ticket to hear Renée Fleming (Yevgeny's ticket) as bait, intended to influence the outcome of the race to bed David. And David bit. Which left Yevgeny slim chances of either hearing the diva or bagging the boy. A stinging setback, surely—but did it measure up to a motive for murder? If so, to my thinking, Yevgeny's target would more logically have been Curtis, whose demise would free up Yevgeny's options with David; it would also allow them to hold hands while basking together in the glorious strains of the diva doing Beethoven. Or was I overestimating the lure of fifth-row center?

Driving out of town on Perkins Road, as I had done the day before, I again came to the intersection of a quiet county highway. Today, however, instead of whisking past it, I turned north on it.

Trundling along the rustic road for a few minutes without another vehicle in sight, I then saw, up ahead, the folksy wooden sign with bent-twig lettering that announced I'd arrived at the practice of James Phelps, DVM. I slowed the car and entered the gravel parking lot.

A split-rail fence separated the gravel from a small, mussy lawn. A path down the middle led to the quaint building, clad in shake shingles, weathered long ago to a silvery gray. Mine was the only car in the lot. I checked my watch—right about nine. In the stillness of the car, I rubbed Mister Puss behind the ears, which always got him purring. I asked, "Ready?"

But I'm fine.

"Come on." I got out of the car, walking Mister Puss on his leash.

A bell on a spring heralded our arrival as we stepped inside. The receptionist looked up from her computer. "Mr. Norris? The doctor was concerned about your message. How's Mister Puss doing?"

"Better than yesterday, I hope. He had a close call. We both had a scare." We passed my credit card back and forth.

She said, "We're not busy this morning, one appointment ahead of you. If you'll take a seat, Dr. Jim will see you soon." As I picked a chair near the window, she asked, "How'd you train Mister Puss on the *leash*?"

Stock answer: "He just took to it."

"That's really something." She got up and retreated to the back of the building to check on something.

Mister Puss hopped up to the chair nearest mine, separated by a small table with a pile of magazines. The waiting room's other accoutrements included an aquarium, which bubbled quietly; a parrot in a cage, which chattered and hacked; and a lethargic but fat brown snake in a terrarium, which creeped me out. Mister Puss seemed bored by these lowlier denizens of the animal kingdom. Instead, he watched TV.

A cable news program played at low volume on an older set—with a picture tube—mounted near the door. When a commercial for a car dealer in Green Bay ended, the screen blossomed with the face of Chad Percy, mister dollcakes himself, looking serious, talking about "…another disturbing incident of anti-gay activity right here in Green Bay. While the city has a working-class reputation and a legacy of passion for football, it's also home to a University of Wisconsin campus, with its progressive mind-set and tolerance…"

I stepped over to turn it up, but by the time I'd sat down again, dollcakes had recovered his usual toothy cheerfulness, talking about his favorite topic. "…since I've partnered with the legendary scentologists at Parfumerie Abraxas for the introduction of a new unisex fragrance you'll want to make your own. You already know what we're calling it. 'Chad!' That's right, with an exclamation point! Isn't it *dynamite*? You'll find it at finer fragrance counters everywhere, coming soon, just in time for—"

Saved by the bell. On the spring. Which rang as the front door opened. And in walked Geoff Lovell, with his big, sickly dog, Cindy. He did a double take when I stood to snap off the television, as astonished to see me as I was to see him. *"Brody?"* he asked. "What are you doing here?" Then he noticed the cat in the chair.

"Small town," I said. "Not many vets, I guess. I'm taking care of a friend's cat."

Geoff stepped over for a closer look. "Awww. Gorgeous. Hope she's okay."

"He," I corrected. "This is Mister Puss."

"Hey there, Mister Puss," said Geoff, twiddling the cat's chin. Mister Puss purred. Cindy limped over to explore the situation, bumping noses with Mister Puss, then offering a big lick. The cat's purr intensified. Geoff looked more presentable than the last time I'd seen him—cleaner, better groomed, more neatly dressed.

I said, "I've been worried about your dog. She didn't look good at the sheriff's office on Thursday. Any improvement?"

"About the same," said Geoff, "so I thought I should get a professional opinion."

I was about to inquire about his girlfriend, Spark, who had looked even worse than the dog, when the receptionist returned.

"Mr. Lovell?" she asked as she stepped behind the counter and tapped at her computer.

Geoff went over to the counter and conversed with the woman in hushed tones. I heard her say, "But we do require payment in advance from new accounts." Geoff hesitated, then asked if she could take a debit card, which she said would be dandy. After passing the card back and forth, she rose and said, "You can come right in."

I told Geoff that I hoped he and Cindy would get a good report. Then he and the dog disappeared down the hall with the receptionist.

Sitting again, I patted my knee, and Mister Puss moved over from his chair and sat in my lap. Thinking about what had transpired, I idly rubbed the cat's neck. Purring, Mister Puss climbed my chest and reached his snout to my ear.

Nice guy.

I had to admit, Geoff's caring interaction with Mister Puss had dampened my suspicion that he might be guilty of fratricide. I told the cat, "Geoff's dog seemed to be in pretty bad shape."

But I'm fine.

I continued to ponder my mixed feelings about Geoff. On the one hand, his kindness toward animals suggested he was not capable of murder. But on the other hand, I now had reason to question his honesty. He had used a debit card to make advance payment for his appointment with Dr. Phelps. The receptionist had run the card, and the transaction, evidently, was approved. Meaning, Geoff had money in the bank. However, the prior week, he had begged cash from his brother, had taken a hundred-dollar handout from me, and had pleaded a complete lack of funds when Mother Hibbard approached him about his brother's funeral.

"Mr. Norris?" said the receptionist from the back hall. "Dr. Jim will see Mister Puss shortly. Can you bring him this way?"

Moments later, she left the cat and me in a cramped consultation room and closed the door. The space was dominated by a stainless steel exam table. An adjacent counter was filled with medical instruments, sell-cards for pet medicines, and a baby scale. The hospital-blue walls were decorated with faded Currier and Ives prints and yellowed charts showing the innards of dogs and cats. Bright fluorescent lighting competed with gashes of sunshine from the venetian blinds.

I assured Mister Puss, "Not much longer."

I'm fine.

Within a few minutes, I heard a door open and close in the hall, a bit of farewell conversation, footfalls retreating toward the front, and then the turn of the knob as Jim Phelps walked in to greet me. "Brody, young man! Always a pleasure. But what's this about Mister Puss? Your message got me nervous."

"Morning, Jim." I shook his hand. Mustering a laugh, I explained, "Maybe I'm overly cautious, but Mary would never forgive me…"

"Well," said Phelps, hoisting Mister Puss from the floor and plopping him on the table, "let's have a look." While chomping on his unlit pipe and removing the cat's harness, he asked, "Where's Mary?"

"Chicago. Book festival. I'm *in loco parentis* for a week."

"That's nice," Jim said vacantly while checking the cat's heart, eyes, ears. He hefted the cat in both hands and stretched him long in an airborne pose resembling that of Superman. Then he bounced the cat gently on all fours, checking his stance on the table.

The vet turned to me with a wink. "He's fine."

Mister Puss turned to give me a deadpan stare.

"That's a relief," I said. "Better safe than sorry."

"Any other issues with him?" Jim stroked the length of the cat's spine.

"Do cats sneeze? Mister Puss seems to do it quite often."

Jim set aside his pipe. "Sure, they can sneeze. Have you noticed what triggers it?"

"Smells. When he smells something he doesn't like."

"Makes total sense. Sneezing can indicate that a cat has a virus or an infection, and we'd want to treat that. But more often—like you describe—it's just something that's irritating the respiratory system. Dust. Chemical vapors. Even pollen."

I suggested, "Or perfume?"

Jim laughed. "You bet. Lots of *people* have a sensitivity to fragrances. Me? I hate the stuff—makes my eyes water. Well, cats have a superhuman sense of smell—about ten times the receptors that we have. Some dogs have way more than that. But cats are even better than dogs at distinguishing *between* scents. Bottom line: doesn't surprise me that strong perfume would make Mister Puss sneeze. Nothing to worry about." He started getting the cat back into his harness.

His mention of dogs led me to ask, "Geoff Lovell's dog—is she okay? I saw them come in."

"Yeah, nothing serious. Poor pooch. Geoff recently put her on a new flea medicine, and the dog didn't react well to it. Sometimes that happens, making the dog lethargic and weak—the limp was just fatigue. So I set them up with a different med. She should improve quickly."

Breezily, I asked, "What'd you think of Geoff?"

Jim shrugged. "Nice guy."

Mister Puss shot me another told-you-so look.

I asked, "Are you aware that Geoff is David Lovell's brother? The choir director."

"Oh, sweet Lord," said Jim, sitting back on a stool at the exam table. "I didn't make the connection, and he didn't mention it. Poor kid, he's got a lot on his mind—his brother's death, sick dog, pregnant girlfriend."

That caught my attention. "Really? Spark's pregnant?"

"No, the *girlfriend* is pregnant. Not the dog."

I explained, "The dog's name is Cindy. The girlfriend is Spark Kavanaugh."

The vet stood, looking bewildered. "Odd," he said.

"Sure is," I agreed. What wasn't odd, though, was Spark's delicate condition. Her queasiness at the sheriff's office should have tipped me off. I stood, clipped Mister Puss's leash to his harness, and moved him from the exam table to the floor.

Jim opened the door and followed as I led the cat out through the hallway. He said, "Give my best to Mary when you see her."

"I will, Jim. Thanks for everything."

He gave a hearty chuckle. "I'll bet she can't wait to get back and have a nice, long talk with Mister Puss." Following us to the reception area, the doctor added, "To hear Mary tell it, he's been working on the Gettysburg Address."

Quack.

"Huh?" said Jim.

I turned to tell him, "You ought to teach that parrot some manners."

Pulling the knob of the front door, I noticed the lazy snake in the tank. It watched with beady eyes as we left.

Out in the car, I phoned Sheriff Simms and explained that I had just left the veterinary office. "But while I was there, who should show up but Geoff Lovell with his sick dog. I saw him pay for the appointment with a debit card, so he can't be as destitute as he claims."

"I may have some insight on that," said Simms. "When we all met Thursday, Geoff gave us the name of the Lovells' family lawyer in Appleton, Stanley Burton. Later that afternoon, I phoned his office, but Burton had been out of town for a few days, returning the next morning. I identified myself and asked to have Burton call me as soon as possible—I said I needed to discuss a matter of some urgency regarding Geoff Lovell."

I asked, "You mean, they hadn't heard about David?"

"No, they hadn't. Burton was absolutely stunned when he called Friday morning and heard the news from me. From my message, he assumed Geoff was in some sort of trouble again. So I filled him in, told him as much as I could. He confirmed that he'd been the parents' estate planner and—guess what—it all goes to Geoff now. I told him how to reach Geoff, who seemed to be flat broke. They must have arranged something over the weekend."

Quick work, I thought. It was Monday, and Geoff had plastic.

Simms asked, "Are you available to meet Wednesday, maybe ten o'clock? Heather Vance will have toxicology results."

"I'll be there," I assured him.

Before hanging up, Simms said, "One more thing, Brody."

"Yes, Thomas?"

"How's Geoff's dog?"

11

Glee Savage was known about town not only as a longtime reporter and editor at the *Dumont Daily Register* but also as the driver of a vintage Gremlin hatchback, which she had custom-painted a metallic shade of fuchsia and adorned with retro whitewalls and baby moon hubcaps. Some forty years earlier, upon graduating from Madison with a degree in journalism and landing her first job at her hometown paper in Dumont, she had celebrated by splurging on her first new car, made in downstate Kenosha. She still had the same job and the same car. Though the car's book value was probably now worth little more than scrap, it was cheap to drive, and tricked out with Glee's no-holds-barred sense of style, it made a statement loud and clear, fetching compliments wherever she went.

She had accepted my invitation to have lunch Tuesday at the Dumont Country Club and, in return, had offered to drive.

The grounds were looking perfect at that time of year, with the summer annuals in riotous full bloom. The golf course, built in the 1920s before the wide availability of heavy earthmoving equipment, was designed to the natural contours of the land, punctuated by rocky outcroppings that had been left by a prehistoric glacier. Immaculate fairways, groomed and green, extended off toward the gentle hills as Glee drove the winding entryway beneath a canopy of oaks. Sapphire splotches of the noontide sky peeked through a matrix of leaves and dappled the windshield with dancing, pristine sunbeams.

When we pulled up to the entrance, the Gremlin was conspicuous among the tony imports in the driveway that circled beneath a soaring porte cochère of fieldstone and timbers. "That is one sweet drive, Miss Savage," said the valet, a hunky college kid, as he opened her door.

Getting out of the car, I said, "Hi there, Victor. Back for the summer?"

"Right, Mr. Norris. One more year of school, then it's time to take my chances in the real world."

"You'll knock'm dead," Glee assured him.

"Thank you, ma'am. Enjoy lunch."

Glee adjusted her big hat, took my arm, then strutted up the flagstone walkway and led me through the double-doored entrance, swung wide as if she owned the place. Actually, Marson and I held a business membership; Glee was a guest. But over the years, she had reported on so many club events in her column, she had doubtless spent more time here than most members.

Inside, we skirted the grill room, which was serving an early lunch to golfers heading out to the links, and walked a long hallway past several banquet rooms, one of which was releasing the attendees of an all-morning breakfast meeting. While wending our way through the yattering crowd, I heard a soft, familiar voice say, "Brody? Glee?"

Turning, I recognized Dr. Teresa Ortiz, Marson's longtime primary physician and now mine as well. It seemed that Glee, too, was one of her patients. Small town.

Glee greeted the doctor with smooches, which made it feel appropriate for me to do the same, even though I had never interacted with her outside her office. Leaning into our hug, I said, "Nice to see you, Doctor."

She grinned. "You're welcome to call me Teresa."

"I'd like that, Teresa. Thank you."

Glee jerked her head toward the meeting room and asked the doctor, "Gallbladder lecture?"

Teresa laughed. "No. Pharmaceutical pitch." Then she turned to me, looking serious. "Brody, my office texted that I had a call from Sheriff Simms this morning."

I asked, "Was David Lovell one of your patients?"

"Yes," she said with a slow, forlorn nod. "When I heard about it last week, I couldn't stop crying. He was such a sweet person. Tragic."

"I imagine Thomas is looking into the background of David's nut allergy."

"That's the gist of it," said Teresa. "He wants me to meet at his office tomorrow morning. I understand you'll be there, too?"

"Ten o'clock. Heather Vance, the medical examiner, will also be there."

Teresa's scrunched features signaled she was weighing things. "I'll come, and I hope I can help. But it makes me a little uneasy—I mean, this is *way* outside my usual line of work." She smiled.

I reminded her, "And I'm an architect. Just being a good citizen."

Teresa nodded decisively.

Glee, hand on hip, asked us, "Shall I hum 'America the Beautiful'?"

"Okay, doll," I told her, "let's get you some lunch."

With parting hugs, Glee and I said good-bye to Teresa. Then we continued down the hall toward the rear of the clubhouse.

We arrived in the formal dining room, which commanded a lofty, verdant view of turf and trees and bitsy distant foursomes of bankers and lawyers at play. On weekend evenings or Sunday mornings, this room would be filled to capacity, but on a Tuesday at noon sharp, only a few of the tables were occupied.

The head waiter approached us. "Miss Savage, Mr. Norris, good to have you with us today."

I replied, "Thank you, Victor." He was the father of the car parker. Victor senior, handsome and refined, had been a fixture at the club for many years, arriving not long after he had immigrated from Mexico. Victor junior, born in Wisconsin, had inherited his father's charms, but the son's upbringing, speech, and wholesome swagger were Midwestern to the core. Both of them were deemed swoon-worthy by all of the ladies at the club—and at least two of the men.

Victor said, "Let me show you to a lovely window table." And he began leading us across the room toward the far wall.

Along the way, I noticed Gloria Simms, the sheriff's wife, seated at a table with her son, Tommy. The lad was adorable in a tiny blazer and dressy shorts, quietly reading a book. Victor broke stride and stepped aside to wait as Glee and I greeted the table.

"Hello, Gloria," I said, approaching her from behind, "what a pleasant surprise."

Turning, she broke into a smile. "Why, Brody—and *Glee*," she said, rising, offering pecks. Then she turned to Tommy with a good-natured scowl. "Where are your manners, young man?"

He rose at once, extending his hand. "Good afternoon, Miss Glee. Good afternoon, Mr. Norris."

We shook his hand, and Glee crouched to tell him, "My gosh, you're growing up fast, aren't you?"

"I just finished second grade."

Gloria added, "He *is* growing up fast. Every time I think of *college*, I break into tears." She laughed as she dabbed at one eye. "School got out a little early this year—they didn't use all their snow days, global warming, I guess—and Tommy had perfect grades, and last week was kind of rough"—she mouthed the word *David* to me—"so this seemed like a good day to have lunch at the club."

Noting the book in Tommy's hand, Glee asked, "Are you reading *novels* already?"

"Yes, ma'am." He showed it to her. "*Stuart Little*. It's about a mouse."

"Oh, that's a *good* one, isn't it?" Glee looked up, telling Gloria, sounding amazed, "I don't think I read that till fifth grade."

Gloria said, "Tommy was reading before kindergarten—he just took to it. Loves school, too. We count our blessings."

I thought of the metal artist, Tyler Schmidt, and his wife, Kayla Weber Schmidt, who weren't so lucky. Tyler had described their four-year-old son, Aiden, as "challenged and challenging." I thought of Mister Puss, nearly killed by Aiden.

Glee's knees crackled as she rose from her crouch.

Victor showed us to our table, from which we could observe the entire room. He asked, "May I bring you something from the bar?"

Glee told me, "I'm working this afternoon."

I told her, "So am I." Then I told Victor, "Maybe a champagne cocktail."

Glee told him, "Make it two."

"Of course, Miss Savage." A slight bob of his head conveyed deference without the theatrics of a lugubrious bow and scrape. He turned to leave, offering a posterior view.

"*Caramba,*" said Glee under her breath.

"Ditto," I whispered back.

Victor's retreat led my gaze back to Gloria Simms's table. The Simmses weren't the only black family in Dumont—granted, there weren't many—but they were by far the most prominent, given the sheriff's position in the community. By all appearances, they were a model couple, smart and involved, raising a bright young son. It seemed they'd succeeded at raising Tommy in a world protected from prejudices they'd probably known in their past. And yet, they hadn't been able to protect him from his first taste of grief, at seven years old, when the meaning of death had become real for him with the loss of his mentor and friend, the choirmaster.

At another table sat Bob Olson, from the St. Alban's vestry, having a business lunch with a dignified older man I recognized as the retired owner of a local company that had manufactured high-end refrigerators—until a year ago, when he sold the business. The deal had netted the owner considerable wealth, but it had also closed the factory he built, moving the jobs offshore. It appeared he had now signed on as a client of Bob Olson, whose accounting and advisory services specialized in wealth management throughout the region.

When Bob happened to look up, he noticed me watching. From across the room he offered a discreet little salute of a greeting, accompanied by a soft smile that I understood to thank me for the kindness shown to his daughter on Saturday at First Avenue Bistro. Hailey Olson, like Tommy Simms, was grieving the loss of their choirmaster.

Who else in the room, I wondered, had been affected by the death of David Lovell? Who else was here now to put on a happy face, to make the best of things, to demonstrate that life goes on?

"Cheers," said Glee, raising her champagne flute.

I had not even noticed that the drinks had arrived or that Victor had recited a few specials. Glee had assured me I wouldn't care for the planked salmon. She had suggested the shrimp Louie instead, to which I had apparently agreed.

Glee was more than a friend. Old enough to be my mother, she had in fact been my mother's best friend, back when they were both growing up in Dumont. Inez Norris and Glee were later college roommates at Madison, but their friendship would end abruptly on a bitter note. Inez, who by then had established the direction of her life's calling as a lesbian activist and community organizer, also had a bisexual edge and an occasional itch. To satisfy this urge, she fled to California with the man Glee intended to marry. Though Inez never married him, he eventually gave her a son.

When I moved to Dumont, some forty years after my mother's betrayal of Glee, the two women had never reestablished communication. Glee, however, instantly recognized in me the features of the guy that got away. Having never married, she now thought of me, in some sense, as the son she never had.

The affection was mutual—and I absolutely loved her style, her flair. Though we shared not a drop of blood, wisecracking Glee had become my surrogate Auntie Mame.

"Yum," I told her, "the shrimp Louie is fabulous. I should always take your advice."

"Then have another champagne cocktail," she suggested.

"Maybe." I dabbed my lips with the big linen napkin before drinking what remained in the bottom inch of my flute. "But first," I said, "you owe me some dirt."

"Aha." She set down her fork and leaned forward on her elbows, resting her chin on her folded hands. "That was the deal, wasn't it? What would you like to know?"

"Saturday at the Bistro, we were discussing how Nancy Sanderson seemed to show an uncharacteristic frostiness toward David Lovell. And *you* said you might know why. Let's have it."

Coyly, she tapped her empty glass. "It's a long story."

I signaled for Victor to bring us another round.

"The story has two parts," said Glee. "The first part goes back about twenty years. Back then, I was already a fixture at the *Register*, having been hired by the paper's founding publisher, Barret Logan. He was starting to think about retirement and ended up selling the paper to Mark Manning. Ever heard of him?"

I shook my head.

"Mark was a hotshot reporter at the *Chicago Journal*. But he had family roots in Dumont. An uncle on his mother's side built that Prairie School house next to Mary Questman's."

"Really? Incredible house, obviously has a pedigree. Taliesin?"

"Right," said Glee, "it was designed by a student of Frank Lloyd Wright's at Spring Green. Mark Manning inherited it, and around that time, he was restless with his career and was looking to take over a small newspaper as publisher. One thing led to another, and he bought the *Register* from Barret Logan."

"And ... what does this have to do with Nancy Sanderson?"

"I'm getting there," said Glee as Victor arrived with the fresh drinks. He cleared the lunch dishes. Glee and I skoaled. Then she continued, "Mark was gay. He moved up here with his lover—who was an architect, as a matter of fact—and also brought along a Chicago colleague, Lucille Haring, to serve as his managing editor. Lucy was damn good. She happened to be a lesbian. And this is where Nancy comes into the picture."

Intrigued, I asked, "Lucy and Nancy ...?"

"Mm-hmmm." Glee sipped. "I'd never questioned why Nancy was single—there are lots of us 'working girls,' wed to our work. I didn't understand that, for Nancy, the right man would *never* come along. But Lucy tuned in to it. And eventually, they were spending time together—like, *overnight*. There weren't many women working at the *Register* in those days, so Lucy often confided in me. Generally, she was reserved, nose to the grindstone, but when it came to Nancy, Lucy went gaga. She was sure they had a future."

"But obviously," I noted, "they're not together now."

"No. It never happened. It was sad. Lucy told me Nancy had 'commitment issues.' Later, when Mark Manning sold the paper, Lucy also left town."

"Commitment issues." I swirled my glass. "Wonder what that was about."

"And *that*," said Glee, "that's part two of the story."

"Need another drink?"

"No, sweets, I'm driving. So here's the dirt. Lucy told me it was a rumor, but if it's true, it explains a lot. As Lucy understood it, way back when—when Nancy was a high-school senior in Green Bay—she was assaulted, maybe raped, by a boy in her class. At the time, she was beginning to acknowledge her attraction to women, and the assault left emotional scars and confusion that still afflict her. But get this: I seem to recall that the guy who attacked Nancy was named David." Glee folded her arms.

I didn't get it. "That's a terrible story, and I feel awful for Nancy. But why's the name David significant? There's a million of them."

Glee raised a finger. "David Lovell, choirmaster, was a 'junior.' I think he grew up in Appleton, which is not far from Green Bay. If his father was from Green Bay, Nancy might have noticed a resemblance. The timeline fits. Nancy is now in her early fifties; David Lovell died last week at twenty-eight. If Nancy's assault happened when she was eighteen, that would be five or six years before David junior was born—not long after David senior finished college. Totally plausible. If so, I can imagine why it freaked Nancy when David turned up in Dumont."

"Wow," I said. "I happen to know for a fact that David's father was a high-school jock in Green Bay."

Glee flipped her hands. "Bingo. Any other questions?"

"Yeah. What happened to Mark Manning?"

Glee grinned. "That'll take another lunch."

Just then, every head in the room turned as Victor ignited a copper skillet of cherries jubilee on a flambé cart at Gloria Simms's table. The flash of orange light, the smell and crackle of kirschwasser, the glittering sparks—it was culinary theater that would impress even the most jaded of diners. To a seven-year-old sprung from school, it was nothing short of magical. Tommy Simms abandoned his book to watch the spectacle with huge, wondering eyes and a gaze of pure enchantment.

"Look at him," Glee cooed. "He was reading *Stuart Little*—and now his world just got a bit bigger. Have you ever seen such a darling child?"

No, I hadn't.

As we strolled out through the main doors together, I saw that Glee's fuchsia hatchback had been parked at the far curb of the driveway, which circled under the porte cochère. The valets had the option of awarding this prime spot as they wished, typically to the richest executive with the snazziest car; other cars were parked out of sight in a storage lot behind a distant berm. But there, front and center, was the old Gremlin—windows spiffed, ready to go.

"Hope you enjoyed lunch" said Victor, the valet, escorting us to the car.

As we were about to get in, a big white Lincoln pulled up—it had the stripped, anonymous look of a rental—and driving it was Marson's college friend, Curtis Hibbard, with Yevgeny Krymov in the passenger seat.

Glee and I greeted them in the driveway while Victor hopped into the Lincoln and spirited it away. "Good Lord," Curtis said to me, leaning near, watching his car vanish. "What a talented young man. Things are looking up, out here in the sticks."

Glee gabbed with Yevgeny, thanking him for the interview that ran the day before.

Curtis explained to me that his and Joyce's membership application to the country club had just been accepted. "When I first suggested it to Mother Hibbard, I thought she might find it too elitist for us to be hobnobbing with the club crowd, but *au contraire*, she told me to go for it. Ho-ho. By the way, did Marson mention that I'd enjoy getting together once more before returning to New York?"

"He did," I said. "We were thinking we could make it a boys' night, so to speak."

Curtis's eyes widened. "What a splendid idea."

"The four of us—Marson and me, you and Yevgeny. Dinner at the loft again, but much simpler than last week. More intimate. Saturday at seven?"

"Oh, dear, that's cutting it close. We need to be back for Renée Fleming on Sunday night, but where there's a will there's a way. Count us in." Low and throaty, he added, "Looking forward to it."

Soon, after saying our good-byes, Curtis and Yevgeny disappeared into the club.

Glee and I buckled ourselves into her car. She checked her hat in the mirror and took a moment to touch up her ruby lips.

We circled the entryway and drove out through the serene, wooded grounds.

Then she punched the gas, goosed the Gremlin, and laughed like a kid in a screaming hot rod.

When Marson had received Curtis Hibbard's email on Sunday, suggesting dinner with Marson and his "charming young man," I dreaded such an encounter and didn't hesitate to say so. Marson himself questioned Curtis's motives for suggesting this, but felt, on balance, that another engagement might be in order. "The dinner party was a crowd," he explained, "and I didn't get to catch up with Curt much. Plus, a second encounter would give *you* a chance to dig a little deeper regarding David Lovell."

He had a point: the group dynamics among David, Curtis, Joyce, and Yevgeny did indeed warrant further exploration.

And another point: though I was ashamed to admit it to myself, let alone to Marson, I welcomed the opportunity to spend another evening in the company of the tantalizing Yevgeny Krymov before he left Dumont, presumably for good.

Now, on Wednesday morning, the day after my chance meeting with Curtis at the country club, I said to Marson as we sat at the kitchen island, "I hope you don't mind that I invited them on the spot, without checking with you."

He laughed. "We're a team. As far as I'm concerned, you're welcome to play social secretary *anytime*. Thanks for setting it up." Marson dropped the *Register*'s want ads to the floor. Mister Puss pounced, adding to the mess he'd already made of the sports section. Quietly, Marson mused, "You know, I'll miss him."

"Really?" I asked. "You'll miss *Curtis*? I know he's an old friend, but—"

"Not Curt. I thought it wouldn't happen, but I'll miss Mister Puss. He has two more days with us—Mary returns Friday."

Things had been hectic since Mary's departure, and I'd lost track of the passing days. Feeling that we needed to make the most of the time remaining, I asked the cat, "Would you like to join me for some crime fighting today?"

Mister Puss rose from the shredded papers and reached his paws to my knee. His wide eyes gleamed. His tail switched.

Mister Puss was already well known at our office, as Mary had brought him in from time to time, so when I arrived with him that morning at nine, he was greeted sweetly, but without surprise, by our receptionist, Gertie, and by the interns and staff accountant.

Shortly before ten, however, when I arrived at sheriff's head-quarters with a cat on a leash, he brought the business of law enforcement to a standstill as I paraded him along the terraz-zo-floored hallways, fetching stares, silencing conversations, and prompting an occasional laugh. Mister Puss could be bothered by none of it. He held his head high and pranced at my heel, steadily approaching Simms's office. We were on a mission.

"Well, now, who's *this*?" asked the deputy as we presented our-selves.

"This is Mister Puss. Is the sheriff admitting cats today?"

"Don't see why not," she said. "Had a dog in here last week."

I reminded her, "I was here."

"You can go right in. He's waiting for you." She waved her fin-gers at Mister Puss as we stepped around the desk and entered the office.

Thomas rose behind his desk. "Hey, Brody. And Mister Puss? Hi there, kit-cat."

"Hope you don't mind, Thomas."

"Had a dog in here last week."

"I was here."

He laughed. "Maybe Mister Puss can help. According to Mary, he whispers in her ear—maybe he'll slip you some clues."

"You might be surprised," I said as Simms led us into the conference room.

Already present were Dr. Heather Vance, the medical examiner, and Dr. Teresa Ortiz, who had been David Lovell's primary physician. They were seated near each other at the conference table, gabbing as we entered. Predictably, the arrival of the cat stole the show, and they were on their feet at once, joining us near the door. After I introduced Mister Puss to both women, Teresa crouched to pet him, saying, "Aren't you just the cutest little monkey?" He broke into a purr.

My eye went to the bare spot on the wall beyond the head of the long table. Again I wondered what had happened to the oddball painting of the man, the horse, and the monkey.

All of us were still standing near the door when it opened again, and the deputy admitted Nia Butler, the city's code-enforcement honcho. She leaned to pet the cat as Simms introduced her to Heather and Teresa, explaining, "I asked Officer Butler to join us today because St. Alban's has a dilemma with building-code issues—which could possibly have a bearing on what happened to David Lovell."

Simms invited everyone to sit, then took the chair beneath the missing painting. The rest of us arranged ourselves around the table; I sat on one side, adjacent to Simms, with Nia Butler next to me; across from us were the two doctors. Mister Puss hopped up to my lap, where he could peep above the edge of the table, keeping an eye on everything.

While Simms made some opening remarks, I couldn't help noting a certain irony in the composition of the group surrounding the table. Here we were in lily-white, working-class Dumont, five professionals (and a cat), sniffing out crime, attempting to right unconscionable wrongs, working for the common good. Conspicuously, however, there wasn't a straight white guy among us. The sheriff, black. The two doctors, both women, one of them Latina. The code-enforcement officer, a black lesbian. And as the only white guy in the room, I was anything but straight.

Not that there's anything intrinsically *wrong* with straight white guys. Not at all. I'm happy to count many among my close friends. But when it comes to toxic masculinity that springs from a wounded sense of privilege, straight white guys own that. I couldn't help feeling amused by any who might feel aggrieved—and therefore distinctly uncomfortable, out of place on their own turf—there in the sheriff's conference room, in a gathering with such overtones of kumbaya.

Simms said, "Heather, let's start with you. It's been a week since David's death. What can you tell us about the postmortem?"

The medical examiner pulled a file from the heavy briefcase that gaped up from the floor. She set the file on the table but didn't bother to open it as she told us, "The results are straightforward, and they're in line with our speculation from last week. To review: my working theory was that David ate nuts, or something with nuts *in* it, and went into anaphylactic shock. In rare instances, the reaction can be sudden and severe—even lethal, as in David's case. His symptoms, you'll remember, included his observed vomiting, swelling, and hives. Swelling of the throat, clogged with vomit, can asphyxiate a victim. The stomach contents were analyzed, as well as the vomit and the macaroons that were found at the scene."

I asked, "And you also analyzed the macaroons later given to us by Lillie Miller?"

"We did."

"And your conclusions?" asked Simms.

"The freshly baked macaroons given to Brody and me on Friday tested negative for any trace of nuts in any form. The macaroons taken from the death scene two days earlier, which we later confirmed had been ingested by David, were identical in appearance and contents to the macaroons given to us by Lillie—with one crucial difference. The macaroons from the church had been infused with a significant amount of almond oil."

"That's it, then," said Simms.

Heather nodded. "I've concluded that the *cause* of death was anaphylactic shock and the *mechanism* of death was asphyxiation. But that still leaves the *manner* of death."

A silence fell over the table. After a long pause, I said, "Looks a lot like murder."

"Sure does," said Dr. Heather Vance.

"Sure does," said Sheriff Thomas Simms.

"*Dios mío*," said Dr. Teresa Ortiz, who had not yet spoken at the table.

Simms asked, "Dr. Ortiz, can you give us some medical history regarding David's allergy to nuts? I assume you knew about it."

"Of course, Sheriff." She cleared her throat, appearing nervous. "When David established himself as a patient—about two years ago, after he arrived in Dumont—allergies were discussed during his initial evaluation. He said he was highly allergic to all tree nuts—but not peanuts, which are legumes—and he invited me to request his files from the Lovells' family doctor in Appleton."

"Did you follow up?"

"Certainly. His file arrived within a few days after I requested it. It was a thin file. He was a young man. Other than the severe nut allergy, which was noted, he had no health issues at all."

Heather asked, "Did David carry an EpiPen?"

"His prior doctor had recommended it and prescribed it—and I did as well—but David seemed cool to the idea. He probably didn't want to bother carrying one around all the time. Plus, they've gotten crazy expensive. But I think the main issue was, he was young and felt no risk. He said to me once, 'The cure is simple: don't eat nuts.'"

I noted, "The fact that he said that underscores that he wasn't being careless when he died last Wednesday. Everyone seemed to *know* about his allergy, so someone must've *tricked* him into consuming almond oil."

Simms asked the two doctors, "Would almond oil produce the same reaction as the nuts themselves?"

They agreed in unison: "Absolutely," said Teresa. "You bet," said Heather.

Simms concluded, "And that's why we're now dealing with a murder case."

Heather said, "I'll complete my report this afternoon and schedule the body for release tomorrow."

Simms turned to Nia Butler. "I'm wondering if you can help us with this—from the perspective of code-enforcement issues."

"Anything to help. What would you like to know, Sheriff?"

"I can't help feeling that David's death might have been related to the city's mandate for St. Alban's to arrive at a remediation plan for the church building: either restore it, or tear it down and build another. The incense fire, the exploding organ, the poisoning death at the keyboard—talk about wacko. Taken as a whole, it seems so staged and ... *gothic*. Which leads me to wonder if the *point* of what happened had nothing to do with David, and everything to do with the future of the building."

Everyone at the table pondered this for a moment. It was a plausible theory, and if it was correct, it made David's death all the more tragic—and utterly pointless.

During the lull, Mister Puss must have tired of keeping watch over the proceedings. He slipped from my lap to the floor, where he curled near my feet for a catnap.

Nia said, "From the city's perspective, nothing has changed. The church didn't sustain fire damage from the burning incense, other than a patch of carpet—but that doesn't mean you can rule out that someone tried and failed to destroy the place. As for the organ, the blown bellows made a hell of a mess, but it caused no additional structural damage to the building. As far as I'm concerned, the parish still has the same options—renovate or rebuild—and they still face the same deadline at the end of the month, six days from now. By then, St. Alban's needs to present a firm plan, or Dumont condemns the building outright and begins proceedings to issue a demolition order."

I shot her a grin. "You're tough, girl."

She slid the granny glasses down her nose and winked. "Better know it, honey."

Half an hour later, concluding a freewheeling discussion of the ins and outs of the case, Sheriff Simms dismissed the meeting, but asked me to stay. I roused Mister Puss from his slumber so the others could coo their farewells, then returned to sit at the table with Simms. Mister Puss hopped up to the cushion of the vacant chair next to me, wound himself into a sleepy knot, and dozed off again.

Referring to a yellow legal pad filled with notes, Simms said, "Okay, it's official, it was murder. So now we need to shift focus. Suddenly it's not a matter of what happened, but why. In other words, motive. Any thoughts?" He turned his notes to a clean page and began to draw a grid, an exercise I'd seen before.

I took a deep breath. "Lots of thoughts. Geoff Lovell, the victim's brother, had a measure of need, greed, and resentment toward his older sibling—all classic motives—and now he's on easy street, but that wasn't the case last Wednesday, when he was with David shortly before he died. Plus, are you aware that Geoff's sickly girlfriend is pregnant?"

"Hngh," said Simms, making note of it, "so Cindy's pregnant."

I reminded him, "Cindy's the dog. Spark's pregnant."

He scratched at his notes.

I continued, "Lillie Miller had a creepy crush on the victim, a much younger gay man. She never got to first base with him and may have felt the pangs of a woman scorned, leading to revenge—

another classic motive. She often baked macaroons for him, which contained no nuts, and he died from eating macaroons, but those were heavily laced with almond oil. Before he died, Lillie needed to leave the church to send some registered mail at the post office."

Simms looked up from his grid. "We're still tracing that. If it checks out, we'll know soon enough."

"And then," I said, "there's Clem Carter, a builder who's in a financial pinch because of a bad investment. He's a member of a parish that's considering the option of building a new church, which could be an easy contract for him to snag, which in turn could get him over the hump. If his situation is bad enough that he'd be willing to burn down the old church, he might be driven by desperation—another classic motive."

Simms underlined something in his notes. "That would be consistent with my theory that the crime might not have specifically targeted David. He could've been 'in the wrong place at the wrong time,' or taking it a step further, the weird circumstances of his death might've been meant to create confusion about the true motive."

"Right. And if you think about it, there's a flip side to Clem Carter as a possible suspect. What about Kayla Weber Schmidt?"

"The preservation gal?"

"Yeah. She's hell-bent on *saving* that church. Frankly, after seeing her in action, I thought she was *nuts*. So who knows what freaky logic she could have invented as a motive?"

Simms drew a large question mark in one of the squares on his grid.

I added, "I talked to her husband on Sunday. Tyler Schmidt—nice guy, talented artist, too. He struck me as honest and forthright. But Kayla? I dunno."

Simms added a new column to his grid. "Any other possibilities?"

"Yes, three. But these are long shots, and they're all connected to St. Alban's. I'm talking about Joyce Hibbard—"

"Mother Hibbard?" asked Simms, a member of the parish. "She's a *priest*, Brody."

"Hear me out, Thomas. You may see her as St. Alban's earthly representative of the Trinity, but she herself is a member of an altogether different—and bizarre—triad. It's an unholy alliance consisting of Joyce Hibbard; her husband, Curtis Hibbard; and her husband's former lover, Yevgeny Krymov."

Simms gave me a lengthy blank stare. "I guess you'd better fill me in."

And I did. I explained the long history of their intertwined involvement, the marriage of convenience, both men's competitive interest in seducing the choirmaster, the flap over Renée Fleming tickets, and the simmering resentment Joyce had displayed at our dinner party. I told Simms, "I know it seems unlikely that any one of them killed David Lovell, but to varying degrees, Joyce and Yevgeny had motives."

"What about Curtis Hibbard?"

I paused to recall my interactions with Curtis before answering, "No motive at all—at least none that I can think of."

Simms filled in three of the squares on his grid. "I hesitate to ask, but anyone else?"

"Not at the moment." But there was someone else. I wanted to explore what Glee Savage had told me about the possibility that Nancy Sanderson, from First Avenue Bistro, had been sexually assaulted in high school by David Lovell's father. For Nancy's sake, however, I was reluctant to dredge up that trauma from her past unless I was able to connect the dots to David's murder. I needed to talk to Nancy before mentioning any of this to Sheriff Simms.

"Well, then," he said, closing his notes, "we have plenty to think about. I assume you'll be at the memorial service tomorrow?"

"Sure. Marson's coming, too. It'll be interesting to see who else is there—and who isn't."

"Exactly." Simms sat back in his chair, weighing something.

"I was surprised when Heather Vance said she'll release David's body tomorrow. I was hoping she'd take a little longer. Geoff told me he was certain David would want to be cremated—David made the decision to cremate their parents after the car crash. But it bothers me that this is moving so quickly now. Cremation cuts off the possibility of future investigation of the physical evidence. Maybe I can convince Jake Haines, the mortician, to drag his feet for a few days."

I asked, "What would you be looking for?"

"At this point, I have no idea."

Out in the parked car, before driving back to the office, I laid Mister Puss in the passenger seat. I'd read somewhere that domestic cats sleep about sixteen hours a day—and I believed it. To my surprise, though, he was now awake and alert. He sat up in the seat and reached his paws to the dashboard to peer out the window as I reviewed the notes I'd typed on my phone.

Feeling perplexed—no apparent logic surfaced from the words I'd written—I reached over to pet the cat's back. He began to purr, which rumbled loudly in the quiet of the car. Soon, he moved from the dashboard to my arm, reaching for my shoulder. His chin brushed my ear.

Switching off my phone, I said, "I'm stumped."

Follow the money.

I laughed. "Thank you, Deep Throat, for that pearl of wisdom."

Half the suspects I'd been considering had plausible motives relating to cash, so the cat's advice had no more value than a coin toss. "Besides," I told Mister Puss, "you slept through half the meeting."

I wasn't the only one. Dullsville, man.

13

The next morning, Thursday, I did not take Mister Puss to the office because Marson and I would be attending David Lovell's memorial service at St. Alban's, scheduled to begin at one o'clock. Since it would immediately follow the noon hour, I assumed the service would not conclude with a catered reception, as everyone would be sated from lunch. I also assumed that the logic for this timing had been based on Joyce Hibbard's decision that the parish would bear the expenses of the funeral, due to Geoff Lovell's plea of poverty, which now rang hollow.

The only other funeral I had attended at St. Alban's had taken place, naturally, in the church. But that was not an option for today's service, as the church had been closed indefinitely by the circumstances of David's death, and I had serious doubts that the old building would ever again serve its intended purpose. So today the St. Alban's community would bid farewell to its choirmaster in the confines of a former gymnasium—an adjunct to the parish school that had also been closed, awaiting its destiny with a wrecking ball.

Marson and I said hello to a few people as we made our way through the grounds to the parish hall. It was the last week of May, nearly June, with a cheery sun shining high in the crystalline sky, a harbinger that the long and languid days of summer lay not far ahead. Today, however, little joy could be found in such a vibrant outpouring by the forces of nature. Today—or at least the next hour—was a time reserved for introspection and sober remembrance.

As we entered the lobby, the quiet din of hushed conversations wafted through the space, an aural potpourri to complement the dabs of perfume and spritzes of cologne that were meant to perk up a sad afternoon but, instead, made me wince. Clumps of mourners stood about, wagging their heads and whispering bromides about the good dying young. Mother Hibbard was stationed near the doors to the main room, greeting people, wearing full liturgical vestments, white and gold, though she had told me on Saturday that it would be a simple service rather than a traditional Requiem.

We greeted the Simmses—Thomas, Gloria, and their son, Tommy—as well as the vestry warden, Bob Olson, with his wife, Angela, and their daughter, Hailey. I spotted Jim Phelps, the veterinarian, and we exchanged a nod. Lillie Miller, the parish secretary, bustled about with a box of printed programs. As I glanced at the outer doors, in walked Glee Savage, dressed for the occasion, looking like a beekeeper in black bombazine.

She hustled toward us and, leaning near, asked, "Can I sit with you guys? I hate these things." I got an up-close whiff of her patchouli.

Marson offered his arm and escorted her to the inner doors.

Joyce Hibbard told us, "Thank you for coming. Pleased you could be here."

I smelled incense burning, but I could not see its source.

After exchanging handclasps with Joyce, we entered the main room.

Some people were already seated, but many mingled front and center, near the altar table that had been set on a low dais. It was draped in white, with three tall candles burning at either end. An enlarged photo portrait of David was displayed on an easel in front of the altar, reminding me of how strikingly attractive he had been in life—but the photo was unable to quash my memory of David's gruesome appearance only eight days before, when I had pulled his lifeless body from the console of the organ. The portrait was surrounded by an exuberant mishmash of floral tributes, some modest, some lavish, all of them expressing heartfelt affection for David, GONE TOO SOON, the ribbons said.

In front of the portrait, a low table bore token gifts and remembrances, lovingly placed by those who had known David and worked with him—a pitch pipe, some scraps of sheet music, a black clip-on bow tie that might have been worn with a prom tux, a few snapshots, and a small plate of Lillie's macaroons. The cookies lent a jarring note, but I reminded myself that their role in his death was not yet a matter of public knowledge.

I noticed Geoff Lovell standing near his brother's portrait and took Glee and Marson over to introduce them. Just as we neared, Yevgeny Krymov approached Geoff with a smile and extended his hand, saying, "I know you, yes? You stay at Manor House with me—with girl and dog."

With a finger snap, Geoff said, "Of *course*. I thought you looked familiar. You were reading in the lounge yesterday when we checked in."

While they introduced themselves, I whispered to Marson and Glee, "Geoff's circumstances *have* improved. They were staying at Pine Creek Suites."

"Yuck," said Glee.

"And now," said Marson, "they're at the best place in town."

When Geoff explained he was the brother of the deceased, Yevgeny expressed condolences. "I met your brother the night before death. Lovely man. I am sorry." Then Yevgeny noticed us standing nearby. "Ah!" he said. "Good friends. Sad day." With a bob of his head, he retreated.

I watched him wend his way toward Curtis Hibbard, who was

gabbing with a group of the nameless vestry members I recognized from the parish meeting.

When Glee and Marson had extended sympathies to Geoff, I did so as well, then said, "I hope your dog is getting better. Dr. Phelps told me he changed her medication."

Geoff brightened. "Cindy's doing great, thanks. Spark still has her queasy spells, but I guess that's part of the drill. They're looking after each other this afternoon."

At the risk of sounding tactless, but wanting to test how Geoff would react, I leaned near, saying, "Well, at least you won't be sweating the expenses."

Unfazed, he shrugged. "I met with the executor of Dave's estate. I'll be fine."

After expressing my wishes that everything would turn out well, I retreated into the crowd with Glee and Marson, looking for seats. I told them, "Geoff's girlfriend is pregnant."

Marson mumbled, "He still looks like a kid, but he'll be growing up fast."

Lillie Miller was making her way down the aisle, passing programs to those who were already seated. Marson and Glee moved on to claim a group of seats near a back corner of the assembly while I lingered in the aisle to talk with Lillie. Giving her a little hug, I said, "The macaroons were wonderful, Lillie. Thanks for sending them home with me." While I am not in the habit of lying to people, I thought the fib was preferable to telling her that her cookies, confiscated by the medical examiner, were now in an evidence bag somewhere, having been dissected for chemical analysis in connection with a murder case.

She said she was glad I enjoyed them, then added, "I'm sorry to be taking so long with your list." I must have looked puzzled. She explained, "Mother Hibbard asked me to prepare a list for you of everyone who has access to the sacristy, but things have been hectic lately—with David's accident, and moving out of the church. I'll get on it tomorrow. I promise."

"Whenever you get to it, I'll appreciate it," I told Lillie as she handed me several programs.

Then I stepped away to join Marson and Glee, who sat at the far side of a back row with an empty chair between them. Rather than climbing over the knees of those already seated, I circled around from the back, but that was a challenge as well, since stragglers from the lobby were entering and milling behind the last row.

"Excuse me," I said, having bumped the back of a young woman in a black jumpsuit.

She turned with a scowl. "Can't you be more *careful?*"

With a flash of recognition, I realized I was face-to-face with the dreaded Kayla Weber Schmidt. Trying to defuse the encounter, I stammered, "I... apologize. And I do want to mention how impressed I was by the sensitive restoration of your Greek Revival farmhouse. I was out there on Sunday."

She looked ready to blow. "So it was *you.*"

"Is something... wrong?" I wasn't sure how to address her: Mrs. Schmidt? Ms. Weber Schmidt? Kayla? Whatever I chose, I was sure to offend her.

"Now Aiden wants a cat!" People were starting to look. She continued, "Do you have any idea what a *challenge* it is, dealing with a child like Aiden?"

"If I didn't before," I said softly, "I do now. Sorry." I wanted her to quiet down. I wanted to escape.

But she saved the best for last: "And you can stay away from my husband."

There was *so* much I wanted to say. But I'd witnessed her making a scene in public once before, in this very room, and the last thing we needed right now was a bitch fight at a funeral, so I zipped it.

Seething, I stumbled across Glee's knees and sat between her and Marson. He leaned to ask me, "What was that all about?"

"Later."

He took my hand, set it on his knee, and patted my fingers.

When everyone was seated, an awkward hush fell over the room. The gathering felt churchlike, but there was no music. Finally, Bob Olson got up from his seat, stood near the side of the altar, and told the crowd, "Please rise."

As we stood, the lobby doors opened. The procession began at a stately pace, led by a sturdy-looking man dressed like an altar boy in cassock and surplice—I flinched when I recognized that it was none other than our builder, Clem Carter—who carried the burning incense. He didn't simply carry the thurible. He didn't just swing it. Rather, he twirled it in full, brisk, vertical three-sixties, shifting it back and forth from his right side to his left, creating showy whirlybirds of smoke, a theatrical display that, frankly, struck me as dangerous. People sitting on the aisle instinctively leaned away as he passed, while the respectful quiet of the room was broken by an outbreak of coughing and wheezing from the gassed assembly.

Clem was followed by a teenage altar boy carrying a staff topped with a crucifix. He was followed by two others, younger, side by side with hands folded in prayer, whose function seemed purely decorative. And last but not least, bringing up the rear of the procession, Joyce Hibbard paraded forward in all her silken regalia.

This was a simple memorial service? Perhaps for Episcopalians.

When the procession reached the altar, Clem passed the thurible to Joyce before he and the kids dispersed. Joyce slowly circled the altar, incensing it and the photo of David. The crackle and the smoke reminded me of the incense fire in the church, now eight days past, when David was killed. Oddly, it also brought to mind the flambé cart and the cherries jubilee, two days ago at the country club.

Setting the thurible aside, Joyce stood behind the altar and raised her palms to address her flock:

"My dear friends in Christ. I welcome you today as we gather to remember David Lovell, who has left this world to join the choir of angels. Though we grieve his tragic passing, we also celebrate his memory, his life, and his many gifts to our St. Alban's community. Having arrived in this parish only recently, I did not have the privilege of David's friendship for very long. But most of you had already come to know him as both friend and family…"

I studied the room. Most of the assembled mourners were parishioners, largely unknown to me, but all of them had known David as their church's choirmaster. Others were there because of their interest in the circumstances of David's death. I saw Sheriff Simms, both parishioner and lead investigator of the murder; Heather Vance, the medical examiner; Teresa Ortiz, the victim's primary physician; Nia Butler, the city's code-enforcement officer. I saw others whose connections to David were tangential at best: Glee Savage, seated next to me, who considered this gathering a newsworthy social event; Curtis Hibbard and Yevgeny Krymov, who had tussled one evening for David's affections; and the abrasive Kayla Weber Schmidt, whose connection to David, as far as I knew, was nil. Why was Kayla there at all? Why had she attacked me in the context of her husband? I felt more sorry than ever for Tyler Schmidt—poor guy. At least he was free of Kayla that afternoon.

Joyce read soothing psalms, filled with sheep and glory and "Thou"s and "Thine"s.

I wondered if the killer was there among us. I had reason to suspect, to varying degrees, that any number of people in the room could have been motivated to murder David.

Greed. Resentment. Jealousy. Desperation. Revenge.

All these shortcomings of the soul had their mortal representatives seated piously around me. If present, did the killer now grieve—or merely pretend?

I continued to study the crowd while Joyce led the gathering in the Lord's Prayer, muttered by some but recited with practiced, full-voiced cadences by the Episcopalians. After the prayer, Joyce shared a few remembrances of her brief association with David; then she invited others to do the same.

At first there were no takers. So Bob Olson got the ball rolling with a few bland niceties about working with David on their "parish team."

This prompted Sheriff Simms to rise, adding his fond recollections as a "choir parent" and thanking David for the legacy of music he had handed down to the children of the parish.

By then, the ice was broken, and many others rose, one by one, to share memories and tributes. I kept waiting for David's brother and heir, Geoff Lovell, to stand and address us—surely others expected this as well—but he never did. He sat quietly in the front row, head bowed, occasionally nodding in agreement with someone else's warm words, but offering none of his own.

I also found it somewhat strange, somewhat sad, that Geoff was there alone. Was there no extended family? Was Geoff's girlfriend, Spark, so sick that she couldn't be there to support the father of her expected child? Maybe. Or maybe she had never even met David. Or maybe Geoff had discouraged her from attending, not because she needed to rest, but because he feared that her goth vogue would be inappropriate to such a setting. I didn't have any of those answers. But I did find it conspicuous that Spark was missing.

And scanning the crowd, I felt that someone else was missing. The people in the room all occupied various orbits that had spun around David's life, orbits that sometimes intersected—the parish, the broader community of Dumont, the world of music, the gay demimonde—but I had the nagging impression that someone expected was not there.

And it clicked. David had been a regular patron of First Avenue Bistro. If only for appearances, Nancy Sanderson should have been at the memorial. But she was missing.

Joyce said, "Before the final blessing, I have a pleasant surprise for all of you, which I hope may help us end this gathering on a happier note. For reasons that are painfully obvious, no music had been planned for this service. But the children of the choir have asked me if they could sing for you a piece that David had been preparing with them. It wasn't intended to be *a cappella*, but they're willing to try. Children?"

The crowd buzzed as Mother Hibbard stepped aside. The children's choir, numbering a dozen or so, popped up from their chairs and moved forward to gather around David's photo at the altar.

Hailey Olson, one of the older, taller members of the group, took the pitch pipe from the table of offerings and sounded a single note. In the hushed space of the former gymnasium, with a backdrop of flickering candles, the choir began to sing.

Amazing grace! How sweet the sound
That saved a wretch like me . . .

A sigh washed over us. Without direction, the kids struggled during the first lines to find their collective rhythm and harmony, but the beauty of their effort, combined with the simple sincerity of the words, had us choking up before the second verse.

'Twas grace that taught my heart to fear,
And grace my fears relieved . . .

David Lovell was truly present that afternoon, having left a living gift to the people of St. Alban's. As the choir's confidence grew, so did the power of their performance, verse after verse.

And a little black kid in the front row, not yet eight years old, led the way.

Through many dangers, toils, and snares,
I have already come ...

Thomas and Gloria Simms beamed, swaying in their seats—we all were—as Tommy's voice rang out above the others.

'Tis grace hath brought me safe thus far,
And grace will lead me home.

The humble song in that humble setting sounded more glorious than the Möller organ surrounded by Tiffany windows. Happy tears were flowing. Glee blubbered at my side. Then the choir parted, humming their lines to let Tommy take it home, front and center.

Yea, when this flesh and heart shall fail,
And mortal life shall cease ...

We knew we were witnessing something unforgettable. People stood to shoot videos with their phones as Tommy nailed the last lines with soul and ecstatic grace.

I shall possess, within the veil,
A life of joy and peace!

Pandemonium. Adding unrestrained bravos to the cheers of the crowd were Curtis Hibbard and Yevgeny Krymov, aficionados who would hear Renée Fleming perform in New York that weekend.

14

Friday, the day after the funeral, was the last day that Mister Puss would be entrusted to our care. Mary Questman and Berta were returning from Chicago later that day and would reclaim custody of the little one that evening.

When Marson and I arose that morning, we lingered longer than usual with coffee and the papers, a ritual that, in a few short days, had evolved into our "family time" with the cat. It now struck me as laughable that I had ever worried that Marson might become annoyed by our visitor's presence. Three days is the oft-stated limit for house guests and fresh fish, so I had feared I was pressing my luck by foisting on Marson (who could be, shall we say, a tad finicky) a full week with a feisty Abyssinian.

Now, though, as that week neared its end, I said to my husband, "You amaze me."

He lowered the newspaper. "I'll take that as a compliment."

"You're far more ... *adaptable* than I would have thought."

His brow twitched. "You mean ... upstairs?" The bed was upstairs.

"Well, *yeah*"—although I recognized he could be a bit of a prig, there was nothing priggish about him upstairs—"but what I meant was, specifically, I'm amazed by how well you've adapted to having Mister Puss around the house."

At the mention of his name, the cat hopped up to the granite top of the kitchen island and gave me a nose bump, purring.

Marson good-naturedly swooped Mister Puss off the counter —his adaptability had its limits—and set the cat in his lap. Petting him, he said, "I've enjoyed having him around. I'll miss him. Elegant little fellow. Seems intelligent, too."

I assured my husband, "*Highly* intelligent."

Mister Puss gave me a look.

Marson said, "Last day together—should we take him to the office?"

"Sure."

We'd developed a routine for the days when we took Mister Puss to work. To spend an entire day there, he needed litter and food, so one of us would haul the supplies while the other transported the cat. Today, Mister Puss rode with Marson in the Range Rover. I arrived ahead of them, and when I watched them enter the office, I was delighted to note that both my husband and the cat had thoroughly gotten the hang of walking together with the leash and harness. I wondered if Mister Puss would later extend this cooperation to Mary Questman—but I still had visions of the cat lying on the floor while Mary tried to drag him.

That morning's arrangement would work well, with Marson busy at the office, looking after the cat. I needed to slip away at ten o'clock for a meeting with Nancy Sanderson at First Avenue Bistro, where Mister Puss would not be welcome.

The premise for our meeting was to discuss some side items Marson and I would need for our "boys' night" dinner at the loft on Saturday. But I also intended to explore Glee Savage's theory that Nancy had felt animosity toward David Lovell because he was a living reminder of a long-ago incident with David's father. While I was walking from the office to the Bistro, my mind reeled at the challenge: How does one make a nonchalant conversational segue from the topic of appetizers to the lingering psychological turmoil inflicted by sexual assault?

When I entered the Bistro, the dining room was empty, as planned. The last of the breakfast patrons had left, and there would be a long lull till lunch. I could hear activity in the kitchen, as well as the scratch of chalk on a blackboard behind the counter, where Nancy stood writing a list of the day's specials, which included clam chowder—no surprise, as it was Friday.

She turned at the sound of the door opening. "Morning, Brody," she said with a smile, setting down the chalk and clapping the dust from her fingertips. With a gesture that encompassed the roomful of empty tables, she added, "Take your pick."

I chose the corner table where Marson and I usually sat, between the fireplace and the windows to the street. Nancy brought over a notepad and sat with her back to the window; I sat with my back to the fireplace, with a view of the room and the street.

She began scratching notes. "Now, the event's tomorrow night, correct?"

"Right." Reviewing a few details I'd mentioned on the phone, I said, "It's dinner for four at the loft, but much less elaborate than the party two weeks ago. We won't need help with serving or cleanup, and Marson plans to prepare his standby tenderloin as well as the salad—he does a fabulous vinaigrette, by the way—so we'll need some cocktail nibbles, a couple of side dishes for the main course, and dessert."

"Easy," she said. "Should I deliver everything late afternoon, or were you planning to pick it up?"

"Delivery would be great, maybe four o'clock?"

"Perfect." She then ran me through the possibilities for each item, which proved to be simple choices, since we'd done this many times before. When we got to dessert, she suggested, "Let me show you something you might like." Rising, she led me over to the display case.

I saw her macaroons and the French *macarons,* as well as trays of pastries and a variety of magazine-worthy cakes propped up regally on white porcelain stands. My gaze slid toward the cash register and the small display of tiny bottles containing gourmet specialty oils and extracts. Even from a distance, I recognized the bottle of almond extract.

Nancy was saying, "I've been working with a new recipe for this honey-almond Bundt cake." She tapped the glass of the display case. "I'm delighted with it, and I think it would be a nice finish for your beef course."

"It's gorgeous," I said.

She smiled. "But this would serve ten or twelve. What I could do—and it should make a great presentation on the table—I could bake small, individual cakes for the four of you." She made a sphere with her fingers, about the size of a baseball. "Finish it with powdered sugar and shaved almonds. You could add a dollop of ice cream, maybe."

I laughed. "Well, *that's* a no-brainer."

"Great," she said. "Let me write this up."

We returned to our table near the window. Nancy reviewed the items with me as she checked her list. While gabbing about payment—she would simply bill us later, as usual—I noticed, through the window, across the street, Curtis Hibbard walking along with the same man I'd seen the prior Saturday while I was seated at that same table with Joyce Hibbard. Curtis and his companion were now walking in the same direction as before. I leaned in my chair to watch them disappear out of view.

Nancy asked, "Is something wrong?"

"I hope not. Did you happen to see Curtis Hibbard out there just now?"

"No." She turned in her chair, from which she could see farther down the street than I could. "Ah. Yes, I think that's him. Stocky build, dark suit. Who's he with?"

"Not a clue."

"He and Joyce come in here often. Every time I've seen him, he's been in a three-piece suit. Always dark, always pinstripes, always a vest. No one around here dresses like that."

I reminded her, "New York lawyer. Wonder if he *sleeps* like that—like he's going to a funeral." We both laughed.

And that was my opening.

"Only yesterday, I was thinking he'd missed his calling. He looked for all the world like an undertaker. Were you there—at David Lovell's memorial?"

"Uh, no. I had too much going on here."

"Ah," I said. "Sorry you missed it. Incredible outpouring for David—seemed everyone flat-out loved the guy."

She said nothing.

"And Tommy Simms—wow. Did you know that kid can *sing*?"

"Uh, no," she said with a tentative smile.

I hesitated. "Nancy, this is awkward, but I couldn't help noticing: whenever I saw you with David, or even mentioned David, you acted sort of cool toward him."

"Was I? I try to be nice to everyone. I'm in business."

"Exactly. That's why I found your reaction to David ... out of character. I was talking to Glee Savage about it, and she mentioned something about an old friend of hers, a former coworker named Lucille Haring."

Nancy froze in her chair, closing her eyes.

One of her helpers walked in from the kitchen, wiping her hands on a gray bib apron. "Nancy? Did that new bouillon strainer come in yet?"

Nancy looked up. "Yesterday, Helen. Still in the box. In my office."

Helen went back to look for it.

Nancy said to me, almost pleading, "This isn't a good place to talk."

"Do you have a few minutes to step outside? The park, maybe?" There was a miniature park across First Avenue, installed by the city a few years earlier, after a fire in an abandoned seventies-era head shop had left a gaping and charred rectangular plot amid a row of storefronts.

Nancy swallowed. "Sure." When we got up from the table, she

crossed the dining room to the kitchen doorway, telling her staff, "I need to run out. Won't be long."

Despite the tainted circumstances of its inception, the little park felt as if it had always been there, as if it *belonged* there, nestled between the brick walls of the adjacent buildings. Quaint lamp-posts. A patch of green, a few lacy honey locusts, a neat square of boxwood hedges. A sputtering little fountain to mask the street noise. Four or five pigeons. A pair of benches.

I sat on the same bench with Nancy, crossing my legs as I turned to her, but giving her space. She sat primly on the edge of the bench, knees tight. With hands folded in her lap, she stared vacantly ahead at the fountain.

Finally, she said, "What would you like to know?"

Speaking softly, I assured her, "It's none of my business, but I'm curious, and I'm a good listener." I meant: I'm gay, you can trust me, we're family.

In the breeze, water petered over the edge of the fountain. A pigeon strutted through the puddle and cooed.

Nancy asked, "What did Glee tell you about Lucille Haring?"

"She said Lucy was a talented editor and great to work with. She said matter-of-factly that Lucy was a lesbian. She also said that Lucy connected with you in what appeared to be a special friendship. But something happened, it didn't work out, and Lucy left town."

Nancy shrugged, breathing the slightest of sighs, which sounded almost like a quiet laugh. Turning to face me, she said, "Then you know. Yes, that happened."

I met her gaze with a wry look, suggesting, "But that's not the end of the story."

She shrugged again. "That *is* the end of the story. It was nearly twenty years ago, and I haven't been in touch with Lucille since she went away."

"Nancy"—I reached to touch her arm with my fingertips—"I'm not talking about what happened in the twenty years since Lucy left, but many years before you met her." I withdrew my touch. Her eyes looked so empty, I felt the need to explain, "In high school."

She lifted a hand to her forehead, muttering, "Oh, Christ..."

Shifting my weight, I moved closer to her on the bench—but still left some space, both physical and emotional. "I can only imagine how difficult this is. If you feel like crying, there's no need to hold back, not on my account."

She looked at me with a smirk. "Don't be silly. I'm not going to *cry*." A tear slid down her cheek, which she brushed away. "Are you sure you want to hear this?"

"Try me." I grinned.

She slumped a bit and planted her palms on her knees, emitting a groan that seemed to rise out of not pain, but resignation. Then she inhaled deeply, as if gathering up memories and strength. Sitting up straight, she pivoted to face me on the bench. As she did, our knees grazed.

"When I was a girl," she began, "growing up in Green Bay, everyone's role in the world was pretty clear. Football was for boys; cooking was for girls. No problem. I *liked* to cook, I liked *learning* to cook, and I *still* love doing it. Didn't give a hoot about football. So everything seemed right on track. And then—*you* know—puberty hit and the world was upside down."

With a knowing laugh, I wondered aloud, "The Prince Charming thing wasn't cutting it, huh?"

"No, it wasn't. But those weren't the easiest times for a kid in the Midwest to put two and two together. I mean, there were *no* gay role models—only jokes and fear. So by the end of high school, I was still a virgin and thoroughly confused: Do I follow my heart and my instincts? Or do I throw in the towel and follow the expected path? Finally, just as I was *beginning* to sort this out, reaching a modicum of comfort with the person I knew myself to be—along came David Lovell—hell-bent on making a decision *for* me."

"That's horrible. I'm sorry."

"It could have been worse," she said, as if resigned to past circumstances that she was unable to change. "He didn't get me pregnant. He didn't get that far, not quite—I had to fight him off. And the scary part was, he was a *friend*, part of my circle, a jock, but nice enough, at least until he attacked me. It was after a party at another friend's house, one weekend that spring before we graduated, with everyone feeling sort of grown-up. The house was a bigger, nicer one, out in a secluded area. David had been drinking—I could smell it—when he pinned me against his car. He wasn't subtle. He was rough, and he wasted no time."

Nancy paused, shaking her head to clear the memories.

"I managed to get away," she continued. "But when I got home, I was scratched and bleeding. My clothes were torn. My parents blamed *me*, even though they had no idea who had done it. 'Boys will be boys,' they told me. Dad said, 'I hope you've learned your lesson.' Honest to God, I think they would've been *thrilled* to know that the revered David Lovell had chosen *me* as his target—everybody idolized him—so I refused to name him. I didn't want to give him the satisfaction. The bragging rights."

I felt sickened by Nancy's story and found myself at a loss for words.

"As you can imagine," she said, "this left an emotional aftermath. College helped. It was a new environment with new people and new values, a good place to start over and grow up. I even had a girlfriend—or two, or three—*lovers*, with deep and real connections, but those relationships didn't last. Back then, I told myself, it wasn't the time for commitment. We were still in *school*, we had no idea where life would lead us. But now, many years later, I know exactly where life has led me, and it's still the same. When someone gets too close, I push them away. It happened with Lucille Haring. I wish it hadn't, but it did. And she's gone."

Tentatively, I reached to take Nancy's hand. She readily grasped mine. I asked, "When David Lovell—the son—arrived in Dumont, did you make the connection right away?"

She nodded. "Not long after David took the job at St. Alban's, while he was still getting settled in town, he came into the restaurant. Even from across the room, I spotted him at once. He was only a few years older than his father was when I knew him, and the resemblance was amazing. So I went over to introduce myself, as I would with any new customer. When he said his name, I winced. He told me he'd just moved from Appleton. He'd gone to the music school at Lawrence, and he'd also grown up there, so I asked if his parents were in Appleton. That's when I learned that they'd died—and that his father was originally from Green Bay."

I blew a low, breathy whistle. "Small world."

Nancy mustered a laugh. "Yeah, tell me. Look, Brody. I tried—I *really* tried—not to let my feelings toward David senior color my feelings toward David junior, and at a purely rational level, they didn't. I knew perfectly well, in my heart of hearts, that David bore no responsibility for his father's crime. Much deeper, though, in my gut, I found it impossible to separate the two. I felt, and will always feel, nothing but rage toward David senior. And now I feel, and will always feel, nothing but guilt for transferring those feelings to his son."

Sitting there with Nancy, I felt her pain. Her ongoing confusion and the tussle of emotions were palpable. She had told me plainly that her rage for David the jock had surfaced as rage for David the choirmaster. Had that understandable transference led her to an indefensible act?

I told her again how sorry I was for the turmoil caused by David's father. "But I can't help wondering," I said, "if attending yesterday's memorial service might've helped bring some closure."

"No," she said decisively, slipping her hand from mine, "it was the right choice, not to go. My therapist agrees."

Back at the loft that evening, I sat at the kitchen island with Mister Puss in my lap, gabbing with Marson while he fussed at the sink, doing a bit of prep work for the next night's dinner. He asked over his shoulder, "Bottom line: Do you think Nancy murdered David?"

"I've been asking myself the same question. She built a credible motive when I talked to her today. She was well aware of David's nut allergy. And basically *anyone* could have entered the church and spiked the macaroons with almond oil. But c'mon, the Nancy *we* know has never come across as a homicidal maniac."

"Do they ever?"

My husband had a point. If the identity of David's killer had been obvious, someone would be locked behind bars by now.

Two days earlier, during my confab with Sheriff Simms at his office, we had compared notes on all the known suspects. While drawing his suspect grid, Thomas asked me more than once, "Anyone else?" And I made no mention of Nancy because I had not yet talked to her and because the possibility of her guilt seemed too remote. Now, though, if I were being objective, I would need to place her near the top of the list. Simms deserved to know this.

I noticed that Marson had unwrapped the tenderloin that would be the centerpiece of tomorrow's dinner, and he was now cutting small pieces of meat from the tapered ends of the raw roast. Mister Puss had jumped from my lap and was pacing the kitchen on high alert. I said, "I'm no culinary wiz, but I don't think a tenderloin needs trimming."

Marson replied plausibly, "I've always found the tips unsightly.

They overcook. And besides"—he heaped the scraps into one of the small Art Deco bowls reserved for His Majesty—"since tonight will be our guest's last supper under our roof, he might as well go out in style."

Marson rinsed his hands and set the bowl on the floor.

We both watched, fawning, as Mister Puss pounced, indulging his inner carnivore.

Grrring.

Around eight o'clock, shortly before sunset, the rusty old bell at the street door of the loft announced that Mary Questman and Berta had returned from Chicago, driving the last leg of their journey from the airport in Green Bay.

We had set out all of Mister Puss's things, and I could tell that Marson was feeling as saddened by the impending loss as I was. He added the canister of catnip to the other treats, and I had already gotten Mister Puss into his smart-looking leather harness. (Hoping the cat would cooperate and dazzle Mary with his newly acquired leash skills, I had taken the liberty of throwing out the cutesy nylon vest.)

When we opened the door, Mary bubbled into the room, thrilled with her trip, thrilled to be back, thrilled to see Mister Puss and us again. Berta, meanwhile, trudged dutifully back and forth to the car at the curb, loading the cat's supplies.

"I had no *idea*," said Mary, "that getting away would be so *stimulating*. The city. The culture. The camaraderie. The *parties*. Good heavens, it gives me half a mind to start *traveling* again! Some of the ladies I met, they were raving about a tour of Sedona. I think Berta and I might enjoy the … what are they, Berta?"

"Vortexes," said Berta, hefting a box of the cat's whatnot.

"Yes indeed," Mary said gravely. "And sometimes, they have this … what is it?"

"Harmonic convergence." Berta schlepped out to the car again.

To my surprise, Marson said, "What a delightful idea. You'd have a ball. And we'd be more than happy to look after the cat again."

"*Would* you? Oh, how sweet. So he wasn't too much trouble?"

"Not at all," I said. "And I have a surprise." I had rolled up the leather leash and placed it in my pocket. I now removed it and let it unfurl. "Mister Puss?"

He obediently stepped over to my feet and let me clip the leash to his harness. Then I walked him about the room, stopping and starting, demonstrating how he heeled.

Mary clapped with joy. "Will he do that for *me*?"

"I think so," I said. I hope so, I thought as I handed her the leash.

The instant she took the leash, the cat flumped down to the floor on his side, looking up at me.

Looking at him, but speaking to Mary, I said grimly, "He's fooling around."

He broke his stare with a wink (or so it seemed). Then he hopped to his feet and let Mary walk him, performing perfectly.

"I can't *believe* it," she gushed. "How ever did you teach him?"

"He just sorta took to it."

Mary offered profuse thanks and smooches. Amid a chorus of cheery good-byes, she, the cat, and Berta headed out into the gathering dusk of the street.

Then Mary stopped in the middle of the sidewalk. Mister Puss heeled as she turned back to look at Marson and me. "I almost forgot," she said. "Did you hear the news?"

"About what?" I asked, concerned by her sober tone.

"Driving here from the airport, we had a Green Bay station on the radio. You know that cable person, Chad Percy, with his perfume or whatever? They were talking about him. They found him *dead* this afternoon. They say he was murdered."

Mister Puss shot me a glance and held my gaze.

It was not a leisurely Saturday morning at the loft. Marson and I were hosting a dinner party that night, which always carried an element of underlying stress, but far more perplexing was the news of Chad Percy's death in Green Bay.

We were out of bed before sunrise, brewing coffee, waiting for the *Dumont Daily Register* to be delivered. By then we had learned details of the story on cable news, but I was curious to read how our local paper would treat it. Having phoned Sheriff Simms the night before, I knew he'd been interviewed.

When we heard the *plop* of the paper tossed at the front door, Marson retrieved it as I poured coffee. He set the paper on the counter, smoothed its creases, threw out the circulars along with the sports section, and then washed his hands as I read the front page.

Was it a hate crime?

*Apparent murder of Green Bay cable star
baffles police in search of motive*

Compiled from *Register* staff reports

•

MAY 28, DUMONT, WI — The discovery on Friday afternoon of cable personality Chad Percy's lifeless body at his luxury condo in Green Bay has left local police searching for a motive in the apparent homicide. The victim was found by his houseman, Nan Yong, when he arrived with a delivery of dry cleaning. A report issued by police on the scene said there was no evidence of forced entry.

The coroner's initial report speculated that Percy's death had occurred at least twelve hours earlier, sometime overnight. The nude body was found in bed, and it appeared the victim had been choked or suffocated. Based on evidence at the scene, the report further speculated that Percy may have been date-drugged with a combination of Ambien and alcohol, but postmortem testing is required for conclusive findings.

Dumont County sheriff Thomas Simms conferred by phone last night with Green Bay law enforcement, as particular aspects of the Chad Percy case are similar to circumstances surrounding the recent death of David Lovell, who served as choirmaster of St. Alban's parish in Dumont. The Lovell death, initially described as suspicious, is now being investigated as a homicide.

Sheriff Simms noted that both of the victims were openly gay men, and suffocation played a role in both of the deaths. Does that mean the crimes are linked? Simms replied, "Look, two gay men have been murdered, nine days apart and 60 miles away from each other. Is that a pattern? Hard to tell."

When asked if he felt the murders were hate crimes, Simms responded, "It's a possibility, but at this point we simply don't know. It all depends on motive, and in both cases, the motive is not yet apparent."

News of Chad Percy's death has sent shock waves far beyond central Wisconsin because of his regular cable cutaway segments, which have enjoyed a ratings surge since first being aired three years ago.

With a personality often described as flamboyant and engaging, Percy had become something of a poster boy for the

"infotainment" trend, building a reputation as a glib racon-
teur as well as a serious commentator.

Demonstrating a keen business sense, Percy had parlayed
his sudden popularity into a budding financial empire that
was built on speaking tours, advice books, a sportswear label,
and most recently, the introduction of a new fragrance line
bearing his name.

Sunny Skyes, station manager and weather hostess at the
Green Bay studios where Percy's broadcasts originated, told
the *Register*, "We're stunned. We're all in tears. Chad put us
on the map. Now what?"

Plans for a public memorial were still pending at press time.

That afternoon, shortly before Nancy delivered the catered items
for our dinner, the mail arrived. I tossed it on the kitchen island
without sorting it, as I'd been busy polishing the stemware for our
meal. When I was satisfied that the wineglasses were as spotless
as they would get, I picked up the stack of mail and stepped over
to the trash bin, since most of the items could be pitched without
opening.

All that remained were a couple of bills and—aha—an envelope
addressed to me from St. Alban's rectory, with Lillie Miller's name
written in tight, tiny cursive above the imprinted return address.

Opening it, I found the requested list of people who had access
to the church sacristy, along with a yellow Post-it note bearing
Lillie's writing: *Sorry this is late!*

The first thing that struck me about the list was its length—
nearly two pages, single-spaced. The next thing that struck me was
that the list contained no surprises. At the top of the list were the
names of Mother Hibbard herself, the executive committee of the
parish vestry, Lillie, a custodian, and "David Lovell, choirmaster
(deceased)." That was followed by a list of "Acolytes"—the altar

boys and several girls—which ran at least twenty names, none of them known to me. Next was a list titled "Adult Choir," with perhaps another twenty names, all unknown, and another titled "Children's Choir," about a dozen names, including Hailey Olson and Thomas Simms, Jr. And finally, there was a list titled "Deacons and Lay Ministers." This one was shorter, with seven names, including one I knew: "Clem Carter, thurifer."

I had to look that one up. A thurifer is "one who carries a thurible, or censer, in an ecclesiastical rite." Okay, got it. Three days earlier, that little tidbit would have proved revelatory, but after seeing Clem's flashy performance at David's funeral on Thursday, it was old news—though no less significant. Clem had a habit of horsing around with burning incense.

G*rrring.*

We were ready. The kitchen was under control. The table was set smartly but simply—without the romantic overtones of flowers. We had mentioned to Curtis Hibbard and Yevgeny Krymov that our evening would be "nothing dressy, just the four of us," so Marson and I had taken it down a notch since the previous dinner; Marson now wore a blazer without a tie, and I had chosen a gray cashmere polo with gabardine slacks. Together, we answered the door.

"*Marson,* old chum, nice of you to ask us over," said Curtis, stepping inside. He wore his usual pinstripes, including the matching vest, with his usual starched white shirt and a proper Hermès necktie cinched tightly under his Adam's apple in a proper Windsor knot. He turned to me, handing me a chilled bottle of Dom Pérignon. "And a good evening as well to *this* charming young fellow. Ho-ho."

"Thank you, Curtis."

Yevgeny followed Curtis into the room, and unlike Curtis,

he had conformed to our suggested dress code, wearing a silky red shirt with tight black pants, both of which highlighted the contours of a legendary body that had routinely fetched standing ovations and tossed bouquets. He greeted me first. "Brody! They have not changed! You still have such *dah*-link green eyes." With a little growl, he playfully hugged my waist, bumping his hip against mine—which had the intended effect. Last time he had been here, he had also come on to me, but then ditched me for David. Tonight, David was gone. I wavered between feeling like sloppy seconds—or the luckiest guy in the world. While Yevgeny greeted my husband, I reminded myself that nothing could come of this.

Moments later, we were gathered in the kitchen, with Marson offering drinks. "Bar's open," he said. "What can I get you? Or if you'd prefer, we could open the champagne."

"Champagne might be nice," said Curtis, "unless the others want something else." Since Curtis had brought the bottle, no one objected to opening it.

When the four flutes were filled, we toasted first to friendship, then to David Lovell's memory, and finally, as something of an afterthought, Curtis added, "And how about that Chad Percy fellow? Talk about a hideous ending." We sipped once again, which left me wondering how news of Percy's death out here in the sticks had managed to penetrate Curtis's aloof New York veneer. Then Marson said to our guests, "If you'd like to get comfortable in the living room, we'll join you with the appetizers."

Marson and I fussed with arranging a tray—Nancy's mushroom tartlets and cheese crisps—as Curtis and Yevgeny strolled to the conversation area at the front of the loft, where two loveseats faced each other over the stone surface of a square low table. I watched as they sat at a diagonal across the table from each other, occupying both of the small sofas. Which meant I would end up sitting next to one of them. I had absolutely no desire to be within pawing distance of Curtis; on the other hand, I didn't quite trust myself flank to flank with Yevgeny. Good champagne can lead to trouble. For that matter, so can the cheap stuff.

Marson carried the tray from the kitchen, and I followed with small plates and our drinks. As we set everything on the table, Marson said, "I think you'll like these. Please, help yourselves." Considering where to sit, he said to me, "Tell you what. Curt and I have some catching up to do, so why don't you keep Yevgeny company?"

"Sure," I agreed with a shrug—couldn't care less—anything to please.

Yevgeny's gray Muscovy eyes twinkled as I approached the loveseat where he waited. The springs of the sofa creaked as I sat. With the additional weight, the cushion sagged in the middle, drawing us closer. Settling in, he lifted an arm to the top of the sofa and stretched it in my direction, fingertips grazing my shoulder; with his other hand, he dangled his champagne flute. Bubbles drifted to the surface like lazy fireworks, exploding between his fingers and thundering in my ears. Or so it seemed.

"Ho-ho," Curtis was saying to Marson, "Felber had it coming. I was surprised they didn't boot him out of the dorm months before *that* little incident."

Marson laughed along with his old college friend. "I guess it's true what they say—*never* trust an ag major." They roared.

Yevgeny turned to ask me, "Where did you attend university, Brody?"

"California. I grew up there."

"Ahhh," he said, reaching to twiddle a lock of hair behind my ear. "The land of fruits and nuts."

I laughed quietly while crossing my legs to mask my arousal—gabardine doesn't hide much.

"Did you also have hijinks like Marson and Curtis?"

"A few," I admitted with a stupid giggle.

He leaned to whisper, "But they are so *old*. At university, *they* studied by gaslight."

I smirked. "I'm no kid. I started college twenty years ago."

"Those were good days—back in school—for all of us, yes?"

"Yes. They were."

"I miss it. I think I go back. To keep me young." He playfully cuffed my chin.

I gave him a skeptical look. "Um, you're joking, right?"

He cleared his throat loudly. "Yoo-hoo? Curtis? Forgive me interrupt your memory lane with Marson. Brody thinks I joke about going back to school."

Curtis looked over to assure me, "No joke. Yevgeny might move to Appleton."

Marson and I asked in unison, *"What?"*

Curtis asked Yevgeny, "Shall I explain?"

With a Cheshire grin, the storied dancer glanced from face to face to face, telling Curtis, "Yes, please explain."

Curtis leaned forward, elbows to knees. "This goes back a bit. Since Yevgeny retired from the stage last year, he's been thinking about what to do with the next chapter of his life, and some sort of teaching gig seemed to make sense."

"Bravo," said Marson. "There's a whole new generation of dancers who could profit from his experience."

"Of course," agreed Curtis. "So I've been poking around for him. Safe to say, any dance school in the country—in the world— would kill to have Yevgeny on their faculty. So it was a matter of weighing all the variables and, most important, finding the right fit for Yevgeny's goals at this stage of his life."

It started to click for me. I said to Curtis, "Joyce was telling me that you planned to visit someone on the dance faculty at the conservatory in Appleton. I assumed that was a courtesy call."

"Ho-ho. It was more than that."

Yevgeny added, "That is why I visit, but I could say nothing."

Curtis added, "And there was so much speculation about what Yevgeny was *doing* here, the dean of the conservatory decided it was too risky for Yevgeny to be seen on campus, where he'd be instantly recognized. If a deal wasn't struck, they'd have egg on their face."

"What?" asked Yevgeny.

"It's an *expression*," said Curtis. "So the dean came to Dumont. He met me at St. Alban's, and I escorted him over to the Manor House for talks with Yevgeny."

"Twice," I said, recalling the sightings from the window at First Avenue Bistro.

"Actually," said Curtis, "there were three or four meetings. Most productive. No announcement yet, nothing signed, but here's the deal: Yevgeny will be appointed as an artist-in-residence for one year, beginning this fall, after which, if both he and the school are satisfied with the arrangement, he'll join the permanent faculty, fully tenured, in a newly instituted program bearing his name."

Yevgeny crossed his arms and turned to ask me, "Not bad, yes?"

"Yes. Not bad at all. Congratulations, Yevgeny." I patted his knee.

"Brody," he said, patting my hand, "you call me Zhenya."

I felt honored—but I would never remember that.

Curtis said, "Congratulations are indeed in order. It's a shame New York will be losing him, but at least he'll be out of the clutches of that horrid old organ-pumper, Fletcher Zaan."

Yevgeny wagged a finger. "Maybe Fletcher come to visit. Meantime, so many adoring students—beautiful young dancers in their prime."

"Ho-ho," said Curtis, returning the finger-wag. "Look but don't touch ... Zhenya."

Moving on to the dinner table, I had to wonder: How could the great Yevgeny Krymov—trained in Russia, mentored by Nureyev, hailed with rapturous applause in all the far-flung cultural capitals of the world—how could he possibly find contentment in central Wisconsin? Perhaps the dean of the conservatory wondered this as well. Perhaps that skepticism had motivated the offer of an initial appointment as artist-in-residence, a trial period that would serve as an escape clause, allowing both the school and the dancer to save face if Yevgeny's new realities fell short of expectations.

For all my doubts, however, Yevgeny seemed happily convinced that he faced a promising future here. As we began dinner, he was saying to Curtis, "Tomorrow will be hectic. Back to New York. Renée Fleming same night. But Monday morning? Time to start planning my move. Much to decide!"

Curtis reminded him, "Not till we get that contract signed."

"Yes, yes, yes." He turned his attention to Marson and me, seated across the table from Curtis and him. "Gentlemen," he said, raising a huge balloon wineglass and swirling the velvety Bordeaux within, "my compliments to the chefs. *Extraordinaire.*"

As we all touched glasses, I told him, "All the credit goes to Marson. He's great in the kitchen."

Yevgeny winked. "But you inspire him, I am sure."

Did I just feel—yes, I did—it was Yevgeny playing footsie under the table with me. My reflexive instinct was to retract my shoe, but … what the hell. I didn't budge.

Yevgeny was right about the meal. It was extraordinary. Marson had outdone himself with the tenderloin, such a simple main course, perfectly prepared and presented with a glistening béarnaise. Not thinking clearly, I cut a good-sized chunk from the middle, where it was rarest, and set it aside on my plate, away from the sauce, saving it as a treat for Mister Puss, but then I realized that he had moved back to Mary's. Having no idea when I might have an opportunity to feed him the meat, I ate it.

Marson said to Yevgeny, "When the story finally breaks about Appleton, Glee Savage will want another interview. It'll be big news out here."

Curtis interjected, "It'll be big news in *New York*."

Marson laughed. "You've been here two weeks, Curt. How the devil have you managed without the *Times*?"

"I read it online." He dabbed his lips with his napkin, then sipped from his wine.

"Soon enough," said Marson, "I suppose that'll be the *only* way to read a paper, if there are any left. At least we won't be getting ink on our fingers."

I reminded Curtis, "Marson can be a bit fussy."

"Ho-ho. Don't I know it. I guess nothing's changed in the forty years since college."

Without a hint of umbrage, Marson agreed, "Probably not."

I asked Curtis, "When you knew him in school, did he have a habit of 'cleaning' the morning paper?"

"*Yes*," said Curtis with a loud laugh. "Threw out the sports and the ads first. Rearranged the sections. Then worked out every fold and wrinkle. I half expected him to *iron* the damn thing."

"Still the same," I said, elbowing my husband.

Yevgeny looked confused. "Why throw away the sports section?"

Marson also looked confused. "Why would I read it?"

Curtis told Yevgeny, "Marson has no interest in sports."

"None," confirmed Marson. "Zero. I find the whole concept unsavory. Tribal."

I explained, "He's talking about team sports."

"Largely, I suppose, yes."

"Marson, old chum," said Curtis, "at a gut level, I'm inclined to agree with you. I mean, here at this table, four gay men, safe to say we all grew up feeling like fish out of water. Safe to say, from time to time, each one of us was taunted as a sissy, or worse."

"*Nezhenka,*" said Yevgeny, nodding.

We all turned to him.

"Russian sissy is *nezhenka.*"

"The point is," Curtis continued, "growing up as we did, it was natural to equate the ethos of sports with an aspect of masculinity we just didn't get."

"Toxic masculinity," I said. "And I still don't get it. Marson picked the right word—it's tribal."

I thought of fist pumps. I thought of aggrieved male privilege. I thought of the jock mentality that had assaulted Nancy Sanderson. I thought of red baseball caps and tiki torches and normalized hate. I thought I might be sick.

Curtis said, "Without dwelling on the heterosexual overtones, there's no need to *read* the sports section." Glibly, he added, "Just browse through the *pictures* to see if there's anything worth ogling before trashing it."

"Well," I had to admit, "there's *that.*"

With a haughty sniff, Marson called us "Philistines…"

I laughed. Then, striking a more serious tone, I noted, "In spite of growing up as 'outsiders,' both of you—Marson and Curtis—you eventually married women, like any normal, red-blooded American male."

Marson turned to me with a warm smile. "That was eons ago, kiddo, when things were different. I married Prucilla because I hadn't found *you.* And once I did find you, everything changed." He leaned over and kissed me.

Curtis coughed, tugging at his necktie, as if it were a noose. "Eons later, as you've surely noticed, I'm *still* a married man. Joyce and I went into this with our eyes wide open. I suppose some people might call it a marriage of convenience…"

No kiddin'.

"…but it works for us, in spite of the fact that I sometimes think of it as a marriage of *in*-convenience. We give each other plenty of space. Talk about 'separate beds'—we generally don't even *dine* together anymore. I came here tonight, for instance, without a syllable of explanation. Odd as it may seem, though, we do love each other."

I thought of the unholy trinity I had described to Sheriff Simms: Joyce Hibbard, her husband, and her husband's former lover.

As our Saturday evening grew late, Marson and I served the four honey-almond Bundt cakes—finished with powdered sugar, shaved almonds, and a dollop of ice cream, as Nancy had suggested—drawing gasps and groans from our sated guests.

"Good God, I couldn't *possibly*," said Curtis as he forked into it with abandon.

"Amazing," said Yevgeny. "You have saved the best for last. How sad that our friend David could not enjoy this."

I asked, "You mean, because he's no longer with us?"

"No, Brody. I mean, because of his allergy. The nuts. That night, he told me."

Which I found strange.

And a few minutes later, we were on our feet, saying good-bye, wishing our guests a safe trip tomorrow and a magical evening with Renée Fleming and Beethoven and a few thousand of their closest friends at Carnegie Hall.

And they were offering hugs, thanking us for such splendid hospitality, asking us to walk them out to their car.

And we were out on the sidewalk, in the dark of a warm midnight, standing next to the rented white Lincoln parked at the curb, gabbing farewells, exchanging stiff handshakes with Curtis

Hibbard and waiting for good-night smooches from the drop-dead Yevgeny Krymov.

And Marson got his.

And then it was my turn. And we held each other for a few moments, smiling. We enjoyed a lingering kiss. I whispered, "Thank you, Yevgeny."

"Uh-uh-uh," he said. "To you, Brody, I am Zhenya."

With a breathy laugh, I was lolling my head back, thinking I would never be able to remember his pet name, glancing over his shoulder.

When I froze. "What the *hell*?"

Everyone turned to follow my gaze.

In the cold, slanted beam of a street light, on the weathered brick of our front wall, we saw scrawled in orange spray paint: RU2 NEXT? GET! OUT! NOW!

"Jesus—Shocking—Horrid—Shit," we chimed.

Catching his breath, Curtis planted his hands on his hips, telling us, "William Maxwell, legendary fiction editor of *The New Yorker*, once decreed, 'Every writer has a lifetime ration of three exclamation points.'"

"Well," said Marson, wagging a disapproving finger at the graffiti, "*this* hack just blew his limit."

They forced a feeble laugh in a lame attempt to defuse the grotesque development.

But I found no humor in it. Not one bit.

PART THREE

Mother Hibbard's Grand Bargain

Sunday morning, Mary Questman slept later than usual.

She had arrived in Dumont from Chicago with Berta late Friday, retrieving Mister Puss from Brody and Marson before returning to the stately old Questman house on Prairie Street. Berta helped Mary and the cat get situated that night, unloading their things from Mary's spiffed-up but unpretentious Buick. The housekeeper agreed to return Sunday morning at eleven to do laundry and the last of the unpacking.

On Saturday, Mary had awoken with the birds, still keyed up from the delights and hoo-ha of her trip, needing to unpack a few things and catch up with mail. By nightfall, however, with most of her luggage still scattered about the bedroom, unopened, her energies had been sapped, exhausted by the sheer weight of her excitement. When at last she tucked herself into bed, she fell quickly into a deep and dreamless sleep.

Now, Sunday morning, Mister Puss lay curled on her pillow, nesting against her hair. Squinting in the sunlight that intruded through a crack in the curtains, he began to purr and reached his snout to Mary's ear.

Time to get it in gear.

Blinking her eyes open, Mary checked the bedside clock. "Good heavens." It was after nine-thirty already.

And I'm hungry.

Throwing back the covers, she said, "Yes, Your Majesty." But rather than heading directly downstairs to prepare their breakfast, which was her routine, she first stepped into the bathroom and quickly performed her ablutions, then poufed her hair and dressed for the day—she wanted to be cleared out of the bedroom by the time Cyclone Berta landed. As a finishing touch, Mary paused at her vanity to apply a dab of L'Air du Temps.

Mister Puss sneezed.

Then he traipsed down the stairs behind Mary and circled her legs while she got busy in the kitchen.

When at last the cat was fed and the coffee was brewing and the toast was buttered and the paper was brought in from the porch, Mary sat down at the big oak table and switched on her iPad to check email. Most of what had accumulated overnight was junk. But one of them was a group blast from Mother Hibbard, sent the prior evening around ten o'clock.

From: The Rev. Joyce Hibbard
To: The St. Alban's Congregation

My dear friends in Christ,

Little more than two weeks ago, on May 12, during an open meeting of our parish vestry, the St. Alban's community was faced with an ultimatum from the city of Dumont regarding the future of the beloved church building that has been our parish family's spiritual home for more than 150 years.

For reasons already thoroughly discussed, we now find ourselves at a crossroads, needing to reach a difficult decision as to how we shall move forward: Do we completely restore and renovate the old church, or do we replace it with a new building?

As you know, subcommittees of the vestry, and committees of the congregation at large, were appointed to study these issues and to report their findings and recommendations prior to the city-imposed deadline of May 31. I am now

writing to inform you that our parish vestry has scheduled
a public meeting to resolve these issues at six o'clock this
coming Monday, May 30, which is Memorial Day. I hope
this timing will prove convenient for all of you, as it falls at
the end of an extended holiday weekend.

Please, please, *please* plan to attend. Your valued input
is vital to these proceedings, as are your prayers for divine
guidance. The decision we must reach has strong advocates
for either of our options, but ultimately, we are called together
as a community of faith to move forward in a spirit of unity.

Offering my blessing for whatever decision will be reached,
I plead for yours as well. As a family, we have suffered
through the recent tragic loss of our beloved choirmaster,
David Lovell, who brought such beauty to our lives and to
our worship through his music. Let us, in his honor, now
strive to achieve a similar harmony as we chart the future
course of St. Alban's.

Yours in Christ,
The Rev. Joyce Hibbard, Rector
St. Alban's Episcopal Church, Dumont

Mary groaned, rising from her chair. The coffee had finished
brewing, and she needed a cup. Mister Puss watched as she poured
it. Having eaten his own breakfast, he then followed her back to
her chair and hopped up to the tabletop, purring, while she pondered the email. Again, she groaned.

What's wrong?

"It's that woman priest, Joyce Hibbard."

Quack.

"You really must stop that." Mary waited for a snappy comeback, but Mister Puss just sat there, watching her with wide, innocent eyes. Mary explained, "There's a big meeting tomorrow night.
Mother Hibbard wants everyone to be there."

Blow it off.

"I managed to avoid the last one. But I don't see how I can get out of this one. They're going to decide what to do about the old church."

Hold on to your wallet.

When Mary had skimmed the remaining emails and the morning paper, she ate the last of her toast and finished her second cup of coffee. Then she carried her dishes to the sink. While taking apart the coffeemaker and rinsing the pot, she fretted over the situation at St. Alban's.

Mary had a generous heart and a caring spirit, but she hated to be taken advantage of. Philanthropy had become one of her greatest joys, but she bristled at the notion that any would-be beneficiary might feel *entitled* to her largess. Granted, St. Alban's and the Questman family had a long history together, but Mary herself, with clear-eyed maturity, had come to view the very premise of her church as a myth. That hadn't stopped Mother Hibbard, however, from trying to put the squeeze on her two weeks earlier at an elegant dinner party hosted by dear friends. And stupidly, Mary now thought, she had cracked the door open that night and volunteered that she *might* be willing to help out if her favorite architect, Marson Miles, was satisfied with the artistic integrity of plans for the resulting project. Instead, she should have kept her mouth shut and followed Mister Puss's advice to hold on to her wallet.

Dingdong.

The perpetually nosy Mister Puss pounced from the kitchen table and scurried out to the front hall.

Odd, Mary thought, checking her watch. Berta wasn't due for half an hour, and she always came in through the back with her key. Who could be calling on a Sunday morning? She dried her hands and walked out to the hall.

When she answered the door, she found a young woman on

her stoop, perhaps thirty years old. She had dark, wiry hair and wore a black jumpsuit. While Mary found the attire a bit odd, she was reassured by the woman's tasteful jewelry, including a sizable wedding ring, and her nice patent pumps.

Mary had opened the door only a few inches, planting her foot firmly against the inside edge, as Berta had suggested she should do when home alone. Mister Puss peeped out from between her ankles. She asked, "May I help you?"

"Mrs. Questman?"

"Yes?"

"I'm sorry to bother you at home on a Sunday, but I've been hoping to talk to you before tomorrow night's meeting at St. Alban's."

"In what regard?" asked Mary. She removed her foot from the door and opened it a foot or two. Mister Puss crept backwards into the hall.

"My name is Kayla Weber Schmidt. I'm on the executive boards of both the Dumont Historical Society and the Wisconsin Preservationist League."

Finding the name vaguely familiar, Mary offered a ladylike handshake. "Won't you come in?" She stepped aside as her visitor entered.

"Thank you, Mrs. Questman."

"Certainly, Kayla. And you're welcome to call me Mary." She didn't feel like tussling with the clumsy kebob of Kayla's surnames.

"My pleasure ... Mary."

Mister Puss followed as Mary led Kayla into a side parlor off the main hall, telling the younger woman, "We can talk in here."

It was a small, intimate space, intended for conversation, but its large swagged window on the front wall of the house, combined with the high ceiling and elaborate cornice, lent a note of cultured formality. Mary perched at the end of a tidy loveseat; the cat hopped up and sat next to her.

Kayla sat across from them in a quilted-chintz armchair. "You have a lovely home, Mary. I've often admired it from the street."

Mary accepted the compliment with a restrained smile and a regal nod. "Now then," she asked, "what would you like to discuss?"

"Two things. The first has nothing to do with St. Alban's, but I think you'll find it of interest. Earlier last week, I was cataloging some of the Historical Society's recent acquisitions—our inventory space is *such* a mess, it's been inadequate for years—but the point is, I ran across something I think you may want to have."

"Oh?" said Mary. The cat's ears perked up.

Kayla proceeded to explain, in intricate detail, what she had found and why Mary might want it.

"As a matter of fact," said Mary, "I'd be delighted to make room for it—and pay for it handsomely."

Kayla grinned. "Contributions are always welcome, Mary, but we'll be happy enough knowing it's found a good home. It *belongs* here."

Mary was thrilled. "I can hardly wait to hear the *other* reason you dropped by."

Kayla leaned forward from the edge of her chair. "This relates to St. Alban's, and it's rather involved. You see, I was in Green Bay on Thursday night, just a personal matter, and while I was there"—Kayla flipped her hands—"it sort of *hit* me."

"What did?" asked Mary.

A few minutes later, the back door slammed as Mary and Kayla were winding down their discussion.

"Mary!" yelled Berta, rushing into the hall from the kitchen. "Mary!" she repeated, spotting them in the parlor, interrupting, breathless. "Driving over here—trouble at Marson and Brody's place. Big commotion. Crowd out front. Cops."

CHAPTER

16

Our loft on First Avenue, our home, felt overrun on Sunday morning.

Since learning on Friday that the cable commentator Chad Percy had been killed in Green Bay sometime Thursday night, a rapid series of events—seemingly unrelated but possibly linked to the earlier death of David Lovell—had heightened my own sense of urgency to solve the choirmaster mystery. When Marson and I found our front wall spray-painted with graffiti on Saturday night, we not only felt the deep emotional sting of having our home vandalized and violated, but far more ominously, we recognized that the scrawled words were tantamount to a death threat.

RU2 NEXT? GET! OUT! NOW!

Prior to Chad Percy's death, his commentaries had made reference to anti-gay incidents in Green Bay, and now those incidents had landed at our doorstep, here in Dumont, which seemed sickeningly out of character for my adopted hometown.

Moving to Wisconsin from California, I had anticipated a measure of culture shock, but I was amazed to discover that my expectations of intolerance were unfounded. With its progressive traditions of the past, Wisconsin had been the first state in the union to adopt any sort of statewide gay-rights protections—a laissez-faire mind-set that had persisted, despite its swing to the right in recent years, riding the same toxic wave that had embarrassed and imperiled a great nation.

And now, it seemed, that rightward tide was beginning to turn, with the redcaps being tested and bested by a different base that was inclusive and energized, showing signs of change for the positive—not only in Washington, not only in Wisconsin, but right here in Dumont.

For example, late Saturday night, after we had discovered the graffiti, Curtis Hibbard left our dinner party and, returning to the St. Alban's rectory, reported the incident to his wife, Joyce Hibbard, the parish rector. Early Sunday morning, Curtis flew back to New York with Yevgeny Krymov. But Mother Hibbard, rather than preparing to celebrate Mass in the gymnasium at ten o'clock, met her parishioners outside the lobby doors, told them what had happened, and then led a caravan of volunteers to First Avenue.

Marson and I were not members of St. Alban's; we weren't even believers. But Joyce had described us to her congregants as "friends of the parish," which was sufficient for two dozen of them to roll up the sleeves of their Sunday best and come over to help with the cleanup. It was almost embarrassing. With cars parked up and down the block, and with a crowd busy at a task that could have been handled by two or three people with a bucket and wire-bristled brushes, the scene attracted far more attention than the graffiti itself would have. But their intentions and fervor were heartwarming.

Another example of Dumont's empathy with our misfortune was the reaction of Sheriff Thomas Simms. When I phoned him well after midnight to report what had happened—and hoping he would not be too disturbed by the late intrusion—his only concern was Marson's and my welfare.

Simms arrived at the loft to begin his investigation within ten minutes, taking pictures and making notes. He assigned patrol cars to keep steady watch on our place, from the street in front and from the alley in back. When he was finally convinced, sometime before dawn, that we were in no immediate danger, he said he would return later that morning, after taking his family to church. Then, since the services were canceled, he came back to the loft an hour earlier than expected.

Not to overstate the obvious: Simms was straight and black. We were gay and white. And his total support was unconditional.

Therefore, on that Sunday morning after we had found the threatening graffiti, Marson and I felt that our home had been overrun—not by any forces of malice, but by a kindly invasion of goodwill.

"I know you haven't had much rest," said Simms, "but I assume you've been thinking about what happened. Last night, you were stunned by it. This morning, any idea who might've done it?"

We were huddled around the kitchen island with coffee and notes. Simms was looking his best, spiffed for church, wearing one of his beautifully tailored suits and a snappy silk tie, which was how he dressed for a regular workday. When we'd seen him over-night, though, he'd looked a bit rough—jeans and flannel shirt, unshaven, leather bomber jacket—and I'd realized he was not only handsome and refined, but fiercely attractive, with the emphasis on *fierce*. Sweet Jesus.

"Not a clue, Thomas," said Marson. "I've lived here most of my life, except for college, and I've never witnessed this sort of hate-mongering, not even once. Can't imagine why anyone would threaten either Brody *or* me." With a chuckle, he added, "Unless it was Prucilla."

Marson was talking about his ex-wife, my mother's sister, who was born in Dumont, still lived in town, and still relished, with operatic flair, the tragic role of a woman whose husband of thirty years had dumped her for her nephew—which was, I admit, a little hard to wrap your head around. Nonetheless, I understood that Marson was joking.

Simms didn't seem to take him seriously, either, turning to ask, "How about you, Brody? Any ideas?" He flipped his notes to the suspect grid he'd constructed the prior Wednesday in his office. It still contained some blank squares.

I slowly shook my head. "Sorry, Thomas. But I've been meaning to ask you about something. Several times in his cable segments, Chad Percy referred to anti-gay 'activity' and 'incidents' in Green Bay, as if it was a growing trend. Disturbing, sure. As far as I remember, though, he never gave any details about those incidents, which struck me as strange in the context of a news program. Granted, as a reporter, Chad Percy was about as hard-hitting as one of those Fox bunnies, but I'm wondering: Do you happen to know what the 'incidents' were that Percy found so alarming?"

"Yeah, I do." Simms blew a long, low whistle. "I got details about that from Green Bay law enforcement. And that's why I hustled over here last night. That's why I'm taking this seriously."

Marson and I exchanged a wary look.

Simms explained, "Percy found the incidents alarming because they were highly personal, directed at *him*. Which is probably why he didn't go into detail, at least not publicly. But he was specific in his reports to police, who concluded there was no evidence the incidents were part of a trend that targeted Green Bay's gay population at large. Bottom line: the only target of this stuff was Percy himself."

"Okay," I said. "And what were the incidents?"

Simms pinched the bridge of his nose, telling us, "Graffiti. The door to Percy's condo. The walls of his parking garage. Eventually, the car itself." He seemed reluctant to add, "Orange spray paint. Looked a lot like your front wall—similar message and lettering. I sent the pictures to Green Bay, and they sent me theirs."

"Well now," said Marson with profound understatement, "how sobering."

Simms continued, "There were a few voicemails, too. Sent from a burner, of course, a prepaid phone that's hard to trace. The messages were short and scripted, with the wording the same as the graffiti. And here's a weird twist: the voice sounded sorta 'Chinesey.' High-pitched and giggly. Obviously fake—that's the whole point—impossible to identify, couldn't even tell if it was a man or a woman."

"That sounds ridiculous," I said with an exasperated laugh. "It would almost be funny—if Percy hadn't wound up dead."

"Yeah," said Simms. He pored over the suspect grid, then tossed his hands.

I said, "At least we know this: There's definitely a link between what happened to Chad Percy and what happened to us. But we don't know why. Going a step further, *all* of this could possibly be linked to what happened to David Lovell, but not necessarily."

Simms told me, "A fair summary, yes."

Marson said, "I'm no sidekick, let alone a detective, but if you'd like my two cents, I think it's all the same ball of wax."

Simms and I held each other's gaze briefly, then nodded. He was drumming his fingers on the suspect grid. I noticed the empty squares again.

"Thomas," I said, "I've been tussling with something for a couple of days. You've asked me more than once if I could think of any other possible suspects—for *David's* murder—and I held back. Actually, there *is* someone else who might've had a strong but irrational motive against David. Trouble is, I don't see how she could possibly be involved with Chad Percy's death—or the graffiti on our front wall."

"She?" said Simms. "I'm listening…"

"Nancy Sanderson."

Simms winced. Then he added the name to his chart.

I told him, "Nancy has some personal history that I'm reluctant to drag into this, but it's highly relevant to David Lovell. Specifically, David *senior.*" I then ran Simms through the backstory: Nancy's confusion with her emerging sexual orientation in high school. The attempted rape by David's father. The psychological aftermath, the commitment issues, the continued therapy. The arrival of David junior in Dumont. And finally, Nancy's inability to quell her bitterness when she recognized in David the man who had assaulted her.

Simms asked, "This is hearsay, right?"

"It was—until Friday, when I asked Nancy about it. Then I heard the entire story from her own lips. The attack by David's father screwed up her whole life."

"In the course of that conversation," said Simms, "I assume Nancy admitted nothing regarding the murder."

"No, Thomas—if she had, you would've been the first to know. But she did say she felt guilty for transferring to David junior the rage she still feels toward David senior."

Simms made a note of it. Then he set down his pen, telling me, "David's body will be cremated after the holiday, probably Tuesday—Jake Haines can't put it off much longer. We need a break."

There was a rap at our front door as a deputy opened it a crack from the outside. "Sheriff? Sorry to interrupt. When you have a minute?"

I saw the bobbing of Glee Savage's big red hat while she tried to look over the deputy's shoulder. "Brody?" she called. "We need to *talk.*"

"Yikes," said Marson. "It's the press."

Moments later, we walked out front, where, ironically, the holiday atmosphere struck me as downright festive. A couple of cops cheerfully directed traffic in the street, exhorting drivers to keep moving. Mother Hibbard dumped a bucket in the gutter as Bob

Olson checked the brushing technique of several volunteers, reminding them of the goal—"like it never happened." Lillie Miller
was pecking about, passing a plate, offering snacks that looked
suspiciously like macaroons.

Grasping Glee's elbow, I marched her away from the crowd,
instructing, "No pictures, doll—understand?"

She smirked.

I tried begging. "*Please?* This has been rough. Marson and I are
feeling victimized. Publicity will only ... spread our shame."

Glee put an arm around me and hugged my shoulders. "Sure,
sweetie. I get it. We'll have to report *something*, but I'll make sure
they generalize it—no pictures, no names, no specifics. Something
about 'petty vandalism downtown' or whatever."

"Thanks, doll."

She asked me, "You okay? And Marson?"

"Everyone's been great." I gestured toward the brick wall, now
clean, still wet.

"But I saw what it said," Glee told me. "You were threatened.
I'm worried."

"Leave that to me—I'm worried enough for both of us." I
squeezed her hand.

She offered a halfhearted smile. Glancing past me, she said,
"Look who's here."

I turned. Chugging up the sidewalk were Mary Questman and
Berta. Walking at Mary's heel was Mister Puss, on his leash.

Marson spotted them at the same time I did, and we converged
to meet them as they joined the crowd.

Mary was aflutter. "I do hope nothing's *wrong*. Why all the
commotion?" She whirled her hands as she spoke. One of her
hands held the leash, jerking Mister Puss back and forth on the
pavement.

I picked him up. He purred as I told Mary, "We had a bit of

excitement. Just some graffiti, probably kids, no harm done." I was stretching the truth—big-time—but there was no point in upsetting her.

Marson picked up the conversation, joking with her, assuring her it was "just one of those things," switching topics to the "glorious weather."

For the first time that morning, I noticed that the weather was, in fact, glorious. Warm and breezy, it was perfect for a Memorial Day weekend. Thoughts of Memorial Day brought thoughts of summer. Thoughts of summer brought thoughts of picnics. And thoughts of picnics brought thoughts of Meteor Lake.

"Mary," I said, "could I possibly 'borrow' Mister Puss for a few hours? I'll get him back to you this afternoon."

Both Marson and the cat gave me a curious look.

Mary said, "Of *course*, Brody. He enjoys your company *ever* so much."

And within an hour—after Mary and the sheriff and the crowd had left, leaving only the two deputies guarding the house—we were in the Range Rover. Marson drove as I sat in the passenger seat with Mister Puss, heading out past the edge of town, where I was eager to show my husband Meteor Lake. Like many others in Dumont, he had grown up there and had heard of the lake, but had never seen it. After a harrowing night and a hectic morning, I thought the serene setting would be an ideal place to decompress—unless it was swarming with holiday picnickers.

But it wasn't. Once again, the tiny county park was deserted. The wooden tables were vacant; the rusty old grills were cold. No one frolicked and laughed along the shore of the little lake. Beyond, no one splashed and rippled the placid surface of the water.

In the fluttering shade of a willow, Marson and I stood alone in the world—with Mister Puss, who circled my feet, purring as he tangled the leash. Marson kissed me and, dropping his hand, touched me. We shared a grin.

And soon we were tearing back to town in the SUV, parking at the curb on Prairie Street, saying good-bye to Mister Puss as we handed him over to Mary Questman's loving arms.

And only a minute or two later, we pulled into our alley and parked with a quiet screech behind the loft. The sheriff's deputy who was stationed there threw us a little salute as we slipped inside through the back door.

And then, under the watchful but unseeing eyes of our armed guards, we traipsed up the spiral stairs.

Monday, Memorial Day, got off to a lazy start, feeling like an extra Sunday but lacking the disruptive excitement of the prior day's cleanup brigade that had purged the graffiti from our façade. Opening the front door to retrieve the morning paper, however, I was reminded that yesterday's troubling episode was not yet resolved when I got a discreet wave from the deputy parked across the street in a squad car. People were bound to notice—and wonder.

Fortunately, Glee had made good on her word. Seeing nothing about the graffiti incident on the *Register*'s front page, Marson and I divvied up the sections to look for a story inside. I finally spotted it, buried beneath the fold in the "Police Blotter" column, making vague reference to "petty vandalism on First Avenue."

While Marson was pouring coffee, the iPad on the kitchen island signaled an incoming email. Marson read it, chortled, and handed me the tablet.

From: Curtis Hibbard
To: Marson Miles

Good morning, Marson, old chum! The Ninth was superb last night, and Miss Fleming made it abundantly clear that she still rules the roost—lest anyone had doubts. The entire evening lived up to all the hype, ending the season with *the* performance of the year. Even Yevgeny (who is not only discerning, but a bit of a snob) was impressed.

I wish you could have been there to hear it. For that matter, I still wish David Lovell could have been there with me, but alas, 'twas not meant to be.

Aside from the cultural update, dear Marson, I am writing this morning to pose two simple questions (partly at my Poopsie's prompting, but also to assuage my own curiosity).

1. Would it be presumptuous of me to ask the nature of your relationship with Mary Questman? I know that the two of you worked together on the design of the performing-arts complex, and I was pleased to be included when you entertained her in your home. But I am wondering: In addition to your professional ties, do you and Mary count each other as friends? Close friends?

2. Back in our college years, you took a dim view of religion, and I presume that hasn't changed. In the course of your career, however, have you ever designed a church? Looking ahead, would you ever consider such a commission?

Clever lad that you are, you may sense a link between the first question and the second.

Best regards,
Curtis Hibbard, Founding Partner
Hibbard Belding & Smith, LLP
New York • London • Berlin

Marson and I had previously discussed, as a hypothetical, the possibility of church design for our firm, so I could guess how he would respond to Curtis in that regard. I also knew that Marson's friendship with Mary was every bit as close and loving as mine was. What I couldn't predict, however, was how Marson might respond to Curtis's suggestion that there was a link between these two issues.

He sat next to me at the island, typing quickly. He sent the message with a decisive tap. Then he passed me the iPad to show me what he'd written.

From: Marson Miles
To: Curtis Hibbard

Good morning, Curt. I'm somewhat rushed today, so allow me to respond to your queries by number.

1. Mary Questman and I are indeed close friends. I have known her forever, but it was during the design and construction of Questman Center that we truly bonded. She gave me the most important opportunity of my career, and I delivered, in return, the project that will seal her legacy. I adore the woman. And I think it's safe to say the feeling is mutual.

2. Le Corbusier was an avowed atheist, and yet he designed the chapel at Ronchamp, which has inspired generations of believers. No, I have never designed a church, but I have designed theaters, and if you think about it, churches and theaters share an uncanny similarity of purpose, scale, and effect. To answer your question, then: yes, I'd consider such a commission.

But also a caveat: I don't need the work, and I am keenly protective of Mary's interests.

Best regards,
Marson

Late that afternoon, while Marson was upstairs, figuring out what to wear to the public meeting of St. Alban's parish vestry, I was down in the kitchen, browsing inside the refrigerator, wondering if there was anything on hand that might serve as a late supper after the meeting, which would begin at six. Nothing—we would need to eat out somewhere. As I closed the fridge, my cell phone rang.

"Hello?"

A squeaky voice asked, "Mista Nollis?"

"Yes, this is Brody Norris."

"He-he-he. Are you two next? He-he-he. Get out now!" *Click.*

I took a deep breath. Then I phoned Sheriff Simms to report that I'd just received a call from the voice he'd described—fake Chinesey, high-pitched and giggly—quoting the graffiti that had been spray-painted on our front wall.

When Marson and I arrived at St. Alban's, Simms was standing outside the doors to the lobby of the former gym, waiting for us. He stepped us away from the stream of people filing in. Arriving near the corner of the building, concealed by the green blob of an unshapely car-sized juniper, he told us, "We tried tracing that call. I didn't think we'd get anywhere—and we didn't. There'll be plainclothes officers in the hall tonight. I hope there won't be any real danger at the meeting, but try to stay alert."

"You can bet on *that*," I said.

Marson asked wryly, "Don't you hate these long weekends?"

Simms winked. "Things should be back to normal by tomorrow, right?"

I was skeptical. But I said nothing as Simms slipped away, around the back of the building, while Marson and I returned to the front doors.

At six o'clock at the end of May, there were nearly three hours of daylight remaining in Dumont. The day had been warm, and now it felt hot as we entered the crowded lobby; back when the school gym had been built, air conditioning was an unthinkable luxury for such a space, at least in sensible, workaday Wisconsin. I unbuttoned my collar and removed my jacket—Marson loosened his tie—as we passed through the lobby and into the main room. Large exhaust fans whirled lazily at either end of the rafters, which made things more bearable, but not much.

The crowd milled and gabbed, but the dour tone of the chatter, punctuated by no laughter whatever, reflected the weighty purpose for which the parishioners had assembled. At the front of the room, the altar table had been moved aside, replaced by the row of folding tables where the vestry members would sit, some of them already in place. As at the earlier parish meeting, almost three weeks earlier, American and Episcopal flags drooped from staffs behind the table, with a small crucifix centered between them on the wall.

We mingled in the wide center aisle, greeting the people we knew, though they were far outnumbered by the rank and file of the congregation—all of whom, I presumed, were in attendance to witness this watershed moment in the history of their parish. I was delighted, and more than a little surprised, to see that Mary Questman had decided to come; she stood near the front of the aisle, surrounded by fellow parishioners who had not seen her in many months. Mother Hibbard hung near her as well, strategizing, no doubt, how best to convert Mary's presence into Mary's signature on a dotted line.

Tommy Simms stood with Hailey Olson and some of the other choir kids, who were joined by passing adults in congratulating Tommy on his stirring rendition of "Amazing Grace" at David Lovell's memorial on the prior Thursday. Among them was David's brother, Geoff Lovell, who shook Tommy's hand. I did not see Geoff's girlfriend, Spark.

Nancy Sanderson was there, which struck me as odd. She had *not* attended David Lovell's memorial service, where I had expected to see her, so why was she present tonight? As far as I knew, she was not a member of the parish. While pondering this, I noticed

Nia Butler, the city's butch code-enforcement officer, mosey over to Nancy and strike up a conversation. As Nia spoke, she removed her granny glasses, smiling shyly as she pocketed them in her olive twill Eisenhower jacket.

And then, Glee Savage arrived.

With her big purse and her huge hat and her mile-high heels, she strutted down the aisle, parting the crowd, leaving in her wake a blinking pack of proper Episcopal stares.

Meeting me, she leaned to peck my cheek. In the warm room, the smell of her patchouli seemed even more intense than usual. She glanced about while pulling a notebook from her purse. "Nice crowd. Dead, though."

Then Kayla Weber Schmidt arrived.

I got a glimpse of her black jumpsuit barreling down the aisle behind Glee, framed between Glee's shoulder and the brim of her hat. I must have looked panicked; Glee asked, "What's wrong, sweets?"

I stammered, "K-k-k-kayla's here." Recalling the scene she'd made at the first parish meeting, not to mention her verbal attack of *me* as we gathered for David Lovell's memorial, I instinctively stepped out of view, as if hiding behind Glee—feeling deflated and stupid.

"Why, that *snip*," said Glee, planting her hands on her hips and turning to face my nemesis. "Kayla!" she said. "Of all people—what brings you *here* this evening?"

We knew damn well why Kayla was here: she came to throw a shit fit.

Glee must have been as surprised as I was by Kayla's buoyant tone when she replied, "It's such an important occasion for St. Alban's—and all of Dumont. It's history in the making. Where *else* would I be?" She answered her own question with a breathy little laugh.

Huh? I leaned from behind Glee to take a peek at the woman, wondering if she'd been possessed by an alien spirit with a wily voice not her own.

She spotted me. Chipper as could be, she said, "Hello, Mr. Norris. I owe you an apology." Glee stepped aside as Kayla moved near, extending her hand. When I offered mine in return, she held it gently. "I was *way* out of line when I saw you here last time. I hope you'll forgive me, Brody. May I call you Brody?"

"Uh, yes ..."

"It's no excuse," she explained, "but I've been under a lot of stress lately."

I asked, "The church issue?"

"There's that, yes." She hesitated. "But really, it's my son. Aiden. He has developmental issues. They were diagnosed early on, but a few months ago, the reality finally set in. He's four. In a year, he starts kindergarten. Maybe. Everything's uncertain. It has me scared ... and feeling guilty."

Both Glee and I assured Kayla that Aiden's condition was no one's "fault," least of all hers.

"That's kind of you," she said. "Kind and generous. But I've been in denial. And I've taken it out on ... everyone."

I reminded her, "Your husband loves you. Tyler will help you work this out."

She smiled. "He's with Aiden now. He told me about your visit. I'm sorry—I understand there was a close call with your cat."

In an instant, I felt the same panic as when I'd feared for Mister Puss's life, but the wave of alarm passed as I quelled the memory. I told Kayla, "That cat isn't mine; he belongs to Mary Questman."

"Really? The brown cat?"

"Right. He's Abyssinian. His name is Mister Puss." I wondered when Kayla had seen Mary with him.

"Oh," said Kayla, as if recalling something. "Tyler asked me to give you his best. He said you liked the totems."

"Loved them."

Glee interjected, "See? Didn't I tell you?"

A gavel rapped, hushing the crowd. Standing up front, Bob Olson said, "We need to begin soon, so please take your seats." Then he moved behind the table, sitting in the center chair behind his nameplate: SENIOR WARDEN.

Joyce Hibbard, RECTOR, sat in the chair next to him. On his other side sat Lillie Miller, SECRETARY. At the far end of the table sat Nia Butler, representing the city. Other members of the vestry filled in the remaining six or seven seats at the table, and the room reverberated with the banging of metal chairs as the crowd got situated.

As before, I sat between Marson and Glee. Mary Questman sat in the front row, as did Clem Carter, our builder. I noticed three doctors in the room: Teresa Ortiz and medical examiner Heather Vance, both of whom had a professional interest in David Lovell's death, and Jim Phelps, the veterinarian, who was a member of the parish. Sheriff Simms stood in one of the side aisles, leaning against the wall with his arms crossed, discreetly scanning the crowd.

With everyone settled, Bob Olson rapped his gavel again and called the meeting to order. "Before we begin," he said, "let us make note in the minutes that today is Memorial Day. As a tribute to those who have fallen in the defense of our nation, let us observe a moment of respectful silence." All heads bowed.

Olson then invited Mother Hibbard to open the proceedings with a prayer. All heads bowed.

Olson then asked Lillie Miller to read from the agenda, which established that the purpose of the meeting was to hear reports from the committees that had been charged with recommending the course of action to be taken by the parish, either repairing or replacing the original church building. Also noted for the record was the presence of Dumont's code-enforcement officer, Nia Butler, whose department had issued the deadline for a remediation plan, due tomorrow, Tuesday, May thirty-first.

Olson then asked each of the five committee heads to give a verbal summary of the written reports, which were submitted to the secretary.

Over the next ninety minutes, one by one, the grim-faced committee chairs stood before the crowd and explained, sometimes tearfully, that their members had weighed all the options, all the pros and cons, and had reluctantly concluded that the best course of action was to replace the beloved old church—which invariably evoked ripples of conversation in the crowd and subsequent raps of silence from the senior warden's gavel.

At the conclusion of the reports, Olson opened up the meeting to comments from the assembled parishioners. Hands fluttered for his attention.

Clem Carter thought the recommendations were just dandy.

Others weren't so sure, but acknowledged the need to move forward.

Someone asked if the new church might look like the old one.

Someone else suggested, no, the parish needed a clean break.

One of the choir parents asked if the organ could be saved.

Another asked about the Tiffany windows.

Someone asked about a timeline for construction.

When would demolition begin?

And by then, the fluttering hands had dwindled to one.

"Ms. Weber Schmidt," said Olson, "we understand that your interest in these issues is keen. However, because your participation in our last public meeting proved disruptive—and contentious— we are limiting comments tonight to members of the parish. This is, after all, a family matter and ours to decide. Therefore, I'm sorry, the vestry does not recognize you to speak."

She dropped her hand, eyeing Olson with a steely gaze.

Uh-oh, I thought. She's gonna blow.

In the dead silence that followed, a hand popped up in the front row.

"Aha," said Olson, sounding pleased. "The vestry recognizes Mrs. Questman. What would you like to say, Mary?"

Because of Mary's age and wealth, her breeding and manners, her perpetually cheery disposition—and the widely gossiped notion that she communicated with her cat—it was sometimes easy to patronize Mary, to dismiss her as benignly out of touch or even a bit dotty. At other times, however, she surprised everyone with her wisdom and shrewd clarity.

Mary stood. "Thank you, Bob. As the last of the Questmans, one of St. Alban's founding families, I'm happy to share my thoughts with the parish regarding its future. But I wish to cede my time to the young lady. I ask that she be allowed to speak in my stead."

Boom.

Marson, Glee, and I exchanged bewildered glances.

"In that case," said Olson with a wary smile, "the vestry is pleased to recognize Kayla Weber Schmidt."

Mary sat.

Kayla stood. "Thank you, Mr. Olson. And thank *you*, Mary." From her chair near the far side of the room, Kayla turned to address the entire assembly.

"As most of you know, I'm on the board of the county's historical society, which has a mission to preserve Dumont's significant historic sites. Your lovely old church is a prime example. We are opposed to demolishing it—and I'm sure that many of you, in your heart of hearts, would find such an outcome tragic.

"Yet, we understand the bind that the parish now faces. I had the opportunity to discuss this dilemma at some length yesterday with Mary Questman, and we concluded that St. Alban's options may not be so black-and-white. Why not, for example, proceed with your need to construct a more modern structure for worship, but at the same time, put the original church to use in some other manner, rather than destroying it?

"For example, many old churches have found new life as restaurants or even bars—a repurposing that you would probably find undignified. As it happens, I have a different idea that may be far more appealing.

"The Dumont Historical Society has struggled for some years with facilities that have been outgrown by its mission. Our current facilities, in a building of no historical significance, afford us no exhibit space at all. Offices, storage, and curatorial space are all inadequate. So my board has authorized me to bring you this win-win proposal:

"Don't tear down your church. Give it to us. We will lovingly restore it, bring it up to code, and put the building to new use as the repository and guardian of Dumont's past. We'll be your quiet and respectful neighbor. Not only will we save you the expense and anguish of demolition; we'll compensate you for the building by assisting with demolition of your abandoned school building, which has little historic or architectural merit. That will free up the land you need for a new St. Alban's.

"Well," Kayla concluded, "what do you think?"

At first, no one spoke. But a palpable wave of excitement rippled through the crowd.

Mary Questman stood. All eyes were on her as she turned. When she spotted us near the back of the room, she looked directly at Marson, raising an inquisitive brow.

Subtly—though everyone saw it—Marson signaled Mary with a thumbs-up.

Mary told the vestry, "I like it."

Mother Hibbard *loved* it.

Officer Nia Butler, speaking for the city, thought it was *perfect*.

Bob Olson asked the assembly for a motion that would advise the vestry to proceed.

"So moved," said Clem Carter.

A dozen others popped to their feet, chorusing, "Second!"

The motion passed by affirmation, with no nays.

"Well, now," said Olson, sounding relieved, "that was what I'd call a productive meeting. Everyone can leave here tonight with a clear sense of direction."

He paused.

"Then again," he added, "we still need to figure out how to pay for it."

As Bob Olson had pointed out, when St. Alban's arrived at a consensus to build a new church, that was only the first step for the parish. The biggest challenges still lay ahead, not the least of which was funding.

Though it was not within the scope of the Monday-night meeting to delve into such issues, Joyce Hibbard wasted no time nabbing Marson and Mary after the adjourning gavel, asking if they could meet at the rectory the next morning to explore options for moving forward. When they agreed, Joyce also invited Nia Butler, for her advice on code-related matters. When Nia agreed, Joyce informed the parish secretary, Lillie Miller, and the senior warden, Bob Olson, that they, too, would be needed Tuesday morning at ten.

Monday night, when Marson and I finally returned to the loft—tired and sluggish after a late meal in a brightly lit burger joint—we noticed that a sheriff's deputy was still stationed in front on First Avenue. When we parked in back, a second deputy was still stationed there in the alley as well. He wished us a good night as we locked the SUV and disappeared into the loft through its rear door.

"I'm sorry I dragged you into this," I told my husband as we stood in the dark kitchen.

He stepped near and put his hands on my shoulders. "You didn't drag me. I practically *goaded* you into getting involved."

"Yes," I recalled with a grin, "you did. But you weren't bargaining on death threats and armed guards."

He shrugged. "Goes with the territory. You'll figure it out."

"I appreciate your confidence. But I'm clueless."

"No, you're not. Lots of clues—just put'm together."

With a snort of laughter, I told him, "Thanks." Standing there in the dark, I wrapped my arms around his waist and contemplated what was known about David Lovell's and Chad Percy's murders. They seemed connected, and at the same time, they didn't. I said, "Your meeting at the rectory tomorrow—mind if I tag along?"

"I was hoping you'd join me." He looped his fingers through my belt and yanked me close, telling me quietly, "Everything's better when *you're* involved."

"Oh, yeah?"

Without a word, he led me to the spiral stairs.

In the quiet, cavernous space of the loft, as our footfalls resonated on the metal steps, I recalled the offhand opinion Marson had expressed to Sheriff Simms regarding the two murders:

It's all the same ball of wax.

Tuesday morning, stepping out the front door to retrieve the rolled copy of the *Register*, I offered a routine wave to the deputy across the street—as if his presence was totally normal and expected, as if I didn't notice that there had been of shift of guards during the night, as if the expense incurred by the county for this extravagance didn't matter in the least.

An hour or so later, when Marson and I left the loft through the back door, it was the same thing—another wave to another guard on another shift—as if I took comfort in this intrusion on the privacy of our ordinary lives. At a purely rational level, I understood that these protective measures were wise, perhaps even necessary, but that didn't stop me from wanting to be done with all of it, and unfortunately, that would depend on solving a crime or two, which seemed unlikely anytime soon.

Marson and I took separate cars to the office that morning. We would attend the meeting at the rectory together, but the rest of the day was unplanned, and it was sure to be busy. The long holiday weekend, coupled with the increasing demands of the investigation, had forced me to let my work slide, with deadlines looming.

As I entered our offices through the street door, Gertie greeted me, asking if I'd enjoyed the weekend, but before I was able to fabricate a sunny reply, she rattled off a chilling litany of items needing my immediate attention.

"Uh"—I halted her midway between the client in Sheboygan and the monthly financials—"maybe you could just take calls for a while. I need an hour at my desk."

And before long, Marson popped over from his office across the hall, jangling his keys, saying it was time to leave for the rectory.

While he drove, I confessed to my growing anxiety: the investigation was pulling needed focus from my work at Miles & Norris. "More than anything, Marson, I *never* want to let you down."

"Impossible, kiddo. We're in this together. When you're under pressure, I pick up the slack. And you'd do the same for me." With one hand on the wheel, he reached over with his other.

I grasped his hand and held it in mine as we circled the downtown commons, approaching St. Alban's.

Gusty winds had picked up on that bright final day of May, as if to signal a precise shift of seasons—a last cool gasp of spring, making way for June. Walking from the church parking lot, we laughed at the blustery assault as we hunkered into our jackets and darted up to the porch of the rectory.

Marson rang the bell as I tried to do something with my hair. He assured me, "You're gorgeous."

Lillie Miller opened the heavy door, welcomed us into the hall, and then thumped the door closed behind us.

We followed her into Joyce Hibbard's office, where Nia Butler and Bob Olson had already arrived. They stood to greet us as we entered, with Joyce leaning to tell Lillie, "We'll need an extra chair."

"Sorry," I said. "I didn't mean to cramp everyone."

"Nonsense," said Joyce. "Delighted you're here. Plenty of room."

But when Lillie wheeled another chair in from her side office, the mishmash of furniture went from cozy to crowded. Settling in, we left one chair vacant. Joyce said, "I presume Mary will be along soon." With a sly chuckle, she added, "No point in beginning without her."

I knew what that meant: the whole point of this get-together was to put the screws to St. Alban's wealthiest parishioner. I noticed a closed manila folder on Mother Hibbard's desk. Did it contain a drafted agreement, perhaps a multimillion-dollar pledge, ready to sign?

Nia Butler wore her usual outfit—I still wasn't sure if it was an official uniform or simply a paramilitary style she had adopted as her own. She sat with a slim zippered portfolio in her lap. Opening it and removing a sheaf of papers, she said, "I did some digging in the city archives this morning. I imagine you've already gone over the plat map of the parish property, but I wanted to have a look. Bottom line: Kayla Whatsername's idea ought to work out fine. Give the old church to the county, raze the old school, and build the new church there. Setbacks are good. Plenty of parking space, if the parish and the county share the lot."

Marson said, "And I like that the school has some frontage on the commons. The parish would want that visibility for the church, and the church would replace some public blight."

Dingdong.

We all sat hushed as Lillie got up to admit the last arrival.

"Woo-hoo, this *wind*," warbled Mary, fussing with her hair as Lillie led her in from the hall. And following at Mary's side was Mister Puss, leashed and harnessed. His unexpected entrance, I realized, gave my sagging spirits a needed boost.

Everyone rose to welcome Mary, also greeting Mister Puss with coos and baby talk—everyone, that is, except Joyce Hibbard, who could barely hide her disdain for the cat.

At our dinner party two weeks earlier, Mary told Joyce that Mister Puss had convinced her that "God is a myth." Joyce also learned that the cat had warned Mary to "hold on to your wallet." And I later saw the email Joyce sent to her bishop, in which she weighed the possibilities that "Mary could be swayed to step forward as a major donor, though the cat does present obvious complications." In that same email, Joyce had derided Mary's relationship with Mister Puss, writing, "It troubles me to realize that the mind is so fragile at our age, that dementia is so indiscriminate, that it can strike such a good and kindly soul without warning." Earlier still, Mother Hibbard's husband had sent a long email to Marson, bragging that his wife "knows how to sniff out the money."

And now, just when Joyce was approaching her moment of triumph—having sniffed out the money, having done all her homework, having finally lured Mary into her den with all the paperwork within reach, ready to sign—just when Joyce had set the stage for a victorious climax, in walks Mary with her four-legged defender and confidant. Joyce sputtered pleasantries while watching her furry antagonist with a deflated look of dismay. Mister Puss, in turn, eyed Joyce with a smirk. Truly: the cat smirked.

The wind was rattling the windows of the old rectory, so Lillie closed the carved pair of sliding doors between Joyce's office and the front hall, which shut out much of the noise, but it also increased the sense of claustrophobia as we crowded around Joyce's desk. The cramped room felt suddenly warm.

As conversation began to swirl around me, so did the sickly bouquet of too many fragrances. Mother Hibbard's secret sauce wafted from behind the desk. Behind her, Lillie Miller sat taking notes while exuding a strong whiff of her Shalimar. In front of the desk, to my right, Bob Olson had doused himself with something, which seemed at odds with his number-crunching personality and bland sense of style. To my left, even Marson's light touch of Vétiver invaded my space. And next to Marson, Mary Questman's lively chatter bubbled forth with olfactory waves of her L'Air du Temps.

In the last chair, beyond Mary, Nia Butler made no discernible contribution to the thick, perfumy potpourri. Neither did I. And neither, of course, did Mister Puss, whose eyes watered as he looked at me from Mary's lap.

Joyce was saying, "So it seems we're in a position to move forward. With the county's offer to take responsibility for the old church, and with the city's approval of new construction on the land occupied by the school, all that remains now"—she flipped her hands—"is to build a new church."

"Easy peasy," I said with a tepid laugh, which the others echoed.

"Yes," Joyce said agreeably, sharing the laugh, "there's a long way to go. As I see it, there are three general components to the project: design, construction, and yes, the ever-important issue of funding."

Mary asked, "Has any thought been given to the design yet? What would the new church *look* like?"

"An excellent question, Mary," said Joyce, "and I know the answer is important to you. Right now, the issue of design is wide open. At last night's meeting, someone asked if the new church would essentially copy the old church. That's one approach, I suppose, but it strikes me as a bit...backward. Then again, who am *I* to judge?" Joyce folded her hands on the desk and leaned forward on her elbows, asking quietly, "Marson? Any thoughts about this?"

"Yes," said my husband. "I agree that it would be a mistake—a lost opportunity—if St. Alban's simply tried to build an updated duplicate of the original church. After all, the old building will remain. Under the stewardship of the historical society, its legacy is assured. To my mind, the parish now finds itself in the enviable position of totally reimagining its spiritual home—from a clean sheet, and with a clean conscience."

Mary Questman nodded. "Yes. Exactly."

I noticed Joyce exchange a poker-faced glance with Bob Olson. They were hearing what they wanted to hear.

Joyce said, "Hypothetically, Marson—if given a clean sheet— what would *you* do with it?"

And I knew that Joyce had followed her bishop's advice regarding Mary: "Make her an offer she can't refuse." By soliciting Marson's design input and then, no doubt, offering him the commission, Joyce would render Mary powerless to refuse funding the project. At the dinner party, Mary had said she might be persuaded to contribute if Marson approved of the project's artistic merits. If he ended up designing it from scratch, all the better— Mary's support would be nailed.

Marson must not have understood the strategy that was being set in motion; if he had, I doubt he would have played along. When he answered Joyce's "hypothetical" question about the clean sheet, he spoke with sincerity and vision and knowledge, waxing eloquent for several minutes about the nature of worship as mystical theater; the shared experience of any gathering place; the role of public architecture as living art in a community; the need to combine respect for aesthetic traditions of the past with an understanding of contemporary forms and an eye toward future functions. Without describing in any detail what the new St. Alban's might look like, without trying to sell himself in the least, he left no doubt that he was the right person to lead the parish on its journey of discovery and design.

When he finished, no one spoke. Then Mary reached over and patted his hand, telling him softly, "Bravo, Marson."

Joyce cleared her throat. "I'm sure I can speak for the vestry, Marson, as well as the entire parish. Would you do us the honor of accepting the commission to design the new St. Alban's?"

"Oh, *Marson*," said Mary, bouncing in her chair. "You *must*."

Hook, line, and sinker. While I felt a measure of discomfort with Joyce's motives, I couldn't fault her technique.

Marson said, "Well, first time for everything—I'm designing a church."

If my husband didn't grasp what had just happened, and if Mary didn't either, her cat seemed to get it. Mister Puss fidgeted in Mary's lap, stood, and gave an odd little yowl, looking directly at Joyce, who stared back at the cat with scrunched features. If the priest could have gotten away with it, I think she would have stuck out her tongue.

Mister Puss hopped to the floor and paced around Mary's feet, tangling his leash.

I offered, "Let me take him, Mary."

"Thank you, Brody. You're so good with him." She lifted the cat from the floor and passed him to Marson, who passed him to me.

I settled the cat in my lap and twiddled his chin, which got him purring.

"And now the unpleasantries," said Joyce, pleasant as pie. "Costs and funding."

Mister Puss turned once or twice, then stood with his paws on the arm of my chair, leaning toward Bob Olson.

"Sorry," I said, tugging the cat down.

Olson laughed. "No problem. I like cats." He offered his fingers for Mister Puss to sniff. Then he rubbed the cat's ears. Purring louder, Mister Puss climbed to the arm of the chair again and reached his paws to Olson's shoulder.

Joyce was saying to Marson, "Last time we met here, you came up with a rough estimate of what the total project might cost."

Mister Puss sniffed his way from Olson's shoulder to his neck.

"That was a wild guess," said Marson, "not an estimate. There are many, *many* variables that will affect the final cost."

Mister Puss sneezed.

"Okay," I said, "that's enough. Sorry, Bob." Pulling the cat away, I lifted him to my opposite shoulder. Olson stifled a laugh, using the back of his hand to wipe the spray from his cheek.

Joyce said to Marson, "For discussion purposes, though, you mentioned a very round number."

Marson ballparked the millions.

Purring, Mister Puss reached his snout to my ear.

He smells like a fruitcake.

"Goodness," said Mary, fingers to lips, reacting to the millions. "I had no idea."

Coming soon ...

I rubbed the scruff of the cat's neck as he nuzzled my shoulder.

Marson turned in his chair to face Mary. Taking her hands, he said, "It's a lot of money. You shouldn't feel pressured."

She wavered. "I suppose I *could* postpone a couple of other projects I was considering." She didn't sound happy with that option.

Joyce said, "What a delightful thought, Mary. Your generosity is nothing short of breathtaking."

Marson said brightly, "I have *another* idea."

Joyce's features pinched. "Yes?"

"First of all," said Marson, "responsibility for the new church rightfully falls to the entire parish. So consider a pledge drive, to get all the members 'invested.' For a project of this magnitude, though, you can't squeeze blood from a turnip, so you'll also need a lead donor—or two—to guarantee the shortfall. Mary seems willing. How about Curtis? They could go halves."

"Curtis?" said the rector, Curtis Hibbard's wife.

Marson reminded her, "He's richer than God."

Mary was effervescent. "Oh, *Marson.* I think you've hit the nail on the head. I can easily manage half. If it would help get the ball rolling, I can commit to that—today." Mary repeated, "Half."

Joyce was not effervescent. But she was practical enough to reply, "That would be splendid, Mary. As it happens, we've taken the liberty of drafting a pledge agreement."

Bob Olson rose from his chair and stepped behind the desk, next to Joyce. He opened the manila folder, explaining, "We drew this up with the expectation there'd be a parish-wide fundraising drive, and the wording reflects that Mary is committing to cover any shortfall, not to exceed an amount of 'blank.' What amount would you like me to fill in?"

Marson stated a figure that was half of the ballparked millions.

"Very good," said Olson. When he finished the notation, he handed the document to Marson and the pen to Mary.

While Marson read through the agreement, Mister Puss hopped up from my lap to the desktop, purring.

"This looks fine," said Marson, passing the paper to Mary. He said to Joyce, "And when you talk to Curt, tell him I said hi."

"Count on it," said Joyce through a tight, wry smile.

Mister Puss watched as Mary signed on the dotted line.

Outside the rectory, the wind whistled.

CHAPTER

19

On that windy Tuesday, one day shy of two weeks since David Lovell's murder, some half-dozen people with an interest in the investigation found their plans for that afternoon abruptly changed when Sheriff Thomas Simms called for a meeting in his office at one-thirty. There had been a breakthrough, he announced, but he needed more input before taking any action.

As requested, I arrived ahead of the others. The deputy outside Simms's office grinned as I approached. "I think you know your way by now," she said, admitting me with a jerk of her head. I entered the sheriff's empty office, crossed to the door on the rear wall, and stepped into the conference room, which had the lingering smell of fresh paint.

Simms looked up from the stack of papers he was arranging at the head of the table. Behind him, the ghosted rectangle of the missing painting had disappeared from the wall, formerly a faded green, now sporting a coat of institutional beige—a slight improvement, much less somber, but uninspired. The medical examiner, Heather Vance, was already there, removing files from her briefcase and placing them on the table, adjacent to Simms. Off to the side, by the wall of bookcases, a police stenographer was setting up his stenotype machine and backup recorder.

Simms and Heather moved over to greet me. Closing the door, Simms asked dryly, "Did you have time for lunch?"

"Barely," I said.

"I didn't," said Heather.

"Me neither," said Simms. "But this was sorta sudden."

Eyeing the table, I asked, "Where would you like me to sit?"

With a gracious sweep of his arm, Simms said, "Be my guest. Anywhere you want."

I stepped over to the table and set down my notebook, claiming the seat across from Heather's; we would both sit adjacent to Simms.

After a perfunctory rap at the door, the deputy admitted Bob Olson, senior warden of the St. Alban's vestry, and his pretty wife, Angela. Then the deputy withdrew and closed the door.

"Hey, Bob," said Simms, shaking hands, "thanks for coming over on such short notice."

"Anything to help, Thomas," said Olson, "but I hope you don't mind—Angela and I were out having lunch when you called, and there wasn't time for me to drive her home, other side of town. I didn't want to be late, so here we are."

His wife quickly added, "I could wait outside, Sheriff, in case this is, you know, 'confidential' or anything. I don't want to butt in."

"Nah," said Simms, "plenty of room, Angela. Always a pleasure to see you. Sorry to mess up your afternoon, though."

As Heather Vance was introducing herself to the Olsons, the deputy rapped again, admitting Joyce Hibbard and Lillie Miller. The deputy then left, closing the door.

"Well, now," said Joyce, taking command, sounding jovial, "we meet again." She, Lillie, Bob Olson, and I had concluded our morning meeting at the rectory only two hours earlier. Noting the presence of Mrs. Olson, as well as Simms, who was also a parishioner, Joyce said, "This seems to be quite the St. Alban's crowd."

"And there's a reason for that," said Simms. "Shall we all sit down?"

Joyce sat next to me, and Lillie filled in our side of the table, sitting next to Joyce. On the other side, Olson sat next to Heather Vance, and Olson's wife sat on his far side. With the seven of us seated, there was still one empty chair—at the far end of the table, opposite Sheriff Simms.

Simms began by pointing out that a transcript of the meeting was being made by the police stenographer. Simms proceeded to read everyone's name into the record, and he then explained, "You're here today because we've discovered some additional evidence relating to the death of David Lovell. Since David was St. Alban's choirmaster, I'm sure all of you have an interest in figuring out what happened. This is personal; I feel the pain as well. David's murder has been a terrible, frightening loss to the whole parish."

At the far end of the table, Angela Olson raised her hand.

Simms said, "Yes, Angela? No need for formality. Please, jump right in."

"Sheriff, I just wanted to ask how little Tommy is doing. The kids in the choir have had *such* a shock."

With a soft smile, Simms said, "Thanks for asking. Day by day, Tommy's doing better. And how about Hailey?"

Mrs. Olson answered, "Better, yes, but I still catch her crying now and then."

Mr. Olson added, "Thanks for your concern, Thomas."

Joyce Hibbard said, "Yes, Thomas. We're *so* grateful to count you as a member of the St. Alban's family. And you've certainly caught our interest with your news of a breakthrough. What can you tell us about that?"

"Let me back up a bit," said Simms. "Because David worked for St. Alban's and died in the church, on the job, so to speak—and given the truly weird set of circumstances surrounding his death, which has since been declared a homicide—in light of all that, from the beginning, we've suspected that David's killer had some connection to St. Alban's."

His words drew a collective gasp from around the table. Joyce asked, "You mean—one of our *parishioners?*"

Simms waggled his hand. "Maybe. Maybe not. It seemed reasonable to assume that the killer was someone within the broader 'orbit' of St. Alban's."

Bob Olson said, "Then the killer could've been just about anyone. St. Alban's has connections all over Dumont. It's part of the *fabric* of the town."

"Yes," Simms agreed, "that's the tricky part. But there were two other threads running through this, intriguing details that could've had a bearing on what happened to David. First, David's death stemmed from an allergic reaction to nuts."

The others looked at each other and shrugged, as if to say: Sure, David had a nut allergy, everyone knew, so what?

"And second," said Simms, "David was openly gay."

Again the group shrug: Sure, David was gay, everyone knew, no problem, so what?

Joyce said, "In the few months since I arrived in Dumont, I've found the community to be remarkably tolerant and enlightened. To be honest, when I accepted the assignment here, I didn't know what to expect, but I was pleasantly surprised. And it goes without saying—the Episcopal Church has long been known as a welcoming denomination."

"True enough," said Simms. "As a person of color, with a wife and child, I'm proud to be building a life here. But being straight, I felt there was an angle to David's life—and maybe his death— where I didn't have sufficient insight. Needing some assistance, I turned to a gay friend."

I waggled my fingers, explaining to the table, "That would be me."

Simms told them, "Brody's been a tremendous help."

At the far end of the table, Lillie Miller had not made a peep since we sat down. She now said to me, "I *wondered* why you came to my house with Dr. Vance that morning."

Heather said, "I hope you didn't find our visit intrusive, Lillie. We needed to get to the bottom of things."

Lillie assured us, "I enjoyed the company. And it was helpful to talk—there were many things that had never been said. Confession is good for the soul."

Joyce and the Olsons exchanged a surprised, curious glance.

I said, "Over the last two weeks, I've heard more than a few confessions." I was thinking not only of Lillie's desperation to know the love of a perfect gentleman, David Lovell. I was also thinking of Nancy Sanderson's hatred of David's father; Heather Vance's "special friendship" with a gay guy in college; Clem Carter's need to find a lucrative construction job that would help him pay off a bad investment; Kayla Weber Schmidt's admission that she had been lashing out at everyone, feeling frightened and guilty because of her son's developmental issues; Tyler Schmidt's understanding with Kayla that love and passion aren't necessarily the same thing; and Curtis Hibbard's stated contentment with an odd marriage that merely "works for us."

All of those confessions bared some measure of personal guilt— the graceless struggle with a shortcoming or with a difficult turn of fate—which can be cleansed, at least partially, by exposure to daylight. With the simple act of admission, such foibles can be atoned for and forgiven. Confession, as Lillie noted, is good for the soul.

However, confessions that are good for the soul don't arise from a rotted core where a dark kernel hides, festering with the motive to kill.

I told everyone, "David Lovell didn't die because of his nut allergy—not exactly. And David didn't die because he was gay—not exactly. Both of those factors played a part in it. What killed him, though, was the motive."

Simms nodded. "That's generally how it works."

"Now, *really*, Thomas," said Joyce, "you're both speaking in riddles. If you know, just tell us: What was the motive? And who killed David?"

"We're working on that," said Simms. "But that's for Brody to tell. He has a strong theory. In fact, he asked me to invite you here."

Joyce pivoted in her chair to face me directly. "You?" she asked with an air of annoyance. "Brody love, I genuinely enjoy your company, but don't you think we've already seen enough of each other today? I realize you younger people are fond of 'taking meetings,' but frankly, I have a parish to run and a church to build. Must we play games?"

Bob Olson added, "And I have a business to run, with clients to meet."

"Won't be much longer," I assured them while checking my watch. "You see, we're not all here yet."

All heads turned to observe the empty chair at the far end of the table. Lillie, sitting adjacent to it, recoiled an inch or two, as if it might bite. Joyce Hibbard and Bob Olson, sitting across from each other, exchanged a look of exasperated boredom. Angela Olson, blond and buoyant, said, "Well, I find it all quite *thrilling*. Not the lazy afternoon I was expecting, not one bit."

I explained, "While we were meeting this morning about the new church, something clicked. I could be way off base, but we'll know soon enough."

Joyce and Lillie compared notes, deciding that the only people at the rectory meeting who were not now in the conference room were Mary Questman, code officer Nia Butler, and my husband, Marson.

Joyce said, "None of them could *possibly* be involved with this. Could they?"

Bob Olson responded, "I hate to say it, but I have a hunch Clem Carter will be walking through that door."

They debated these possibilities, as well as other random theories—suggesting murderous intent on the part of everyone from the church custodian to a disgruntled groundskeeper who'd been sent packing nine years earlier with a booze problem. While they passed the minutes searching, in their minds, the closets and cellars and belfries of St. Alban's, I waited.

As two o'clock approached, gusts of wind raised bits of gravel and whorls of dust from the service drive beyond the big window looking out toward the brick wall of the jail. Pebbles and grit pecked at the glass.

And then came the rap at the door.

It opened. It closed.

Into the conference room walked Geoff Lovell, brother of the deceased choirmaster. Seeing everyone quietly settled in, he said, "Gosh, am I late? I thought you said two."

Simms told him, "Right on time, Geoff. Have a seat."

As he approached the table, Geoff acknowledged Joyce Hibbard and me, whom he'd encountered several times already. Then, sitting, he noticed Olson. "Well, *hi* there, Bob. Didn't realize you'd be here." Geoff reached over the table to offer a handshake, adding, "Thanks for setting everything up. All set."

"Great," Olson mumbled, "happy to help."

That was it. Geoff's handshake had marked Bob as surely as the kiss of Judas. I asked, "You know each other?"

"Well, *yeah*," said Geoff. "Bob is executor of Dave's estate."

At David Lovell's memorial service, I recalled, Geoff had mentioned meeting with the executor of his brother's estate, expressing relief that his financial worries were over. I knew that Geoff had been dealing with the Lovell family's lawyer in Green Bay, Stanley Burton, who had set up his parents' estate plan. Because lawyers are not generally named as executor of wills or trusts they have written, I had wondered if Geoff was now dealing with someone other than Burton.

Geoff added, "Bob was our parents' executor as well."

Offhandedly, Olson reminded us, "I serve wealth-management clients throughout the region. And beyond—new account in Milwaukee last week."

With a finger snap, Geoff recalled, "Unless I'm mistaken, Bob, didn't you get Dave the choir gig at St. Alban's?"

Mother Hibbard asked, "Really? I didn't know that. David came to St. Alban's well before I did."

Olson explained, "It was shortly after David's parents died. He was alone and adrift in Appleton, and unemployed—though money was the least of his concerns. Then, by chance, we had an opening at St. Alban's, so I put David in touch with Father Sterling. And sure enough, it all worked out. Part of my service. I enjoy helping my clients."

I said, "And that kind of personal service pays off, Bob, doesn't it? Glad to know both you and your clients are thriving. Pardon a snarky question, but if things are going so well, why do you wear such cheap perfume?"

I don't know whether it was my non sequitur—or the bitchy tone of it—that elicited a round of quiet, uneasy laughter from the table, but Bob played it safe and joined in. "Beg pardon?" he asked, as if he must not have heard me right.

"This morning at the rectory," I said, "Mary Questman's cat, Mister Puss, was getting spunky. He climbed your shoulder, sniffing your neck—and he sneezed."

"So?"

"Two weeks ago tonight, David Lovell had dinner at our loft. Mister Puss was there. Same thing happened. David's fragrance made the cat sneeze."

True, many things had been making Mister Puss sneeze lately, but there was an additional detail I was not inclined to share at the conference table: Mister Puss had purred to me that both David Lovell and Bob Olson "smelled like a fruitcake," a crack that applied only to them.

I told the table, "I was looking after Mister Puss last week, and I took him to see the vet, Jim Phelps. The doctor mentioned that cats have a superhuman sense of smell—about ten times the receptors that we have. Some dogs have way more than that. But cats are even better than dogs at distinguishing *between* scents. Fascinating, huh?"

Olson tossed his hands. "So what?"

"So I think you've been wearing the same fragrance that David was wearing the night before he died. He told me it was new. It's called 'Chad!'—with an exclamation point."

Angela Olson's eyes bugged as she choked back a sob. Everyone else at the table appeared mystified—everyone except Bob.

I asked, "Where did you get the Chad!, Bob?"

"I *bought* it. There's been a lot of advertising lately—thought I'd try it."

That morning, Mister Puss had reminded me that the new fragrance was "coming soon." A week earlier, while we were in the vet's waiting room, Chad Percy was hawking the stuff on TV. At the time, it didn't register that Chad! was still "coming soon" because my attention shifted when Geoff Lovell walked in with his sick dog. That was six days after David Lovell had worn it to the dinner party.

"No," I now told Olson, "you didn't buy it. Neither did David. After I left the rectory today, I phoned a few department stores—one in Green Bay—asking if they carried it. Same answer everywhere: lots of demand, wished they had it in stock, not available till next month. But somehow, Bob, you already have it. Was Chad Percy one of your clients? Did you do a bit of so-called wealth management for him?"

He glared at me.

Simms reminded him, "We can easily find out."

"All right," said Olson. "Yes, Chad Percy was a client."

I asked, "Did you also provide him with 'personal services'?"

"How *dare* you?"

Angela turned to him, livid, spitting her words: *"Well? Did you?"*

"Of course not."

"Thursday," Angela told him, "after David's memorial, you said you had to drive to Green Bay to see a client. Fine, I know you keep some odd hours. But this was different—you didn't get home till dawn."

I asked him, "Why did you take Ambien with you? Trouble sleeping? I assume you have a prescription."

Simms added, "We can find out."

Angela turned to the sheriff with steely resolve, telling him flatly, "Yes, Bob has a prescription for Ambien."

Olson shot his wife a look of utter hatred. Mimicking her earlier enthusiasm for the proceedings, he quoted her in a high-pitched voice: "I find it all quite *thrilling*! He-he-he. Not the lazy afternoon I was expecting!" He sounded an awful lot like the Chinesey voice on my phone. Then he dropped to his normal register: "What the hell was *that* little performance?"

She explained, "When they started talking about the empty chair, I was excited—because I thought I must have been *wrong*. I was hoping they'd prove it was someone else who ... did these things. Guess not, though." A tear slipped from her reddened eyes. Snot glistened on her upper lip. "Why *ever* did you marry me?"

He countered, "Why did *you* marry *me*? You knew what you were getting."

"I knew you were into men. I knew, to some extent, I'd have to overlook that. But not *this*."

"What *this*?"

She couldn't say it. She looked away.

I said to Bob, "I believe your wife was referring to murder. Two murders."

He told me calmly, "That's fucking insane."

"Yeah," I agreed, "insane. Nevertheless, here's what happened: A closet case with a beautiful wife and a lovely daughter had the perfect cover for indulging in his yen for men with a few choice clients—two in particular, both of them exceptionally attractive, openly gay, a bit flighty and naive. Both of them, in recent years, had come into some sudden wealth, and both were more than happy to entrust their money-management needs to Bob Olson, who took care of all those pesky details for them, did all the bean counting—and robbed them blind while providing other 'personal services.' Along the way, Bob was even given a few advance samples of his Green Bay client's new unisex fragrance, which he shared with his other special client in Dumont.

"But something went wrong. Maybe Bob had gotten too greedy. Maybe one of his clients had grown suspicious or had simply gotten bored with him. Maybe there was talk of 'moving on,' which would have exposed Bob's malfeasance to the probing eyes of a new accountant, initiating a domino effect of investigations that would reveal a long history of greed that rose to crime. Needless to say, this was an untenable prospect for a proper Episcopalian senior warden.

"So those two clients—the linchpins in an elaborate scheme on the verge of collapse—those two needed to be rendered permanently silent.

"David Lovell was easy. He had a deadly nut allergy, and everyone knew about it, especially the father of a girl in the children's choir—there were parties and potlucks, and David always warned about the allergy. So Bob waited for the right time to slip David a lethal dose of almond oil, drizzled on a plate of homemade macaroons. Bob knew, or had access to, everyone's schedule at St.

Alban's. He knew when to find David and Lillie practicing in the church. He was well acquainted with the sacristy, which made it convenient for him to set the bizarre incense fire, clouding the cause of—and the motive for—David's murder.

"One down.

"The other client proved more challenging; he would need to be dispatched by more direct and reliable means. So, following the funeral of the Dumont client, Bob drove up to visit the Green Bay client, meeting for dinner and some after-hours horseplay. Chad had been on edge because of threatening graffiti and voicemails— guess where *those* came from—so it was easy for Bob to convince Chad to relax with ample booze that night, followed by a dash of Ambien and a pinch of deadly intent. With Chad finally unconscious and helpless, Bob did what he needed to do."

I concluded, "Two down."

I then turned to Mother Hibbard, suggesting, "If you've been wondering why St. Alban's has suffered such a financial slide over the past few years, it may be time to call in a forensic accountant. Someone might've cooked the books."

Mother Hibbard, pallid and ashen, looked blankly toward the ceiling.

Angela Olson dabbed a few more tears from her eyes.

Sheriff Simms recited Bob Olson's rights.

Olson admitted nothing.

As a dead stillness took hold of the conference room, the soft tapping of the stenotype machine fell silent.

20

By evening, the armed guards at our loft had disappeared. Marson cooked, opening a rare vintage of Château Lafite Rothschild that he'd tucked away for a special occasion. Together, we celebrated the end of a harrowing two weeks—and my unlikely role in bringing a killer to justice.

The next morning, the first of June, it was a pleasure opening the front door to an empty street, without the ritual of acknowledging a salute from a squad car. Birds twittered—apparently they'd been cued up for the happy ending—as I retrieved our rolled copy of the *Dumont Daily Register* and took it inside. The front page displayed the expected headline story:

Two murder victims linked

Charges filed against alleged killer
of gay men in Dumont and Green Bay

Compiled from *Register* staff reports

•

JUNE 1, DUMONT, WI—The mystery surrounding two recent deaths, which had baffled law enforcement in Dumont and Green Bay, came to a dramatic close Tuesday afternoon when the alleged killer was named and apprehended in the Dumont offices of Sheriff Thomas Simms.

Robert Olson, 44, was charged with two counts of murder. Further investigation could produce additional counts of fraud and embezzlement, stemming from Olson's financial services provided to victims David Lovell and Chad Percy, who were both gay.

At a press briefing where Sheriff Simms announced these developments, a reporter asked if Olson had confessed to the alleged crimes.

Simms responded, "No, but I'm confident we've arrested the guilty party. And I'm confident a jury will agree."

Simms also said, "I want to assure the gay communities in Dumont and Green Bay, as well as those cities at large, that the danger has passed and justice will be served."

The accused is well known within Dumont business circles for his wealth-management services. As a parishioner at St. Alban's Episcopal Church, Olson has served for several years as...

Pouring coffee, Marson asked me, "What do you think, Sherlock? Were they crimes of passion or just garden-variety greed?"

"Greed," I answered without hesitation. "Sure, there was sex involved—apparently lots of it—but when Olson killed David and Chad, it wasn't blind passion. It was calculated, and it had one purpose: to hide the secret of Olson's ill-gotten gains."

Marson nodded. "Follow the money."

With a laugh, I recalled Mister Puss purring those exact words into my ear. I had razzed him about it, calling him Deep Throat and facetiously dismissing his advice as a "pearl of wisdom." But as things turned out, he was right. Was it a lucky guess? Or common sense? Or was there another, more rational possibility: Had I simply imagined those words from the cat, intuiting for myself the root of these crimes?

Ping.

"Uh-oh," said Marson. An email had arrived on the iPad at the kitchen island. "It's from Curt. He must've found out that he's building half a church." Marson slid the tablet toward me, and we read the message together.

From: Curtis Hibbard
To: Marson Miles

Good morning, old chum. I understand there was a good deal of excitement in Dumont yesterday. Poopsie tells me she was there in the sheriff's office when your charming young man ferreted out the murderer of our late, beloved choirmaster and that other gay goose up in Green Bay. And to think—the culprit had been right there all along, like a viper in Mother Hibbard's nest, a slave to his insatiable taste for filthy cash.

The darkness of the soul can be *so* appalling, can it not?

Bad enough—but there's more to this narrative.

While Poopsie had me on the phone last night, she said there was another matter of some urgency that we needed to discuss, but I told her it would have to wait. What I did *not* tell her was that she had caught me at an inconvenient moment in the back of my car, being driven home from dinner, in the company of a fine specimen of a young man named Jürgen, in town this week with the Stuttgart Ballet, which is on tour.

As you've surely noted, I have always been drawn to dancers. Not only are they svelte and athletic, but they often tend to be shorter than I am, which I find appealing—a nice, tidy package, so to speak. More to the point, I enjoy kissing shorter men, the way they need to lean back the head to reach my lips. Not that I'm into a dominance scene (ho-ho), but I love that image of a hungry bird, a hatchling seeking my sustenance.

Such was the case last night, in the car, when Jürgen and I were interrupted by that untimely call from Joyce. It thoroughly jinxed my well-laid plans, with the result that Jürgen ended up back at his hotel. And I (boo-hoo) went home alone.

Speaking of dancers, Yevgeny—or Zhenya, now that he counts you among his intimates—can't seem to stop talking about your young man. He asked me to let both of you know that his upcoming relocation to Wisconsin is proceeding as planned. He looks forward to seeing you again once he is settled.

Best regards,
Curtis Hibbard, Founding Partner
Hibbard Belding & Smith, LLP
New York • London • Berlin

I said to Marson, "Seems your old chum hasn't heard about the 'grand bargain' you brokered between Joyce and Mary."

"He'll find out about it soon enough—when he's not busy cheating on his wife, or trying to."

I set aside my coffee, pondering something. "In their case, is it cheating? Sure, they had a la-di-da wedding with the presiding bishop—ten thousand nights ago—and there must've been vows involved, but they didn't have blinders on. They struck a 'grand bargain' of their own, and they're still married."

"It's *their* choice." Marson flipped his hands. "Marriage of convenience."

Though the concept was anything but novel, marriages of convenience had played an outsize role in the events of the last couple of weeks. The Hibbards—Curtis and Joyce—had blown into

Dumont with their unconventional relationship, raising more than a few eyebrows and not giving a damn; they'd been at it for a long time.

Then there was the artist, Tyler Schmidt, and his wife, Kayla Weber Schmidt. Their arrangement seemed more subtle, less premeditated than the Hibbards'. The Schmidts were still finding their way, or their separate ways, while also defining what was understood and expected. In the sense that their marriage was an equation, their troubled son was the variable—and the challenge. But something told me that Kayla and Tyler would make the best of this.

On the other hand, there could be no silver lining to the marriage of convenience between Bob and Angela Olson. How do you begin to "fix" something like that? You can't. You don't—not after all the deceit, not after two murders.

That same day, Wednesday, the day after Bob Olson's arrest, we learned that Angela and her daughter, Hailey, had already left Dumont. They had fled to a remote summer cabin owned by Angela's parents along the upstate shore near the Apostle Islands, where they could hide for a while, grieve, and think about what to do next. Come fall, Hailey would need to be back in school. But I felt certain they would never return to Dumont.

Over the next couple of days, Marson and I found that life got back to normal. We had a house to build—the perfect house—and fortunately, Clem Carter seemed to have the project back on track.

There were also *paying* projects at Miles & Norris that needed our attention, and now we were able to focus again on doing the jobs we loved. Demand for our design brand had spread far from Dumont, but even there at home, we had plenty to keep us busy. Completion of the new county museum was at the top of Marson's list. As for me, I was gearing up to take on a design commission for the county library system's new main facility; their board had just voted final approval to proceed.

With Memorial Day behind us, with schools closed, and with the days heating up and growing longer, it now truly felt like summer. On Thursday, Mary Questman phoned, inviting us to an impromptu cookout the next evening in the backyard of her home. She suggested arriving around six, when there would be plenty of daylight remaining for relaxed conviviality.

On Friday, Marson and I decided to stay at the office past five, using the extra hour for some quiet catch-up, undisturbed. Leaving at six, locking up, I said to my husband, "This is a cookout, remember." He removed his jacket and tie as we climbed into the SUV.

Prairie Street, the graceful old boulevard where the members of Dumont's early elite had staked out their turf, looked serene and welcoming that evening as we cruised beneath the arching elms, which transformed the warm gold of low-slung sunlight into long, cool shadows of dusky blue.

As we approached Mary's house, I noticed familiar cars parked up and down the block—there could be no mistaking Glee Savage's vintage fuchsia hatchback. I briefly studied the distinctive lines of the Taliesin-designed house Glee had told me about, where a prior publisher of the *Register* had lived. Marson slowed the Range Rover as we drove by; then he parked only a few steps from Mary's driveway.

Although our hostess had insisted there was nothing we could bring, Marson was the type who could never show up empty-handed, so earlier that afternoon, I had fetched a showy arrangement of big summer flowers—tiger lilies, snapdragons, gladiolas—which now bobbed and swayed as I carried them up the long driveway, under the porte cochère, and around the rear corner of the house, emerging into the expansive backyard, where the festivities were already under way.

Mary spotted us at once and rushed over to greet us. Mister Puss strutted at her side on his leash, looking exotic and wild (even more so than usual) as he stalked through the tall grass.

Mary handed me the cat's leash and offered smooches as I passed the flowers to Marson, who presented them to Mary, who then passed them off to Berta, standing nearby. Mary told her, "Find a nice spot for these on the serving table."

Berta took the flowers and made a facetious show of a curtsy before heading off with them.

Mary told us brightly, "I think we're going to *do* it. We've been home from Chicago for a week now, and I thought the urge might pass, but it seems I've caught the travel bug. We'll be going to *Sedona* in a few months. To find the vortexes—or whatever."

I wondered if Berta had been baking peyote treats.

"It's a mystical place," said Marson. "So much history and legend."

While Mary and Marson gabbed, laughing, I picked up Mister Puss and rubbed his ears. He purred.

Bar's open.

Mary said, "Now, I want you boys to make yourselves at home. I think you know everyone. One of the girls will get you a drink, or you can help yourselves in the kitchen. And I hope you came hungry—the food won't be long." The air was scented with grilling meat. Mister Puss purred.

Marson and I drifted into the amiable crowd while Mary moved away to mingle.

The "girls" Mary had mentioned were employees of Nancy Sanderson, who was working the party as well as attending it. I noticed that Nia Butler, the code enforcer, had cornered Nancy for a quiet conversation, much as I had seen her do at David's memorial service. Unless I was mistaken, their giddy chitchat appeared to have flirty overtones. My, my.

Marson asked one of the girls for a gin and tonic—very summery. Still holding Mister Puss, I declined. I couldn't juggle a cocktail and a cat.

Marson broke away to talk shop with Joyce Hibbard, who stood—rather imperiously, I thought—at the center of the large flagstone terrace, where she could see, and be seen by, everyone in attendance. Cicadas had begun to buzz from the heights of the surrounding trees.

"*Brody*, sweets."

I turned to find Glee standing behind me, posing with a champagne flute, wearing mostly white—with a big red hat, big red purse, and big red lips.

"Hi, doll." I offered a peck, avoiding the lipstick. Mister Puss stretched to my shoulder.

"Well, love, I understand you did it again. Maybe it's my news sense, but I think you ought to get at least *some* of the credit."

I shook my head, assuring her, "I don't want it. Not being modest—just thought I should help. Plus … well, I myself had a bit of help." I petted the cat. He hadn't stopped purring.

Good job, kiddo.

Glee asked, "What sort of help?"

Coyly, I replied, "That's a secret."

She smirked.

"Hey, Brody!" It was Sheriff Simms, approaching with a smile. He shook my hand, then gave me a hug—which may have been a first. "Thanks, man. You oughta get a *medal* or something."

"Thomas, don't go there."

"Okay," said Glee, "I've heard this song." She raised her glass as a parting gesture before moving off into the crowd.

"Know what?" said Simms. "We did a voiceprint analysis of the Chinesey phone threats left for Chad Percy before he was killed.

And we did another of the recording made in my office Tuesday, when Olson mocked his wife with that high-pitched voice. You were right: they matched. That alone won't convict Olson, but combined with all the other evidence—the accountants are having a field day—Olson's cooked."

"Glad to help."

Simms gave me a slow, deliberate wink of gratitude. Then he moved off to join Gloria and their little Tommy.

I watched as the Simmses spoke with Geoff Lovell and his girlfriend, Spark Kavanaugh, who tried to put on a happy face for the gathering, but she seemed to be dealing with another bout of early-pregnancy nausea. I hoped the crackle and smell of charred bratwurst wouldn't be too much for her. They had Cindy the dog with them, romping with Tommy Simms. Cindy appeared to be totally cured of whatever had ailed her.

And then the dog and Tommy were joined in play by Aiden Weber Schmidt, the four-year-old son of Tyler and Kayla. His parents strolled through the crowd looking content with life and with each other. I reminded myself to nab Tyler later and discuss his steel totems—I was working on a library and a perfect house and any number of other projects that his artwork might complement.

Three doctors huddled near the grill—the medical examiner, the vet, and my own physician—breathing smoke and inhaling the evening while speaking of life and death.

Lillie Miller, the parish secretary, drifted waiflike, smiling now and then at someone but looking lost, tippling from a glass of pale wine while the chattering locusts grew louder, pleading for the sun to set.

With his chin on my shoulder, Mister Puss purred.

"I want to show you something," said Mary Questman, appearing out of nowhere.

"Oh?" I said. "What is it?"

I've seen better.

"Come along and find out." With a wag of her finger, she led me across the terrace and into the house.

In the kitchen, after the screen door swung closed, I set Mister Puss on the floor and unclipped his leash, which I rolled up and stowed in my pocket. The cat followed at my heels as Mary led me out to the front hall and then entered the small parlor.

From the middle of the room, she turned, gesturing back toward the doorway.

I turned—and gaped. There, on an expanse of the refined brocade wallpaper, hung the ugly old painting of the man with a horse and a monkey. Mister Puss gazed up at me with a smart-alecky look. "I, uh"—I struggled for something to say—"I've seen this before."

With a chuckle, Mary asked from the side of her mouth, "Isn't it *hideous?*"

"In fact," I agreed, "it is."

She explained, "The man is Quincy Franklin Questman, my late husband's grandfather, lovingly known in the family as Quincy the First. He had a perverse sense of humor, I'm afraid. Back in those days, there wasn't much culture in Dumont. One of those itinerant portrait painters from back East rolled through town with his wagon and an assortment of unfinished paintings. You could buy the one you liked, then have your head inserted. Quincy, *naturally*, snapped up the monkey. His wife couldn't *stand* it—said she couldn't sleep with that little demon in the house—so Quincy made a big show of 'donating' the picture to the courthouse, where it hung for many years. But eventually, it was put in storage, and later still, it ended up in the sheriff's offices. Recently, I'm told, they were doing some remodeling and almost threw the painting out—perhaps they *should* have—but then they called in the historical society. Their staff hauled it away and did the research. Then the young lady, Kayla, came to see me and offered to return the portrait to the Questman family. I'd often *heard* of the painting, so I was thrilled to accept it." Mary paused. "Then I saw it."

"Well," I told her, only half joking, "it's a striking conversation piece."

She squeezed my arm. "You're too kind." With a hoot, she strolled out of the parlor and headed back to her guests.

My phone vibrated. I glanced at the screen. "Uh-oh," I told Mister Puss. Marson had forwarded to me an email from Curtis Hibbard. I sat to read the message in one of the quilted-chintz armchairs. The cat hopped up to perch on the back of the chair, peering over my shoulder.

From: Curtis Hibbard
To: Marson Miles

So you convinced Mary Questman to cover *half* the funding for a new church, did you? And *I'm* on the hook for the other half?

Honest to God, Marson, I don't know whether to throttle you—or thank you.

It could have been worse, I suppose.

I might have been stuck with the whole nut to crack. From that perspective, I got off easy. And now, moving forward, my Poopsie will be busy as a bee out there, leaving me more room to maneuver. (Yes, it's true what they say: happy wife, happy life.)

Although my last visit turned out to be far more costly than planned, I must admit that it was awfully good to see you again.

So I'll be back.

And during that next visit, ho-ho, I *do* hope to spend more time with your young man.

Best regards,
Curtis Hibbard, Founding Partner
Hibbard Belding & Smith, LLP
New York • *London* • *Berlin*

Ugh. I deleted the email and flumped back in the chair. Mister Puss touched his nose to my cheek. I reached up to twiddle his chin.

The doorbell rang.

Mister Puss leapt from the chair and shot out of the room, into the hall. When I arrived a few seconds later, the cat was sitting within an inch of the door, switching his tail in curious anticipation of the new arrival. The chime sounded again.

I looked down the hall, but there was no one in the kitchen; everyone was out back. So I picked up the cat and opened the front door. "Well, *hello* there," I said brightly.

"Hi." He was handsome (very), probably late-thirties, about my age. Great smile, nicely dressed, with a solid sense of style. Not a blip from my gaydar, though; he was straight. And although he looked familiar, I was sure we hadn't met. He asked, "Is Mrs. Questman in?"

"No, but she's in back. She has some people over."

"Yeah, I saw the cars. Hey, beautiful cat."

"This is Mister Puss. He's Mary's cat. Please, come in."

"Thanks." The visitor stepped inside and patted the cat's head; the purring began. "You see, I used to live next door—while I was in high school—gosh, can't believe it was almost twenty years ago."

I closed the door, feeling confused. "I seem to recognize you, but

I haven't been in Dumont that long."

With a modest shrug, he said, "I've done some film." Then he added, "And a soap."

"Really?"

He extended his hand. "Thad Manning."

Adjusting the cat, I shook his hand—nice grip. I said, "Brody Norris."

"Pleased to meet you, Brody." Again the smile. The perfect, veneered teeth.

I heard Mary bustle into the kitchen from outdoors. She tootled, "Did I hear the door?"

Thad Manning called to her, "You sure did, Mrs. Questman."

She stepped into the hall and stopped short with a gasp. "*Thad?* Oh, my God!" I stepped aside as she rushed forward and greeted the new arrival with a full embrace. Then she held him at arm's length, asking, "You remember Glee Savage, don't you? She worked for your uncle Mark."

"Of *course.* You mean, she's here? Glee's *here?*"

"You bet. Come on." Mary took Thad by the hand and led him out through the kitchen.

Rubbing the cat's ears, I wondered aloud, "What was that all about?"

Not a clue.

Then I set Mister Puss on the floor and crouched to clip the leash to his harness. "We should get back to the party."

He trotted at my side as I walked through the kitchen and went outdoors.

Standing on the terrace, I watched a dreamy scene unfold, in which the deep azure sky of evening slipped quickly to the indigo of dusk. Planets peeked through the blackened foliage, while underneath, Mary's guests mingled, ate, and drank, taking pleasure in the simple joy of their togetherness.

On that warm Wisconsin night, from the far side of the lawn, my husband broke into a smile as he spotted me across the gathering of our friends and neighbors. Marson blew me a kiss, which took flight like a lazy moth, fluttering toward me, buffeted by eddies of conversation and gentle laughter.

The buzz of locusts swelled from the canopy of trees.

A summer song of crickets pulsed from a living Earth.

And at my feet sat Mister Puss, watching, hearing, wondering. His primal purr...

blending with the chorus of the night...

                    spoke to me.

•

ACKNOWLEDGMENTS

When I set out a year ago to introduce the reading world to Mister Puss in *FlabberGassed*, I had no idea whether the idea would fly or not. I wasn't even sure how to explain the concept: "It's a gay cat mystery. I mean, the amateur sleuth is gay, not the cat. And the cat talks. Sort of." Somehow, the seeming absurdity of that premise proved to be the very aspect of the story that drew so many readers to the book. And their ringing enthusiasm is what gave me the confidence to proceed with this unlikely series.

First, then, I would like to acknowledge and thank *you*, my readers, for wanting this next installment, *ChoirMaster*, Mister Puss Mystery #2.

Further, I could not have brought *ChoirMaster* to publication without the help of many friends and associates, including David Grey, Richard Strattan, and Bruce Wilkin, for their guidance with various plot details. For their keen attention to the words on the page, I thank James Karela, Amy Knupp, Barbara McReal, and Larry Warnock. A special note of gratitude goes to Lynn DeTurk, who contributed her evocative poem, "Gregorian Cat Chants," which serves as the epigraph to this volume.

Looking much further back, I want to extend an overdue thank-you to Allan W. Osborne, my high school English teacher and theater director, known to all as Oz. Both in the classroom and onstage, he not only taught me the workings of a plot but also inspired me to write.

As always, my agent, Mitchell Waters, has been generous with his encouragement and wise counsel. And my husband, Leon Pascucci, has been a steady font of patience, support, and good cheer. My sincere thanks to all.

— *Michael Craft*

Michael Craft is the author of sixteen novels, including the acclaimed "Mark Manning" mystery series, from which three installments were honored as finalists for Lambda Literary Awards: *Name Games* (2000), *Boy Toy* (2001), and *Hot Spot* (2002). In addition, he is the author of two produced plays, and his prize-winning short fiction has appeared in British as well as American literary journals.

Craft grew up in Illinois and spent his middle years in Wisconsin, which inspired the fictitious setting of this book. He holds an MFA in creative writing from Antioch University, Los Angeles, and now lives in Rancho Mirage, California.

In 2017, Michael Craft's professional papers were acquired by the Special Collections Department of the Rivera Library at the University of California, Riverside. A comprehensive archive of his manuscripts, working notes, correspondence, and other relevant documents, along with every edition of his completed works, is now cataloged and available for both scholarly research and public enjoyment.

Visit the author's website at www.michaelcraft.com.

The text of this book was set in Adobe Caslon Pro, a 1990 digital revival designed by Carol Twombly, based on the original specimen pages produced by William Caslon between 1734 and 1770 in London. Caslon is a serif typeface classified as "old style."

William Caslon's enduring typefaces spread throughout the British Empire, including British North America, where the family of fonts was favored above all others by printer Benjamin Franklin. Early printings of the Declaration of Independence and the Constitution were set in Caslon. After a brief period of decline in the early nineteenth century, Caslon returned to popularity, particularly for setting body text and books.

Numerous redesigns of Caslon have reliably transitioned the face from hot type to phototypesetting to digital. Among its many conspicuous uses today, Adobe Caslon is the text face of *The New Yorker*.

Made in the USA
Middletown, DE
29 May 2020